This book is dedicated to my

father, Walter Edward Piatt, whose

constant encouragement and support

have been a great blessing

throughout my life, and to my

friend, Angela Kleimola, who stood

beside me all

the way. I love you both very much.

SWEET,

SWEET

JUSTICE

By Nancy Jane Piatt

PROLOGUE

As he sat on the bed, he picked up the gun that was lying on the small night stand. Gingerly, he turned it over and over in his dirty hands, thinking about justice. He closed his eyes and drew in a long, deep breath. The metal was hard and cold in his hands, hard and cold like his heart. But it wasn't his fault. Not really.

He placed the gun back on the stand and walked over to his desk. Gently he ran his fingers over the place where he had spent hours reading newspaper articles that glorified these greedy people, people who had turned their backs and their fortunes away from him.

He took a small knife from the drawer in his desk. Tenderly, deliberately, he cut the tip of his little finger until blood was running down the side, threatening to spill over onto the floor. He placed the knife on the desk and walked over to his masterpiece.

With the blood from his finger he traced over the faces of the family who had tried to erase him from their lives. They couldn't deny him now, he thought to himself, as he moved his finger along the outline of their images. Now they were bound together forever.

He placed his wounded finger at the top of his face near his scalp. Slowly, he guided the bloody pinky down his face, with his eyes closed, a twisted smile on his face. He stopped at his lips and outlined his smile in blood, then continued down to his chin.

Justice, he thought to himself. *Sweet, sweet justice.*

CHAPTER 1

The late night sky was bright with the glare of flashing lights. One by one emergency vehicles and police cruisers raced to the house to respond to the call. There was no real hurry now. The last radio transmission indicated that there was only one survivor. Medics were already on hand to take her to the hospital when she was in stable condition.

It was nearly midnight, but dozens of spectators lined the streets, looks of horror frozen on their frightened faces. They were too scared to speak, too much in shock to understand how this could have happened in their quiet little neighborhood.

Uniformed officers were walking through the crowds, gathering statements from the bystanders. No one had heard or seen anything unusual. No one knew who would want to hurt the people who lived in the beautiful home with the meticulously landscaped yard. No one admitted to making the mysterious 911 call to report the crime.

A police photographer was also walking around, taking pictures of the onlookers as well as snapping shots of the perimeter of the home. He was careful to pay attention to the gathering crowd, hoping to capture clues that would help to determine what happened here.

Several plain clothes officers mingled with the bystanders, hoping to either see something unusual or to overhear conversations that would lead to a break in the case. Quiet panic filled the air.

Detective Jack Russell pulled in just as the last ambulance arrived. He was a tall, thirty-something man, with his six foot frame, and easy smile. It was true he could be a little gruff, but he got the job done. In his nineteen years, he had solved every case that found its way to his desk.

His reputation for flawless police work was due to his passion for detail. That was one of the things his wife, Shelby, had loved about him. Jack never forgot a birthday or an anniversary. Even the details of how, when and where they first met were as clear as the day it happened. Nothing escaped his watchful attention.

As he stepped out of his car, a rookie cop ran out of the house and vomited in the front yard. Jack shook his head as he recalled his first homicide. He drew a deep breath as he walked towards the house.

"Jack. Good to see you," Detective Dan Meyer said as he reached out to shake Jack's hand. "Better get ready for this one. I've never seen anything like it."

Dan was a seventeen year veteran of the squad and a first rate detective in Jack's opinion. They had been partners for over ten years and worked together on numerous cases. He was glad to see Dan was already on the scene.

As he and Dan walked to the front door, Jack noticed that Dan had already used several pages in his detective's notebook. Jack was pleased. He admired Dan's thoroughness, and knew that his notes would be valuable during the investigation.

Jack drew in a deep breath as he stepped into the foyer. When he looked into the living room, he winced at the sight of all the blood.

Memories of his first crime scene poured into his mind.

It had been ugly. A woman was brutally beaten to death with a baseball bat by her jealous husband. Thinking of what he saw when he first entered that home still made him nauseous even after all these years. Jack shivered, and then tried to get his focus back on the situation at hand.

He stepped aside as the medics wheeled out the lone survivor. When they first arrived on the scene she was going into shock from all the blood she lost. Thanks to their prompt actions the victim was finally stable enough to be transported to Meadowbrook General Hospital.

His eyes followed Dan as his partner walked with the medics to the waiting ambulance to get the transfer details for their report. When Jack and Dan finished at the house their next stop would be the hospital to interview the woman – if she survived.

When Jack stepped into the room, he could barely breathe. Blood was spattered over nearly every surface of what had once been an elegantly designed living room. Not even the ceiling had been spared the assault. Clearly rage was one of the driving forces behind this blood bath.

He closed his eyes, and drew in a long, slow, deep breath. He let it out slowly, and then opened his eyes. Nothing had changed. It was clearly the most gruesome crime scene he had ever been involved in.

He noticed three overturned chairs, chairs that seemed out of place in this designer room. Bloody ropes were twisted and lying loosely around the legs. Was this a robbery gone wrong? Jack did not think so. This was too personal, too brutal for it to be a stranger.

There was no sign of a murder weapon. The curtains were closed, and stained with streaks of deep, crimson blood. A lamp had been knocked over, and the bulb was missing. He could not tell if it had been shattered when the lamp fell or if it had been missing all along.

Jack considered the possibility that there had been more than one attacker, more than one weapon. He even wondered if there might be more victims. He had never seen this much blood. It was hard to comprehend how anyone could inflict this amount of cruelty on other human beings.

The grandfather clock in the corner of the living room by the windows was not working. Jack doubted that it had been working at the time of the attacks, but he made a mental note to have that checked by the crime scene investigators.

There were objects Jack could not identify because of the amount of blood that covered them. He sighed, running his hand through his dark, brown hair. It would be weeks before everything was processed from this vicious attack.

"What'd I tell you? Awful, isn't it?" Dan asked as he slipped into the room behind him. "We've got two bodies over here. Third victim's on the way to Meadowbrook General, but it's too soon to know if she'll make it."

"Any ideas about what happened?" Jack asked.

Dan responded to Jack's question by shaking his head and lifting his hands slightly as his eyes moved around the room. Jack was gazing at the two women who were sprawled on the floor near the fireplace. One looked vaguely familiar, but Jack could not quite place her.

"Don't recognize them, huh?" Dan asked. "Can't say I blame you. Who can see anything through all this mess?"

Dan tried to step around the dark, sticky pools of blood. It was nearly impossible to avoid any contact. He cursed softly as his foot slid when he stepped on the dripping wet carpet. Slowly he knelt down between the bodies, and with his gloved hand he gently lifted the hair from the face of the closest victim.

Jack stared at the woman's blood-smeared face in total disbelief. He clenched his fists and shook his head in anger. For a brief moment he closed his eyes and drew in a deep breath of air, as if he were hoping that the nightmare in front of him would vanish.

"This can't be happening!" he exclaimed. "Not the Swanson sisters!"

CHAPTER 2

Meadowbrook, Virginia was hardly the kind of place where a crime like this would occur. The homes were upscale, and most residents had more money than they and their heirs could spend in three lifetimes.

Everyone in Milford County knew of the Swanson's. An affluent family that was once known for their philanthropy and generous nature had been torn apart piece by piece. Tragedy descended upon them suddenly like a storm in the night.

Michael Swanson was a self-made multi-billionaire. He achieved great success in the computer technology industry, and retired at the age of fifty-two to a life of community service.

His wife, Melody, was a gracious woman whose generous spirit complemented her husband's passion for helping those less fortunate. She was a vision of loveliness, with her dark brown hair and coffee brown eyes. Few would have guessed the petite mother of four grown children had just celebrated her fiftieth birthday.

Michael and Melody were extremely proud of their family. Each of their daughters was as beautiful as their mother inside and out. They were reflections of her kind nature, and served others in the example set for them by their parents.

Beth, the eldest daughter, followed in her father's footsteps in their computer software corporation. She shared her mother's beautiful brown hair and dark eyes. By her twenty-sixth birthday she had become the Vice President of Sales, mostly on her own merit.

Two years after Beth was born, Stacey arrived. Her fair complexion, light blond hair and blue eyes proved she was clearly her father's daughter. As she grew into a young woman, her own talent for business became evident. She chose to forge her own way through the world of graphic design and was president of her own firm.

The third daughter, Madeline, celebrated her twenty-first birthday by accepting a full time faculty position at Milford University. Her exceptional gifts in science and technology enabled her to complete her Master's Degree almost a year ahead of schedule. Like her mother and sister, Madeline was a vision of beauty and grace with her dark hair and deep brown eyes.

It was their fourth daughter that proved to be the greatest challenge for Michael and Melody. Born over two months prematurely, Megan was always physically much smaller than children her own age. She was a bright child, but a little slower to learn.

Her dark blond hair and light green eyes set her apart from the other girls. When they all stood together, it was difficult to see the family resemblance in Megan.

Melody worked hard with Megan to overcome the physical and mental challenges of her premature birth so she could master her own talents and abilities. The little wonder, as her father lovingly called her, was naturally gifted in music, and by the age of nineteen played the harp, the piano, the silver flute and the cello.

Michael and Melody were extremely grateful for the many blessings in their lives, but most especially for their children. From all appearances, they were the perfect family.

The summer after Michael retired, they all gathered at their summer home on the Virginia shore. They were celebrating Madeline's twenty-first birthday and acceptance of her new job with the university.

The family had enjoyed many vacations there basking in the pleasures of Virginia summers at the beach. The plan was to spend the month of July together as a family, treasuring their time together.

During the day they swam, walked on the beach, shopped and enjoyed the sun. At night, they feasted on the cuisine from local restaurants, or shared meals they made from the spoils of their fishing trips. They reminisced about growing up and their family adventures over the years.

Then, three days before they were to return home, the course of the Swanson family was changed forever.

That morning, Michael woke up with the desire to go deep sea fishing. He tried to charter a boat, but there were no charters available at such short notice. They could get a reservation for the next day, but Michael was too impatient to wait. He decided to rent a sailboat and just drop lines from the sides. That decision would prove to be a costly one.

Melody was still tired from shopping the day before, and decided to stay home with Stacey, who wanted to spend the day out of the sun. Stacey and Beth helped Melody prepare food and drinks while Michael, Madeline and Megan gathered the fishing gear they would need for the day.

The sky was bright blue, with only a hint of a cloud hovering over the house. Beth wondered why she felt so apprehensive about going, but shook it off quickly. After all, it was a perfect day. What could possibly go wrong?

After loading the car and saying goodbye to Melody and Stacey, the adventurous group drove down the driveway and headed for the marina. They finally boarded the rented thirty-two foot sailboat at about nine o'clock.

Michael was confident his years of sailing during college would be all he needed to captain the vessel. The girls were quick learners, so he was sure they could handle the sails with a little guidance from him. He masterfully maneuvered the boat away from the dock and they began their journey out into the open sea.

The morning conversation was as uneventful as the fishing. Not a bite - not one – for any of the four.

"Should have waited," Michael said sheepishly. "Tomorrow might have been better."

The girls laughed, and Madeline handed out sandwiches. They chatted excitedly as they moved along in the water, not really paying attention to their surroundings. Suddenly, Beth looked up and noticed the darkening sky.

"Dad," she said.

Michael glanced towards the sound of her voice, but was more focused on untangling his fishing lines. Beth called to him again and he turned his head in her direction.

"The sky is getting a little dark. Do you think we need to head towards shore?"

Beth shared her mother's tendency to worry. Michael looked at the sky then shook his head.

"We have plenty of time, honey," he said, waving his hand towards the sky. "The morning weather report didn't mention any storms. We'll be fine."

He turned his attention back to the fishing lines he was trying to unravel. Beth kept a worried eye on the clouds, but decided her father was right. The waves were getting a little rougher now, and the wind was picking up, but she trusted her father.

A short time later, a powerful gust of wind tossed the small sailboat and almost knocked Michael off of his feet. As he regained his balance, he noticed the menacing clouds that had begun to consume the sky. The waves were higher as well, and were becoming increasingly stronger.

He cursed softly as he dropped the fishing pole he had in his hand. He knew he had to get the boat moving quickly back towards the shore. Michael made his way to the stern of the boat. He started the small engine used to steer the boat into and out of the marina.

Gusts of wind were making the boat hard to control. The sailboat began to rock wildly as the waves grew stronger and higher. Fear kept the girls from crying out, but their eyes spoke loudly to each other as they frantically worked at getting the sails down.

The pounding waves slapped roughly at the boat. They were brutal, and water was rapidly washing into the vessel. They slammed into the boat relentlessly, tossing it this way and that. With one final assault, the angry waves capsized the sailboat, trapping Megan and Madeline underneath it.

They were all strong swimmers, but the waves were forceful. Michael cried out frantically for the girls, trying to account for them all. Beth finally surfaced next to him. They grabbed onto each other and clung to the boat, screaming for the other girls. The waves were too powerful for them to try and search for them.

The Coast Guard arrived within minutes, but it was too late. They pulled Michael and Beth onto their vessel and covered them with blankets. It seemed like hours before the water had finally calmed down enough for divers to get under the capsized sailboat to search for Madeline and Megan.

They found Madeline just a few moments after they entered the water. Her body had become tangled in some of the lines, trapping her under the boat when it capsized. The divers cut away the lines and brought her to the surface. Once she was pulled onto the rescue boat, a medic immediately began CPR.

He was able to revive her, but Madeline had been submerged for an extensive period of time. There would most likely be brain damage. How much would be determined at the hospital. Worse still, after searching for nearly an hour, there was no sign of Megan.

Michael crumbled to the deck when the ship's officer gave him the devastating news. Beth began to cry and shake uncontrollably.

Ambulances were waiting to take them to the local hospital when the Coast Guard vessel reached the shore. Melody and Stacey would meet them there, they were told.

Mercifully, the sedatives they were given at the hospital worked quickly. Soon they were both asleep, finding temporary relief from the overwhelming agony.

The months following the accident were a blur to Michael. Losing his daughter was the hardest thing he had ever faced in his life. He blamed himself. He should have been paying attention. The family they had so carefully cultivated was now in ruins, and it was his fault. *His* fault.

He was certain Melody blamed him, too. She would sleep for hours during the day, and take sedatives to help her sleep through the night. He knew she was overusing the medication their doctor had prescribed. Who could blame her? How else could she live with the pain he caused her?

Megan's body was never recovered. The current was so strong that day that according to the Coast Guard officer, she was probably whisked out to sea. It was highly unlikely that her body would ever be found. She was officially listed as missing and presumed drowned.

Michael was haunted by the thoughts of what his girls had suffered that day. He imagined them crying out for him, begging him to rescue them. He had let them down. He had let them *all* down.

Finally, the grief became too much. On a quiet, warm night in October that year, he collapsed at his desk in the library of their home.

A massive heart attack ended his life that day, according to the death certificate. They all knew differently. The Michael Swanson they knew had really died back in July with his daughter.

Melody suffered a complete breakdown when Michael died, and was hospitalized for several months. She finally returned home the following February, only to die of an accidental overdose of antidepressants a few days later.

Beth and Stacey were left to care for Madeline and carry on the family legacy. The girls tried, sometimes successfully, to go on with their lives. They treasured the outpouring of support from their friends, but they slowly drifted away from each other.

In less than a year, the privileged young women went from living an enviable life to losing both of their parents, and one of their sisters to death and another to mental incapacity. Life as they had always known it was over. They would have to begin all over again, together, but alone.

CHAPTER 3

Several weeks had passed since the bodies of the Swanson sisters were discovered at their home in Meadowbrook. Jack ran his fingers through his hair as the notes from that gruesome day stared silently back at him.

The only sister that survived the murderous assault was Madeline. Unfortunately, she died two days after the attack, and never even regained consciousness. It was probably for the best, Jack thought. Living with the memories of that horrific day would have been torture for the already traumatized socialite. Still, he wished he had gotten the chance to talk to her before she passed away.

The coroner determined that each of the women had been shot multiple times with a .22 caliber pistol. Seventeen slugs were removed from Beth's body. Madeline was shot nineteen times, and Stacey's body was riddled with twenty-two bullets. There were no signs of sexual assault on any of the victims.

Jack grimaced as he wondered why anyone would have such a grudge against a family who had done nothing but good for the entire community. How could anyone be this hateful?

And why, oh why, was it such a brutal slaying? The coroner had a difficult time determining which bullet entered into which body first, last, or in any order at all. They were tortured, one cold bullet at a time. The massacre must have taken hours.

As near as the detectives could tell from the scene, the women were bound by rope and their mouths taped shut. Pathology results revealed that each of the women had trace amounts of Rohypnol in their systems.

The illegal drug renders people unconscious and leaves them vulnerable to the desires of any predator sick enough to take advantage of helpless victims. That might help to explain how all three women could have been subdued so easily, and why no one heard any screaming. But there were still so many questions left unanswered.

Someone hated them. Maybe it was jealousy. After all, the Swanson sisters were listed as Virginia's wealthiest heiresses in the local newspaper. Some people can't handle the good fortune of other people – if you could call it that, considering all they'd been through in recent years.

The police considered the possibility of a mob connection. However, careful scrutiny of Michael Swanson's financial records proved only that he was one of the most upstanding citizens Jack had ever come across.

There were no hidden mistresses, no ties to organized crime, not even a parking ticket as far as anyone assigned to the investigation was able to determine. The rest of the family appeared to be just as clean, leaving the detectives with lots of speculation, but no true direction in the case.

Jack was exhausted. He and Dan had been working on the murders for more than twelve hours a day nearly every day since it happened. They were no closer to finding the killer today than they were back when it all started.

He closed his eyes and leaned back in his chair. Thoughts of Shelby came to his mind. He smiled wistfully, knowing what she would say if she were still alive.

"You need a break, babe," she would say gently. "Let's take a picnic lunch to the park and watch the boats."

Shelby was the love of his life. Her auburn hair framed her pretty face. The sparkle in her green eyes was the first thing he noticed about her. She glowed with her love for life, and her gentle way won over many a dark mood for Jack. Even the long, demanding hours of a police detective could not sway her. She was his rock.

Cancer took his beautiful bride just eighteen months after they were married. He did not leave her side during the last three months of her precious life. He could still picture the tender way she looked at him. She'd made him promise to marry again. He agreed, because it gave her peace.

It was a promise he wasn't sure he would be able to keep. Some people say time heals all wounds, but Jack did not agree. The last seven years had been the loneliest and saddest years he had ever experienced. Even still, he could not imagine himself with anyone but his treasured Shelby.

Jack never understood why watching the children sail their toy boats cleared his mind. Somehow, after a few hours in the park with Shelby, he would come back to his desk and find another clue for a pending case.

It's worth a shot, he thought to himself.

He stood up and put on his jacket. As he was walking towards the door, Dan popped his head in.

"Heading out for lunch?" Dan asked. Jack nodded.

"Join us, then," he said. "Jennifer and I are going to that new little Thai place. She's waiting for me now."

"Sounds good to me," Jack replied.

The two men walked to the elevator and rode down to the lobby. As they stepped out into the sunshine, the cool breeze felt good on Jack's warm face.

Dan and his wife, Jennifer, had been great friends all the way through Shelby's illness. They even orchestrated the details of her funeral service, which Jack was eternally grateful for. He simply did not have the emotional energy to do it himself.

Dan's large six foot three inch frame next to Jennifer's petite, five foot two inch stature made them an unusual looking couple. Jack knew he could not find better friends. He remembered watching Jennifer and Shelby laugh as they talked at the hospital. It was a memory that carried him through some of his darkest moments in recent years.

A brisk walk found the men at the entrance of the newly renovated restaurant. Dan opened the door and allowed three ladies to enter in front of them, then motioned for Jack to go in.

Once inside, Jack's eyes adjusted to the darkened room. When his eyes met Jennifer's, he could not help but smile. Her face brightened up any room she was in. She turned and spoke to the woman standing next to her.

Oh, no! Jack exclaimed to himself. *I've been ambushed!*

He glared at Dan, who smiled sheepishly and pointed at Jennifer. Jack sighed. If it were anyone else, he would have turned around and gone back to the office. For Dan and Jennifer, he would bite the bullet.

The new restaurant was crowded with hungry patrons. They would have to wait for ten minutes before they could be seated, according to the hostess. Dan and Jack made their way over to where the women were standing. Jennifer reached up to kiss Jack on the cheek.

"What have you been doing with my husband all those late nights?" she chided with a stern voice.

Jack saw the sparkle in her eyes. He knew a smile would be quick to follow. He laughed and scooped her up in his arms to return the kiss.

"Jack, I'd like you to meet Sara Bronstein. She works at the hospital with me. Sara, this is Jack Russell – the man who keeps my husband on his toes."

Jack laughed a little nervously then shook Sara's hand. He could not help but notice how soft her skin was.

"It's nice to meet you, Sara," Jack said politely.

She smiled back sweetly, and replied in a cheerful voice, "It's very nice to meet you, Jack."

Jack could not think of a single thing to say. His mind went completely blank. Anxiety rose up like a fountain in his chest. He looked for an escape, but there was nowhere to go. All he could do now was engage in polite conversation and hope for an excuse to duck out early from this obvious set up.

The hostess came over and walked them to their table. Sara and Jennifer chatted along the way so, for the moment, he was off the hook. Jack took several deep breaths.

You can do this, he said to himself. *You talk to dozens of people every day. She's just another person.*

His sweaty palms said something different. As the foursome sat down at their table, Dan seemed oblivious to Jack's plight. He teased his wife as she tried to say the names of the various menu items.

Jack noticed how Sara's blue eyes seemed to sparkle, catching the glimmer of the candles that were burning on tables all around them. Her shoulder length blond hair was pulled back in a pony tail. Jack found himself wondering what she would look like with it down. Finally, the waitress took their orders. Jack listened to the preciseness in Sara's voice as she spoke.

Confident, he thought. *Self-assured.* Those were things he had loved about Shelby. Jack was sure Shelby would have loved this place. For a moment, sadness filled his soul.

Lunch was pleasant but uneventful. The conversation had been animated, and Jack even managed to laugh a little. He made a mental note to be suspicious the next time his friend invited him out to lunch with his wife. As the four made their way out of the restaurant, Sara turned to Jack and smiled.

"I enjoyed meeting you, Jack," she said as she held out her hand.

"It was a pleasure," Jack replied, shaking her hand gently.

He turned and thanked Jennifer for inviting him. When Dan kissed his wife goodbye, Jack noticed Sara watching him out of the corner of his eye. The women waved as they walked back to the hospital.

"You owe me for this," Jack said gruffly to his friend.

Dan just laughed.

"It was Jennifer, honestly!" he exclaimed. "I'm innocent! Besides, Sara's nice. You really ought to get to know her."

Jack stared hard at his friend, which only made Dan laugh again. They walked the two blocks back to the police station in a comfortable silence. A black sedan pulled up and parked in front of the building just as the detectives rounded the corner of the building. When the driver opened the door a distinguished looking gentleman stepped out of the car.

"Isn't that the Swanson's lawyer?" Dan asked Jack.

"It sure is," Jack replied. "I wonder why he's here."

The tall man made his way into the building as the driver pulled away. Jack and Dan hurried into the station. As they walked to the front desk, Jack became more excited with each step. He was hoping the attorney found something that would lead to a break in the case. The officer at the front desk motioned towards Dan and Jack and the lawyer turned around and greeted the detectives.

"Gentlemen," he said boldly.

He smiled and reached out to shake Jack's extended hand.

"Where can we go to talk?"

CHAPTER 4

Miles Winston was a genuine but formidable man. Word throughout the legal community was that he was no one to fool around with. He was a straight shooter who relentlessly pursued what he thought was in the best interest of his clients.

The fifty-four year old lawyer represented his good friend Michael Swanson in all of the business tycoon's financial dealings for as long as Swanson had been in business. As tragedy slowly stole Swanson and his family, the aging attorney had become consumed with the complicated legal affairs left behind.

The Swanson wills were in probate. Michael and Melody left the bulk of their assets to their girls, who were now also deceased. Since none of the sisters had wills, all of the estate assets were vulnerable.

Distant relatives stepped in to make claim to the estate. Miles never ceased to be amazed at how ruthless people could be when money was involved. It could take years before everything was finalized.

Jack and Dan first met with Miles the day after the murders. Jack was impressed at the attorney's obvious devotion to Michael Swanson. Miles appeared to be fully cooperative and desperately wanted the case to be solved quickly. The information he provided during the initial investigation had been helpful.

Jack led the men into a conference room. As they sat down, he closed the door and slid into the chair next to Dan. He watched Miles as he pulled several books out of his briefcase. Jack noticed the circles under his eyes.

He looks worn out, Jack thought to himself.

He knew how the attorney felt.

"As you know," Winston stated matter-of-factly, "I'm responsible for resolving the affairs of Michael Swanson and his family. The task is monumental, to say the least."

His voice was deep, and he looked directly at Jack and Dan as he spoke. Both Jack and Dan nodded. Collecting evidence from the house and property took over three weeks after the murders. Given Swanson's involvement in so many affairs, they could only imagine the burden Miles faced.

The attorney slid the three books across the table towards Jack. They appeared to be journals of some sort. The books were old and somewhat worn, but in reasonably good shape. Jack picked up the top book and opened it. The pages were yellowed with the passage of time, but the beautiful handwriting was still legible.

"My assistant came across these journals while we were reviewing paperwork from one of Michael's offices. They were buried deep in a chest we found in one of the storage rooms."

Jack frowned as he glanced at Dan.

"Storage rooms? We didn't find anything like that when we were conducting our investigation. What part of the house are these storage rooms located in?"

Jack could feel frustration rising at the thought that they would have missed something so crucial to the investigation. Miles cleared his throat.

"They are not in his home, Jack. His main office is located down on Kensington Street not far from the wharf. Michael ran all of his charity work from there. When he sold his business he kept the buildings that housed his offices. Mostly they are now used to store old records."

"The information in these journals is extremely sensitive," Miles continued. "The family's reputation has come under close scrutiny since the sisters were murdered. I don't want any of this information released to the public. There is no reason to tarnish this good family's name any further."

"Wait a minute," Dan said as he waved his hand. "Why weren't we given the location of these offices before now? His financial records were supposed to be made available to us – *all* of the records, not just his personal ones."

Miles sighed. He rubbed the brow above his right eye slowly.

"Michael's charity work was extensive, as you know. He was careful to keep it separate from his personal and business lives. As far as I can tell, there is no connection between his philanthropy and the murders."

"That isn't your decision to make, counselor," Jack retorted gruffly. "We'll need a complete list of all facilities that house records concerning the Swanson's. *ALL* of them!"

He slapped a tablet of paper on the table and slid it towards the attorney. Dan took a pen from his shirt pocket and handed it to Miles. Jack was livid, and Dan shared his anger. One of these facilities might hold the key to a crucial piece of evidence that could very well give them the break they needed to identify the killer.

After all this time, something could have been destroyed or removed, making it even more difficult to solve this high profile case. The attorney was not moved by their obvious anger. He pushed the tablet aside and pulled a typewritten list from his briefcase.

"I thought perhaps it was time to turn this over to you," he said calmly.

Jack glared at Miles then began to read the information on the paper. There were three addresses on the list, none of which Winston had made the detectives aware of during their previous conversations. When he was done reading the information, Jack passed the list over to Dan.

"Exactly what other information are you withholding, counselor?" Jack demanded.

He looked hard at the aging attorney, who seemed slightly smaller than he had when he first entered the room.

"Detective," Miles said sadly. "I know this has been a difficult case for you. It has been a nightmare for everyone who ever knew the Swanson family, and even for many who only knew *of* them."

Miles closed his brief case then looked back at Jack.

"Michael Swanson was my friend," he continued sadly. "Perhaps the best friend a man could ever have. Forgive me for wanting to protect his reputation and the reputation of his family. I did not believe that anything you might have found at any of these places would have helped you find a murderer. Until we found the journals, that is."

He gestured towards the books on the table that had momentarily been forgotten.

"Please," he pleaded, his eyes looking Jack square in the face. "Please promise me you will proceed as delicately as possible. There is no need to cause this family any further heartache."

Jack could sense the sincerity in his voice, but right now, he was furious at Winston for keeping this information hidden. Jack stood up and stormed out of the conference room. As he walked down the hallway to his office, Jack could feel his blood pressure rising.

He shut the door behind him, and slumped into his chair. Five months had passed since he first received the call about the gruesome scene in Meadowbrook. The case was growing colder by the day, and this arrogant attorney was sitting on a critical piece of information that he should have supplied from the very beginning.

Hindering an investigation is a crime, Jack thought to himself. *Why would an attorney keep such important information to himself?*

As he continued to ponder that question, the phone rang. Jack briefly considered letting it go to his voice mail, but reconsidered and took the call.

"Hello, Detective Russell? This is Lisa Vick with the Meadowbrook Daily News. I'm calling to follow up with you on some new information I received regarding the Swanson family."

Jack immediately sat up in his chair. He took a deep breath before responding. The press was always looking for a scoop, whether the information they discovered was true or not.

Jack knew he had to be careful how he responded, or risk that a full blown media circus would erupt again over this unsolved case.

He remembered this reporter. She was new to the paper and was looking to make a name for herself. She was constantly calling his office, pressing him for details of the murders that they were not going to release. Vick was relentless, and arrogant to boot.

Her last article was critical of the investigation and of Jack specifically because the Swanson murders were still unsolved. He dreaded talking to her, but knew if he did not, she was likely to speculate that he was hiding something from the public. The last thing he wanted was her creating "facts" that did not exist.

"How can I help you, Miss Vick?" Jack's voice was calm and steady.

The reporter spoke rapidly in response.

"Can you confirm that Melody Swanson had an affair?"

CHAPTER 5

For a brief moment, Jack felt as though he had just taken a blow to his gut. When he finally caught his breath, he spoke slowly and evenly into the receiver.

"I'm sure you realize, Miss Vick that I can't comment on an ongoing investigation. If you have facts that you believe may be helpful to the investigation, our Community Relations Director would be happy to speak with you. Would you like me to transfer you?"

The sharp "click" on the other end of the line was how their conversations usually ended. Jack sighed as he placed the receiver back in its cradle. He rubbed his temples, trying to stave off the headache he was sure would be coming on very soon.

Jack wondered how they could have possibly missed something as significant as an affair. He thought back to his notes on Melody Swanson. Could it really be true? Is it possible that such an elegant and dignified lady would have been unfaithful?

His mind wandered to Shelby. The memory of her beautiful smile made his heart ache. He still missed her so much, even after all of these years. Losing the most valuable person in his life made Jack acutely aware of how precious love and commitment were.

What went wrong in the Swanson fairy tale that Melody would have strayed? What could possibly have been missing? And when did it happen? Was it connected to the murders?

This reporter seemed to have a knack for uncovering information that people deliberately tried to hide.   If Melody did indeed have an affair, Jack was sure Lisa Vick would do whatever was necessary to expose it for the sake of another front page story.

There would be repercussions all the way to the Governor's mansion if this information was released to the public. Swanson had been a big contributor to the Governor's early campaigns for public office. Jack could not recall a time in recent years when he had felt so pressured. Discouragement was creeping in, trying to rob him of the confidence that he had in his ability to solve this crime.

Dan tapped on the door as he looked in through the glass. Jack glanced up and waved him in. As he sat in the chair directly across from Jack, Dan laid the journals the attorney had given them on Jack's desk. He knew his friend was upset. Dan's jaw dropped open as Jack shared the details of his conversation with the reporter.

"That can't be true!" Dan gasped, as he tried to absorb what Jack had just shared. "Did she say how she found out? Does she know who it was?"

Jack shook his head.

"She wouldn't have told me even if I had asked," he said flatly. "She never does - won't reveal her sources and all that nonsense."

Dan rubbed his eyes and slowly moved his head from side to side. He quickly sat up and slid the journals he had placed on Jack's desk towards him.

"Maybe these will help, then," Dan said. "Maybe a little late night reading will give us some clues."

Jack had momentarily forgotten about the journals. He picked up the top one and began to slowly turn the pages, hoping something would jump out at him as he scanned the words.

The writing was elegant and very legible, which would make for an easy read. The first entry was dated over twenty-five years ago. The graceful strokes indicated that the book belonged to a woman. Although there was no name, Jack surmised that they belonged to Melody Swanson.

Dan sighed. They had been so careful to go over every detail of the Swanson's lives. How could they have missed something as significant as an affair? As he looked at Jack, he could see fatigue starting to paint the lines under his friend's eyes with dark shadows.

Jack took his work to heart. This was the longest one of his cases had remained unsolved. Dan knew that bothered him, more than Jack would ever say.

"We need to start over, Dan," Jack said thoughtfully. "In the morning, let's review all of the notes we have on the family, especially Michael and Melody. I'll work on these tonight."

As much as he dreaded the long hours of going over details they had already reviewed over and over again, Dan knew Jack was right. Starting over at the beginning often gave them new perspectives on old information. Dan stood up and ran his hand through his hair.

"I'd better head home, then," he said.

Dan knew they were in for some long hours. He wanted to spend the evening with his wife and their three children. He also knew he needed a good night's sleep before the grueling hours began again. Dan walked to the door, then turned around and spoke reassuringly to his friend.

"We're going to get whoever did this, Jack. You know that, right?"

Jack sighed. He shifted in his chair and gazed thoughtfully at Dan's large frame.

"I know, Dan. I know. Something just doesn't fit in this one, you know? Something is just not right."

Dan nodded his head in agreement.

"We'll figure it out. Go home and get some rest. And eat something, would you? Jennifer says you're too thin!"

He laughed as he left Jack's office, leaving the detective lost in his private thoughts.

The loud bang of a door slamming from somewhere down the hall woke Jack with a start. The stiffness in his shoulders told him that he had fallen asleep at his desk reading – again. He sat up slowly, trying to let his eyes adjust to the office lights. The time on the wall clock was almost four thirty in the morning.

Jack rubbed his neck as he leaned back in his chair. His muscles ached, reminding him why he wasn't going to do this anymore. He turned his chair around and scooted over to the corner that housed a small refrigerator. Jack opened the door, looking for something that might not be spoiled.

I don't even know what that is! Jack thought to himself, as he smelled the contents of the carton he had pulled from the top shelf.

He tossed the container into the trash then moved his chair back to the desk. He stood up and fished change out of his front pocket, then walked to the door to go to the vending area.

As he passed his desk, his gaze fell on the picture of Shelby and their dog, Buddy, on the patio the summer before she got sick. A wave of loneliness filled him as tears touched his eyes briefly. How she loved that dog.

Buddy died not long after Shelby. He was an older dog, so it wasn't a surprise, but Jack missed that crazy animal. Shelby found him in the park, running free with no collar, covered with mud and too thin from not eating for who knew how long. He would never forget how excited she was over that mutt.

Buddy quickly won over both of their hearts and became a member of the family in no time. Their new companion had earned his own bed in their bedroom, and his own spot on the sofa. Jack smiled as he thought about Buddy and Shelby running together in the park.

The hallway was bright, but no one was around. At this hour, not many people were in the police station. Jack wondered what he might find edible in the vending machines. He rounded the corner and nearly collided with one of the night officers.

"Whoa! Sorry about that, sir!" the robust man exclaimed.

"I'm sorry," Jack replied. "I should have been watching where I was going."

"No harm done!" the man exclaimed. "I was just on my way to deliver this letter to you."

He held out a small, flat brown envelope, and Jack accepted it curiously. He turned it over to see the return address. Nothing was written on it except his name.

"Where did it come from?" Jack asked, looking into the desk sergeant's smiling eyes.

"I'm not sure," the office replied. "It was here when I got in at midnight. I thought I'd drop it off on my way to the break room."

Jack thanked the man and continued on until he arrived at the vending area. He searched the rows of food for something that looked reasonably nutritious. Settling for a ham and cheese sandwich and an apple, he dropped change into the machine and pressed the buttons until his food dropped.

He eyed the snacks lined up neatly behind the glass in military-like rows. Jack finally settled on a bag of chips and a soda to wash it all down with.

Jennifer just said I should eat, he thought to himself, smiling. *She didn't say it had to be good for me!*

He made his way back to the office with his food in his hands and the envelope under his arm. As he laid his early morning cuisine out on his desk, the envelope dropped to the floor. Jack bent over to pick it up, and set it off to the side.

He slid into his chair and began to eat his sandwich. His mind wandered to the Swanson family, and the accusation made by Lisa Vick. Jack had finished reading most of the first journal before he fell asleep. He just couldn't see it.

The author of the journal was certainly Melody, as Jack had suspected. She seemed happy, writing about her family and their trips, Michael's work and their charity activities. There was no indication of discontentment that he could discern from her notes.

There were no years in the dates, however, so Jack was having a hard time figuring out when the words had been written. As far as he could tell, the journal he was reading was written after their oldest daughter Beth was born, but sometime before Madeline, the third child arrived.

Jack was trying to pinpoint any detail, however small that would give him some idea as to what Miles was so concerned about. Nothing stood out so far. The first book seemed like any other diary Jack had ever read. So much information was floating in his mind that he could hardly keep it all straight.

By the time Jack finished his meal, the gym in the basement of the police station was open. He took a clean shirt from his desk drawer and snatched his gym bag from the back of his office door. A good workout was just what he needed to clear his mind and prepare for what was sure to be another long, grueling day.

CHAPTER 6

Two hours later, Jack was back at his desk reading the remaining pages of the first journal. Dan tapped on the door and popped his head in.

"Ready to go, chief!" he exclaimed, his eyes laughing as he saluted.

Jack smiled and replied, "Great! Let's wrap this up by lunch then, shall we?"

Dan laughed as he sat down.

"You stayed here last night, didn't you?" he asked.

Dan could see the exhaustion in Jack's eyes. He knew his friend wanted closure for this case, for the family and the community. Jack nodded, and shrugged his broad shoulders.

"A lot of good it did me," he replied gruffly. "I feel like I'm reading a fairy tale. I hope the next journal has a little action!"

Dan laughed. He had spent hours reading diaries from other cases. He knew they could be downright boring – until you get to the good stuff, which could be never.

"So what's the game plan?" he asked, eager to begin the daunting task that lay ahead.

He watched Jack carefully, trying to read the thoughts that he knew were swirling around in his friend's mind. Jack paused then sat up straight. He pulled out the list of addresses that Miles Winston had given them the day before.

"Here," Jack said confidently as he pointed to the first address on the list. "We need to get into these buildings to see what's there. We'll start at the one near the wharf, the one that the journals were discovered in."

Dan nodded in agreement. It would take time to secure the warrants and dispatch the teams of uniformed officers they would need to begin examining everything in each of the offices. Dan sighed. He really disliked paper work.

His eyes fell on the small brown envelope lying on Jack's desk. Jack's eyes followed Dan's gaze. With so much on his mind he had forgotten about the letter. He pulled some latex gloves out of his desk drawer. With his hands protected, he scooped up the envelope and began to tear it open.

"This was delivered to the front desk sometime last night," Jack said as he tilted the envelope to examine its contents.

He turned the envelope to allow a small, tarnished brass key to fall onto his desk. From its size, he guessed it was a key to a safety deposit box. The number 737 was written in black marker on one side. Jack raised the envelope to his eye to see if there was anything else in it, but the envelope was empty. He frowned. He had no idea what this was about.

"What do you think it goes to?" Dan asked, just as puzzled as his friend. "Is it related to the Swanson case?"

Jack shrugged his shoulders.

"I have no idea. Let's send it down to the lab. Maybe they can pull some prints off of either the key or the envelope, or at least figure out what it might open."

He pulled an evidence bag from his desk and prepared the label. He buzzed his secretary, who promptly responded to his page. Stephanie Bright was the best secretary he had ever had. She was very young but extremely capable. She could almost read his mind. She had been with him for three years now, and she was fiercely loyal.

Although she had never told him, Stephanie considered it an honor to work for him. Jack Russell was one of the most honest and decent men she had ever known.

As she entered Jack's office, her blond hair swayed when she rounded the corner. Stephanie smiled as much with her bright blue eyes as she did with her plump red lips. After listening carefully to the instructions Jack gave her, she promptly left with the bag to complete the task. Jack smiled, glad to have someone so easy to work with on his team.

Returning their attention back to the task at hand, the two detectives divided up the paperwork to gain access to the offices Michael Swanson used for his numerous ventures. With any luck, they would be able to obtain warrants by lunchtime.

Once the requests for the documents were completed, Jack and Dan began the painstaking task of scrutinizing their records from the beginning of the investigation all over again. They listened to the tape of the 911 call over and over, making new notes each time. The call came into the dispatch office at approximately 10:37 P.M. The caller sounded strangely calm.

With a soft, raspy voice, the caller indicated that there was a disturbance at 1733 Harmony Lane in Meadowbrook. Before the dispatch operator could utter a sound, the line was disconnected.

The call had been made with a phone card, so no telephone number appeared on the caller ID. Using the phone card also made it impossible to trace. They felt confident that the caller had been a man, although both Jack and Dan acknowledged that a woman with a deep voice could also have placed the call. They also both suspected that the caller was most likely involved in the murders.

The men scrutinized all of the family members, friends, and business associates over and over, looking for anyone who would have any reason to hurt the girls. Once again, they came up empty handed.

Neither of the detectives could find any sign of anyone with a grudge against any of the Swanson's. There had been no credible threats against the family. The family owed no money, and indeed, they had never been involved in anything that wasn't completely above reproach.

Nothing appeared to have been stolen from the home. There was no evidence of anything being disturbed, other than the furniture used during the bizarre attacks. None of the files containing personal records had been rifled. In fact, with the exception of the room where the crime had taken place, the home could have appeared in a designer magazine.

After three hours, Jack sighed as he pushed the notes away. He was frustrated, and Dan understood why. The murders had been too brutal to be random. Someone wanted to hurt those girls. Who could it be?

"What are we missing, Dan?" he asked his friend. "We have to be missing something!"

Dan leaned his arm on the desk and held his chin in his hand. He shook his head slowly as he tried to make sense of it all. He stared blankly at the mountain of paperwork on the desk, just as perplexed as Jack was.

"I don't know, Jack," he replied. "I just don't know. Maybe what we need is in one of those offices."

Almost as if on cue Stephanie Bright popped her head in, breaking the somber mood.

"Lunch, anyone?" she asked brightly.

Stephanie knew they were troubled by this case. She would be happy when this one was finally solved. She walked over to the desk to collect the money for their orders.

"Oh, by the way," Stephanie said. "The warrants should be ready by two o'clock. A courier will be bringing them by as soon as the judge signs them."

"Excellent!" Jack exclaimed. "Maybe we'll accomplish something at the wharf."

Stephanie smiled and waved as she walked out of the office. Jack appreciated the way Stephanie supported him when he was under the gun. She had an uncanny knack for knowing when to appear. Her pleasant demeanor helped to take the edge off at times. Jack knew he was lucky to have her.

He called the sheriff's office and requested a team of uniformed officers to meet them at the office on Kensington Street. Once all of the contents from the building were logged, everything could be moved to headquarters for closer evaluation. It would take days, possibly weeks to examine the evidence from the three buildings.

By the time Stephanie returned with their lunches, the detectives had already gathered up their records. They were discussing the contents of the first journal, a conversation that continued over pulled pork sandwiches, chips and soft drinks.

Just as they finished eating the courier from the courthouse appeared with the warrants they had been waiting for. Jack scooped them up with excitement. The two men headed to the office on Kensington Street, hopeful that the afternoon would expose the answers that the morning had so fiercely concealed.

CHAPTER 7

The evening sky had stolen the daylight as the teams of uniformed officers finished logging the contents of the first office building. While they had been able to briefly scan the evidence neither Jack nor Dan believed anything they had found held the answers they were searching for.

Boxes of files were loaded into two police vans and the teams of men headed back to headquarters to unload them. It would be after midnight before they were done. Exhausted, Jack and Dan sat down at a table in what had once been a lunchroom for Michael Swanson and his employees. They polished off the last of a cold pizza left over from dinner as they tossed around thoughts on what their search had revealed.

"I don't believe there's anything useful here, Dan," Jack said with disappointment.

"First, I went through the storage room where the other journals were found but I came up empty-handed. I did find a number of other books, but they weren't what I was hoping to find today. Combing through the contents of the other storage rooms proved to be a waste of time, too."

Dan nodded as he listened to Jack.

"Well, I didn't come up with anything new after reviewing the financial records in his office, either," Dan stated. "Swanson was meticulous with his records. Nothing is out of the ordinary as far as I can see."

"To tell you the truth," Jack confided in his friend, "I'm not all that excited about reading the last two diaries. Miles Winston seemed to think something in the journals would help us with the case, but I haven't read anything useful so far."

"I know that there is always the possibility of some hidden secret being revealed in Melody's personal notes," he added. "Once the other two office buildings are cleared out, I will finish reading the remaining two journals for more clues into her life."

"We've got two more buildings to go," Dan said wearily. "We'd better head back to headquarters so I can pick up my car."

The tired men knew they were in for several more long days. As they walked out of the empty building, their footsteps sounded hollow. Jack thought about the energy that had once driven the activities of a thriving corporation. He couldn't help but feel a little sad at all that had been lost because of a cruel twist of fate towards a family that had once been so full of life and love.

After dropping Dan off at his car, Jack glanced at the time. Almost one o'clock in the morning. He decided to stop at the supermarket near his house to pick up a late night snack. As he casually glanced at the frozen dinners, he heard a cheerful voice exclaim, "Well! You *do* leave the police station once in a while!"

He turned around to look into the smiling blue eyes of Sara Bronstein, the nurse who worked with Jennifer at the hospital. Seeing her erased the tiredness he was feeling in his own eyes.

"They do let me out from time to time," he replied, smiling back. "And what brings you out here at this time of night?"

Sara smiled as her cheeks flushed ever so slightly. He could tell she was embarrassed. It made his heart jump a bit.

"Ice cream," she said, giggling like a school girl. "I just had to have ice cream!"

Jack shook his head. He thought of the time he had to brave a freezing rainstorm just to get a quart of mint chocolate chip for Shelby. He couldn't help but smile.

"And what a sensible thing to do at this hour of the morning!" he responded, pretending to be stern.

Sara giggled again and shrugged her shoulders.

"What can I say? It's a weakness!"

She motioned towards the contents of her shopping cart. Jack took a mental inventory as he casually glanced in the direction of her hand. One loaf of multigrain bread, butter pecan ice cream, strawberries, blueberries, and a roll of paper towels.

"I just got off of work a short while ago. I thought I'd pick up a few things on my way home. Do you live near here?"

Sara's eyes sparkled in the florescent lights as she tilted her head. Jack tried not to seem too interested, but he was. She was a beautiful woman, so full of energy.

"Not far," Jack replied. "I'm on Walnut Street. What about you?"

He was trying to figure out how old she was. Late twenties, maybe, or early thirties, he guessed.

"I live on Winchester Street. It's a great place, and I can ride my bike or walk to the hospital if I want to. Not at one o'clock in the morning, of course!"

She laughed again. Jack couldn't help but notice how easily laughter came to her. They chatted for a few more minutes then walked to the check out counter together. Sara placed her items on the conveyor belt and paid the cashier while Jack bagged her groceries. As they walked out, she stopped suddenly.

"Wait!" she exclaimed. "You didn't buy what you came for!"

Jack stopped, and they both laughed. He had become so caught up in their conversation that he had completely forgotten to buy anything at all.

"I have plenty to eat at home," he said, his cheeks flushing slightly. "I'll just grab a bite of something there!"

"Well, I have plenty of ice cream and fruit," Sara said shyly.

Jack could see in her eyes that she was enjoying his company. He was enjoying hers, too. His thoughts turned to the huge amount of work that lay ahead for the next few days.

"I can't," he replied, reluctantly. "We're working on a big case. There's a lot to do and we have to get started early in the morning. Will you take a rain check?"

He held his breath hoping she would say yes, which she did with a grin. They walked out to the parking lot, still laughing. He loaded the groceries into her car then took a moment to get her phone numbers, home, work and cell.

After they said their goodbyes Jack watched her drive off as he walked to his car. He opened his door and climbed in. He stared at the scrap of paper with Sara's phone numbers written on it.

His thoughts turned to Shelby. She would be laughing at him right now, he knew. He smiled sadly as he thought of his beautiful wife. He slipped the paper into his jacket pocket. Jack tried not to dwell on the sadness he felt as he made his way down the narrow streets to his house. He missed Shelby. There was no denying it. But maybe it was time..........

He let his thoughts fade away as he pulled into the driveway and parked his car. When he walked into the house, his eyes fell on the wedding portrait hanging above the fireplace. Shelby had been a beautiful bride, her auburn hair elegantly styled, and playfully peaking out from under her veil.

She wore it down that day just for him. He loved the way her shoulder length hair wove its way daintily around her face. He could picture her deep green eyes twinkling in anticipation of every adventure that came along.

Jack closed his eyes. He could almost smell the perfume she used to wear. Lovely Lady. It was called Lovely Lady. And that described his beautiful bride perfectly, inside and out.

He sighed as he made his way into their bedroom. The house seemed empty now that she was gone, and way too big. But he couldn't leave. It would be like losing Shelby all over again, and he just couldn't do that.

He stepped into the bathroom and glanced at the tired face staring back at him. Jack turned on the water and began to brush his teeth. When he finished, he held the washcloth under the running faucet, hoping to wipe away his fatigue with the warm water.

As he dried his face, the grandfather clock in the living room announced that it was two o'clock in the morning. Jack groaned out loud. Six o'clock was going to come early. He turned out the bathroom light and walked to the bed. He sat down and set the alarm clock. Tenderly he stroked the picture of Shelby that adorned his nightstand.

"Goodnight, my love," he said gently, sorrow piercing his heart for a brief moment.

He turned out the light and climbed wearily into bed. Darkness covered him like a warm blanket. Jack closed his eyes and tried to sleep, but thoughts of Shelby and Sara kept flowing through his mind. Finally, he drifted off into a deep, peaceful sleep.

CHAPTER 8

Collecting the records from the remaining two office buildings took the better part of five days to complete. When they were finally done, Jack and Dan were both exhausted and relieved.

Box after box had been loaded into vans and transported to the evidence locker next to headquarters. Now the task of scrutinizing the contents of each box consumed them.

Day after day they examined phone logs, schedules, calendar entries, and miscellaneous documents hoping to find clues that would lead to a break in the case. Night after night, they went home, wondering when that break would come.

After nearly three weeks of twelve hour days, Jack and Dan eventually finished the painstaking task of going through all of the records, only to come up empty handed in their quest for new clues.

It was beginning to look like Miles Winston had been correct in his initial assessment. Nothing in these offices appeared to be guiding them towards a murderer. When they finally returned the last of the boxes to the evidence locker, Dan slapped Jack on the back.

"It's time for a break!" he exclaimed. "Let's go to Madelyn's for a beer!"

Jack agreed. They stopped at his office briefly so Jack could pick up the second of Melody Swanson's journals. Jack did not look forward to reading more of the intimate details of Melody's social events. He was, however, anxious to find out if there was anything useful hidden in the elegantly penned pages. *Was* she hiding something?

They left the building and walked to their favorite watering hole around the corner from headquarters. Dan called his wife on the way to let her know their plans. The weary men sauntered into the bar. Sonya, their favorite waitress, waved at them as they found a seat near the flat screen TV. She already knew what they wanted.

When she finished with the table she had been attending to, the petite brunette made her way to the bar and put in an order for some chicken wings and two draft beers. The waitress skillfully made her way to their table through the crowded bar, and cheerfully greeted them as she gave them their drinks.

"Where have you been, boys? I've been missing you!"

She put her hands on her hips and pretended to be irritated. The men laughed, and she grinned as she handed them menus.

"We've been working hard, Sonya!" Jack said. "We sure could use some of those wings!"

"On the way, sugar!" she said with a wink.

She glanced back at the kitchen.

"They'll be up soon!"

The men ordered some sandwiches as well, and Sonya was on her way to turn their request over to the cook. They sat silently for a few minutes, relishing the chance to think about something other than the Swanson case. The bar was busy tonight, but the flurry of activity was a welcome distraction.

By the time the wings arrived, they were ready for a second round of drinks. Finally, Jack relaxed. Dan watched him as he munched on the wings. He knew Jack was exhausted. The frustration was taking its toll on both of them.

They kept the conversation light, talking about the Meyer's three kids, cars and what teams would be in the play offs. When she delivered their sandwiches, Sonya was quick to offer more beer, but both men declined. She disappeared into the crowd, only to appear a few minutes later with two tall glasses of ice water.

"This will help you wash down that late night dinner, boys!" she exclaimed with a twinkle in her eye.

She placed the check on the table. The tired detectives thanked her and gulped down the cold liquid. When they were done, they decided it was time to head home.

"I'll get this one, Dan," Jack said, snatching the check off the table before Dan could pick it up. "I appreciate all of your hard work these last several months. I know it's been rough."

"Thanks, Jack," Dan said gratefully. "When we catch this guy you owe me a steak – a really big steak!"

They both laughed. Jack dropped a ten dollar bill on the table for Sonya and the tired men left the bar. As they walked back to the parking garage, they discussed their next steps in the investigation. Dan was contemplating which witnesses to interview again and Jack was planning on reading the second of the three journals.

"I don't remember an investigation that baffled me as much as this one does," Jack lamented. "High profile cases are never easy, and this one is certainly no exception."

"That's for sure," Dan agreed. "One saving grace is that Lisa Vick decided to hold off on going public with the story about Melody Swanson's alleged affair. Who do you think is responsible for reigning in her poison pen?"

His partner just shook his head. Jack had been relieved when he heard that, mostly because he didn't need any more pressure from the governor's office. He was also concerned that there was no evidence to substantiate the accusation.

"I don't know but I'm glad they did. I'm not convinced that, even if Melody *did* have an affair, it had anything at all to do with the murders," Jack said passionately. "The memory of the family should not be disgraced with innuendo. They have suffered enough."

"You are so right," Dan agreed.

It was only nine o'clock when they reached the parking garage, much earlier than they had left the office for the last several weeks. The men said their goodbyes when they reached Dan's car, and Jack headed down the aisle towards his own.

Dan was hoping to catch his wife before she headed off for bed. Jennifer had been friends with Melody Swanson. Her heart was still grieving the loss of her friend. She desperately wanted this case solved, and Dan longed to give Jennifer the closure she needed. He was sorry that he would have to tell her they had hit another dead end.

This case was starting to wear on him, too, and he, like Jack, would be glad when the perpetrator was behind bars. Dan headed home, trying to find the words to tell his wife that they still didn't have any answers.

As Jack rounded the corner to his car, he reached into his jacket pocket for his keys. His hand fell to the piece of paper with Sara's phone numbers on it. He thought about their brief encounter a few weeks ago.

He considered calling her, but decided it was too late. He would definitely call her in the morning, though. After all, she owed him ice cream and fruit. The thought of seeing Sara again gave Jack a good feeling. It was strange yet pleasant to think about another woman this way.

In all of the years since Shelby had been gone he never once thought about being with anyone else. He knew his wife would not have wanted him to be alone. He just hadn't been able to open up again. Somehow, Sara seemed safe. Like Shelby.

When Jack arrived at home, he settled onto the sofa with Melody Swanson's second journal. As he continued to read the worn pages of her life, he tried to picture what the world must have been like for the beautiful socialite.

The pages were filled with more stories of parties and trips, of fund raisers and charity balls. The ink brought to life events from their family adventures and their children's lives. Jack could almost picture their faces as he read about people she obviously adored.

He estimated that this part of the journal was written about a year before their youngest daughter, Megan, had been born. Towards the end of the book, however, Jack was beginning to notice a different tone in Melody's writing.

He was trying to determine what her state of mind was. Was she feeling discontented, or possibly unfulfilled? His gut was telling him that something had definitely changed.

As Melody continued to pen her story, it was as if she had shut her emotions off completely. She had begun to record her world as if she was an outsider looking in on her own life. She seemed to be distant, not the same vibrant, compassionate woman Jack had come to admire.

Her words did not explain the subtle transformation, but it was clearly there. Jack wondered if this was what Miles Winston was referring to. He read on, hoping to gain more insight into what was transpiring in Melody's life.

Michael seemed to be working more at this time in their lives. Jack noticed fewer entries about things Michael and Melody did together. Perhaps she was lonely, Jack thought. It must have been difficult to take care of the girls with Michael away from home so much.

The couple always seemed to spend every free moment together before this, but she wrote less of those happy times now. Surely she missed spending time with him. Eventually, Melody began to write about being pregnant with their fourth child. These entries, however, did not contain the same excitement as when she was carrying their first three babies.

"Will Michael ever forgive me for going through with this?" she wrote. "Will he ever accept this baby and love it like our other girls?"

Jack was confused. Michael seemed to adore all of his children. Why would Melody think he would not love their fourth child? Even if the pregnancy was unplanned, would Michael really be angry with her, or resent the baby?

This doesn't make any sense, Jack thought to himself. *What is causing her anxiety about this baby?*

Suddenly, he sat up.

"Is this it?" he blurted out loud. "Is *this* what Miles was referring to?"

He searched the pages carefully, hoping for an explanation, but there was none. Jack's experience kept him from jumping to conclusions without some kind of proof. However, if the pregnancy was the result of an affair that would definitely explain her torment.

Jack continued reading until he finished the diary, but he didn't find the clues he was hoping for. If Melody did have an affair, she hadn't revealed it in her writing.

The first two journals did not shed any real light on the case, but Jack was hopeful that the third journal would. He was sorry he'd only brought one of them home with him. He yawned as he glanced over his shoulder at the grandfather clock. Four thirty in the morning. Jack stood up and stretched, trying to decide it if would be worth it to try to sleep before the alarm rang at six.

The thought of lying in his bed was too inviting to pass up, so he headed off to the bedroom for a short nap before going back to the office. He was excited about what he had learned from this journal. He knew Dan would be, too.

Sleep overcame him quickly as his head hit the pillow. Images of the Swanson family danced through his dreams, chased by the shadow of an over-sized man looming over them. Jack pursued the intruder in his dream, but the elusive menace evaded capture only to threaten the family over and over again. The alarm rang just as the shadow was consumed by the bright morning sun.

CHAPTER 9

When the alarm rang, Jack bounced out of bed as easily as if he had slept soundly all night. The sun seemed to welcome him as he walked to his car for the short drive to headquarters.

While Jack navigated his way through the morning traffic a surge of adrenaline was racing through his body. The thought of what might be contained in the pages of the third journal gave him energy that had escaped him for the last several weeks.

He was anxious to talk to Dan about what he had read a few hours ago. Could this lead to the break they had been searching for all of these months?

Jack pulled into the parking garage at seven sharp. Dan's car was already parked precisely in its space. He wondered what time Dan had arrived. It wasn't like his friend to be this early.

On his way to the elevator, Jack stopped at the front desk to check for messages. The sergeant greeted him with a smile and a wave as he spoke with a caller. Jack peered around the counter to check the slot where his messages were stored. He was slightly surprised that it was empty.

Walking briskly he arrived at the elevator just as the doors opened. The elevator was running extra slow this morning, but Jack was not deterred. He was sure they were close to a break in this case, and nothing was going to distract him today.

He rounded the corner to his office. He noticed Dan sitting in the conference room surrounded by the pictures from the initial crime scene. Curious, the detective ducked his head into the room and greeted his partner.

"You're here early! Need some coffee?"

The expression on Dan's face caught Jack off guard. He walked to the opposite side of the table and looked squarely into Dan's face.

"What's going on, Dan?"

He sat down slowly, waiting for Dan's response. The dark circles under Dan's eyes confirmed that he had had very little sleep. He was staring at pictures of the overturned chairs from the living room of the Swanson house.

"Jack, we have a problem," Dan said quietly, as he motioned for Jack to shut the conference room door.

Jack complied and returned to his seat. He waited anxiously for Dan to continue. Dan sighed and rubbed his brow.

"Jennifer and I talked for a long time last night," he said. "She told me of a rumor that was going around the hospital many years ago about Melody Swanson. It was never confirmed, so it's only a rumor, but………."

Dan stopped, shaking his head. Jack held his breath. Dan was not one to take gossip seriously. He, like Jack, had been thoroughly trained to deal with facts. Unless a piece of information could be positively confirmed, it had no place in their investigation.

"Jack, Melody Swanson may have had an affair with the Governor!"

The color drained from Jack's face as he tried to absorb the words. He let out a soft whistle. This was huge. If that was true and it came out, many lives would be changed forever, and potentially even ruined.

The two men sat silently for a few moments, trying to take in the magnitude of this situation. They would have to proceed very cautiously. Investigating someone like the Governor of Virginia was a career ender if it wasn't handled with absolute discretion.

"Do you think Lisa Vick knows this?" Dan asked.

His knuckles were white as he clenched his fist. Jack knew he was deeply troubled. He wished he had the answers that would ease his concern, but he did not. Jack thought about Dan's question then shook his head firmly.

"I don't think so," he said slowly. "She would have jumped all over this if she had anything implicating Governor Langford. Her reporting during the last election was anything but friendly towards him."

Jack wondered if there was history between the crafty reporter and the Governor. He knew the media was anything but fair when they had an agenda. Perhaps her aggressive tactics were just her way of breaking into national reporting.

The abrasive reporter had rubbed Jack the wrong way on a number of occasions and he did not like dealing with her. He let out a deep sigh as he thought of trying to navigate around her with this kind of information. She was like a shark, elusive and silent. They would have to be very, very discreet.

Jack told Dan about what he read in the journal and Dan agreed that an affair was a real possibility. The third journal could confirm what they both desperately hoped to be not true.

Jack and Dan sat for almost two hours discussing how they should proceed. They still weren't sure that this information was related to the murders. However, it would definitely be motive if it was.

"Governor Langford was the Mayor of Meadowbrook at the time of the alleged affair," Dan observed. "News of marital infidelity, especially if a child had been conceived as a result, would be devastating to his family, his career and his bid for a White House run."

"I don't like this, Dan," Jack said solemnly. "After all of this time, it looks like we might have a person of interest. We can't say anything about this to anyone until we can investigate these allegations further."

Dan bobbed his head up and down quickly.

"You've got that right!" he said. "Governor Langford will be my new focus in the investigation. I don't like the idea of this but I know it has to be done."

"Okay," Jack replied. "I will finish reading the third journal to see if Melody recorded any details that might confirm what Jennifer heard. In the meantime, we say nothing about this to anyone."

Dan solemnly gathered up the photographs he had been reviewing and the two men walked down the hallway to their respective offices. Neither one looked forward to the tasks at hand. As much as they wanted to solve this case, they weren't happy about where the investigation appeared to be heading. Disaster seemed to loom over them from every direction.

While neither of them said it out loud, Jack and Dan were both hoping the rumor wasn't true. The ramifications would be far reaching, and nothing good was going to come from this. Jack rounded the corner and stepped into his office. His somber mood was shattered when his secretary greeted him with her bright smile.

"It's about time you got here!" Stephanie said, pretending to be irritated because he was late.

He smiled back and accepted the folder she was holding out towards him.

"This is the report from the key you sent down to the lab a few days ago. It was misplaced and has been floating all over the place!"

Stephanie turned and left his office, closing the door behind her. Jack sat down and began reading the report. Nothing conclusive was determined from the forensic examination. The key did not match the records from bank deposit boxes in the immediate area. There were no fingerprints on the metal.

The handwritten number 737 on the key did not appear to be significant. Jack had no idea what this key was for and no clue why it was sent to him in the first place. He placed the folder in his *'to do much later'* pile, which seemed to have multiplied significantly in his absence.

Jack picked up the third journal apprehensively and began reading. After only a few minutes it became obvious that this journal was from a time period much later in the Swanson's lives.

Megan was now almost four years old. There was a large gap of information between this journal and the last. Jack laid the book down slowly. They were missing a journal, one that could contain critical and damaging information.

He picked the book back up and scanned through the pages of the entire journal. He had hoped that something of use would jump out at him, but to no avail. Melody was back to her happy life. Any anxiety she had been feeling when she was pregnant with their fourth daughter was clearly gone.

A journal was missing. Nothing like that was documented by their team when they inventoried everything retrieved from Michael Swanson's other offices. Where was it?

Jack grew more concerned as he thought about the information that might be contained in that book in the hands of someone who would use it against the family. Or more specifically, against the Governor. He had to go back to the original source. He set the journal off to the side of his desk. Jack picked up his phone and buzzed his secretary.

"How can I help you?" she asked.

"Would you get Miles Winston on the line for me?" he responded.

CHAPTER 10

According to his secretary, Miles Winston was in court and would not be returning for several hours. Jack felt the frustration of the case gnawing at him as Stephanie gave him the news.

He decided to head out to the park to clear his mind. He asked Stephanie to hold his calls, and made his way to the elevator. When Jack saw the stairs, he changed his mind and walked the five flights to the ground floor instead.

As he left the building, he wondered just what his next step should be. If Miles had the missing journal, why would he have kept it? What would be the point of only giving him three of the books? Since the police had not even known about the journals, Miles could have simply kept his mouth shut. Jack grew more and more disturbed as he thought about what this could mean.

Did Miles know about the alleged affair? Who was he trying to protect – Melody Swanson or the Governor? Perhaps he was trying to protect both of them. Jack glanced at his watch, wondering when the attorney would be out of court.

He turned onto the sidewalk leading into the park. Almost immediately sounds of laughter caught Jack's attention. He turned his head in the direction of the happy voices. A mother and her two small children, all of them laughing, were chasing after a bright yellow ball. Jack smiled. It was a happy day for them.

He thought about Melody Swanson and her girls. From reading her journals he knew how much she loved playing with them. In his mind Jack could picture them here, running and laughing, drinking up the sunshine.

His thoughts turned back to the missing journal as he continued walking through the park. He grew pensive once again. Did Miles know who might have wanted to hurt the Swanson girls? Was he trying to cover something up?

Jack prided himself on reading people. He did not want to believe that Miles would withhold any information that would help them solve this case. After all, the lawyer was held in high regard throughout the community. Miles was extremely loyal to Michael Swanson and his family. A friend like that was extremely rare.

Dan and Jennifer were those kinds of friends. Jack knew he was fortunate to have them in his life. He would die for them and was sure they would do the same for him. Did Michael Swanson appreciate the friendship he had with Miles Winston? Jack was confident that he did.

While he walked through the park, Jack thought of more questions than he could find answers for. He was growing more and more anxious about the possibility of having to interview the Governor.

He finally arrived at the pond where he and Shelby used to come to watch the children sail their boats. A food vendor was just starting to serve hot dogs. Jack walked over to the stand to grab a bite to eat.

After deciding on two hot dogs and a soda, he walked over to a wooden picnic table and sat down. As he laid his lunch out on the table, a gust of wind snatched the napkins out of his hand and blew them in every direction. Jack jumped up to collect the fluttering papers, and nearly collided with the reporter from the Meadowbrook Daily News.

"Here you go!" Lisa Vick said cheerily as she handed him the napkins she had managed to rescue.

Jack accepted them from her outstretched hand, trying not to show his disdain.

"Thank you," he managed graciously, forcing a smile. "And how are you today, Miss Vick?"

"Lisa," the tall brunette said. "Call me Lisa. I'm fine. And how are you?"

She looked directly in his eyes through her gold rimmed sunglasses.

"Quite well, thank you," he responded.

He looked down at his waiting meal, hoping she would take a hint. He was not really surprised when she did not. Instead, she sat down uninvited across the table from him. She quickly started to launch questions at him about the Swanson investigation. How was the case coming? Did they have a suspect? Are they close to making an arrest? When would they be updating the press?

Jack finally stopped her with a wave of his hand and a feigned smile. He wiped his mouth with a napkin and laid it on the picnic table.

"I'm so sorry, Miss Vick. I'm sure you understand that I can't talk about the case with you. The Chief of Police has made it very clear that only he or our Community Relations Director can speak about this investigation. Have you contacted either of them?"

Jack tried to sound remorseful, but he wasn't sure he was pulling it off. Lisa Vick was scrutinizing his face as if she was expecting the tired lines to reveal what he was thinking. She stood up abruptly.

"Are you hiding something, detective? You know I'll figure it out, don't you?" the reporter retorted sharply.

Her words were harsh and accusing. She glared at him through the tinted lenses that camouflaged her eyes. Lisa turned on her heel and walked off in the direction of the park entrance that he had come from.

"And have a nice day," Jack muttered sarcastically to himself.

She must have followed him from the station. What was she hoping to find? Jack knew that he and Dan would have to proceed very carefully. This reporter was clever. She went after what she wanted with a vengeance, and she usually got it regardless of what debris was left in the process. Jack did not want to be on the wrong end of her lethal pen again.

After he finished his meal, Jack stood up and threw his trash in a nearby receptacle. He started to walk slowly around the glistening pond, gazing at the ripples on the glassy surface. He came upon a young boy navigating his battery operated sailboat gently through the water under his father's watchful eye.

Painfully, Jack's thoughts returned to Shelby. They had just begun talking about having children when they found out about the cancer. In a way, he was glad that they never had any. He wouldn't have wanted to raise a child without her.

By the time he finished walking around the pond, he found himself at the entrance of the park nearest the station. A glance at his watch showed the time was almost two o'clock.

Good, Jack thought to himself. *Maybe Miles Winston is back in the office!*

He left the park and briskly walked the rest of the way back to headquarters. He was anxious to speak with the attorney and get to the bottom of the missing journal. He arrived at the building just as Dan was walking Jennifer out. Her face lit up when she saw Jack.

"Where have you been, handsome?" she asked as she threw her arms around his waist.

"Waiting for you, gorgeous!" he answered back, smiling down at her and returning her embrace.

"You need to come for dinner very soon," she said. "We can cook out! You can grill those famous ribs of yours!"

They all laughed, remembering how he had nearly set the house on fire the last time he grilled out. They agreed that it had been too long since they had gotten together. Jennifer would not let him get away without promising to call her to set up a date.

She mentioned that she might invite her friend Sara Bronstein. When he did not protest, Jennifer winked at Dan and he smiled back.

"I saw that!" Jack said sternly.

Jennifer just laughed. They said their goodbyes and she left the station to return to the hospital. While Jack and Dan walked back into headquarters Jack described his unexpected meeting with Lisa Vick.

"She's a piece of work!" Dan exclaimed, after Jack finished his story.

"Don't I know it!" Jack replied. "She's clever and I don't trust her. We have to find a way to keep her occupied."

Their conversation turned to lighter topics as they walked through the halls towards Jack's office. Dan headed towards the records department to continue his research on the Governor after leaving Jack at his door.

Stephanie was away from her desk. Jack flipped through his messages, hoping to find one from Miles Winston. He was irritated that the attorney had not returned his call.

By the time four o'clock rolled around, Winston still had not called back. He asked Stephanie to contact the law office again. This time, his secretary informed her that Miles Winston was gone for the day.

Jack wondered if that was truly the case, but decided against calling back. He took out the folder that contained the original interviews of the family and friends of the Swanson family and began to scan the pages.

Stephanie stopped in to say good night before she left at five o'clock. When she disappeared down the hall, Jack returned to his reading. After studying his notes for another two hours, he gathered the pages together and placed them in the folder on his desk. Jack was exhausted.

He rubbed his eyes and wondered how many more nights he would go home without solving this case. A good night's sleep was what he needed. He decided to go home and find a way to put the Swanson family out of his mind until the morning.

He placing the folder in his desk drawer and locked it. Jack walked to the door of his office. He grabbed the gym bag that was hanging on the back of the door and turned out the office light.

He pulled the key ring out of his pocket and singled out the one he needed. While he was locking his office door his thoughts turned to Sara Bronstein. He'd been meaning to call her but the case had kept him preoccupied.

A smile crept onto his face as he remembered their brief encounter at the market a few weeks ago. Suddenly, the Swanson family was the furthest thing from Jack's mind.

CHAPTER 11

Shadows from the candlelight haunted the panels of the dimly lit room. Stacks of papers bound by rope lined the back wall. A twin bed with an old, dirty mattress occupied the space next to the door.

Candles lined the side of a tiny wooden desk that was under the only window in the room, spilling wax onto the unprotected wood. A table lamp placed carelessly in the far corner of the desk was the only source of electric light in the small, musty smelling alcove he called home.

One chair, one desk. One wall to hang his masterpiece. One of everything. That was all he needed. That was all anyone needed. Excess was wasteful. That's what Mama always said when he was growing up.

He looked at his masterpiece, the collage that told the story of his life, the life he *should* have had. Day by day for years he diligently worked to put the pieces together one by one. The project had taken a long time, but it had made him whole. Finally, he had made it right. Mama would be proud.

Not one spot was left open on the walls that his life story called home. Every cinder block and every speck of paint that covered each one was hidden under newspaper stories of the family that robbed him of his legacy, denied him his rightful place in the world.

As he sat on the bed, he picked up the gun that was lying on the small night stand. Gingerly, he turned it over and over in his dirty hands, thinking about justice. He closed his eyes and drew in a long, deep breath. The metal was hard and cold in his hands, hard and cold like his heart. But it wasn't his fault. Not really.

He placed the gun back on the stand and walked over to his desk. Gently he ran his fingers over the place where he had spent hours reading newspaper articles that glorified greedy people, people who had turned their backs and their fortunes away from him.

Wincing, he remembered the day Mama told him where he really came from. He was only eight, but he was old enough. Old enough to understand that he had been abandoned. Old enough to know that, one day, he would repay them for the evil they did to him.

He took a small knife from the drawer in his desk. Tenderly, deliberately, he cut the tip of his little finger until blood was running down the side, threatening to spill over onto the floor. He put the knife on the desk and walked over to his masterpiece.

With the blood from his finger he traced over the faces of the family who had tried to erase him from their lives. They couldn't deny him now, he thought to himself, as he moved his finger along the outlines of their images. Now they were bound together forever.

He placed his wounded finger at the top of his face near his scalp. Slowly, he guided the bloody pinky down his face, with his eyes closed, a twisted smile on his face. He stopped at his lips and outlined his smile in blood, then continued moving it down to his chin.

Justice, he thought to himself with a twisted smile. *Sweet, sweet justice.*

CHAPTER 12

When Jack arrived at his office the next morning, Dan was waiting to brief him on what he had learned about Governor Langford. They carried their coffee and bagels to the conference room where Dan had organized the photographs and other documentation he obtained the day before.

Fortunately, a significant amount of information on prominent figures like the Governor was stored in the precinct research files. Dan focused on the early years of the Governor's political career to establish a connection between the Governor and the Swanson's. He had been able to trace their relationship from early in Langford's first political campaign.

After winning the last election by a landslide, Lawrence Elliott Langford became known as the 'People's Governor'. His commitment to his personal beliefs along with his kind way with people made him overwhelmingly popular with the citizens of Virginia.

He grew up under the protective guidance of his father, William Langford, a three-term member of Congress and his mother, Martha Wilson Langford. The influential and affluent family was native to Virginia, dating all the way back to Langford's great, great grandparents.

Both William and Martha's fathers had also served in Congress. The political roots of both families ran deep throughout the country. Langford attended prestigious private schools with his two older brothers. Like his father and brothers he excelled in sports and student government. He followed in their footsteps when he attended one of the most prestigious military academies in the country.

After graduating from the Academy with highest honors, he enlisted in the US Navy, where he earned the rank of Lieutenant. Langford received the Navy and Marine Corps Medal before being honorably discharged after six years of service to his country.

Shortly after leaving the Navy Langford married his high school sweetheart Diana Winthrop. The union was a perfect blend of romance and political correctness. Diana's father was a Navy Admiral with close political and personal ties to the Secretary of State. Photographs from their fairytale wedding made international newspapers and magazines for weeks following the glamorous affair.

No one was surprised when Langford threw his hat into the political ring and ran for Governor of Virginia after serving briefly as the Mayor of Meadowbrook. The first of many carefully guided steps to the Governor's mansion was just another chapter in the political lineage of the Langford legacy.

Dan had accumulated hundreds of photographs of the early years in the personal and political lives of Lawrence and Diana Langford. His research revealed that the Governor and his wife initially met the Swanson's at a fundraiser during Langford's first mayoral bid.

From all appearances the two couples had become fast friends. Jack and Dan spent the morning scrutinizing photographs searching for evidence of a personal connection between Lawrence Langford and Melody Swanson.

There were only a few photos of Melody Swanson with the Governor when Michael wasn't present, but Diana Langford was always close by. They examined facial expressions and body language but could not find evidence of anything out of the ordinary.

Michael Swanson was a prominent figure in Langford's campaign. However, there was no evidence that Melody participated in the process. With the exception of accompanying Michael as he attended various campaign events, Melody did not appear to be as deeply involved as her husband.

As the pictures progressed into the later years of Langford's campaigns, Jack and Dan noticed that Michael Swanson had become less and less involved. They compared the dates to the birth of Megan Swanson.

The remaining photographs screamed of Swanson's absence. The last time they could find proof that Michael Swanson was associated directly with Langford was about three months before Megan was born. Is that a coincidence – or is there more to the story?

The two detectives sat quietly for a moment. If Michael discovered that Melody and Langford were having an affair, the timeline made perfect sense. What husband would continue to support a man who threatened his marriage and family?

There was no longer any question in their minds that they needed to meet with the Governor. They would have to tread lightly. Not only could they not risk offending Langford; they also had to find a way to distract Lisa Vick.

After discussing their options, they decided that before they spoke with the Governor they would need to get the third journal from Miles Winston. Jack called his secretary and asked that she call Winston's office again.

He and Dan gathered the evidence and carried it back to the file room. After placing the material in the properly marked cabinet, the hungry detectives made their way to the cafeteria in the basement.

The clamor of the lunch crowd had begun to wind down as Jack and Dan stepped up to the food line. They each picked up a dark green tray and carefully selected the condiments and napkins they would need.

As they made their way slowly down the serving lines, Jack snatched up the last roast beef sandwich. Dan settled on ham and cheese on rye and they each grabbed a bag of chips. Jack opened the drink cooler and took out two bottles of iced tea.

He placed one on Dan's tray and leaned over his friend to pick up two straws. Dan grabbed a banana for himself and tossed an apple onto Jack's tray.

"Pretend this is from Jennifer!" he said, chuckling.

Jack smiled. Jennifer was always trying to make sure he ate well. Jack could almost hear her laughing when Dan tossed the fruit onto his tray. After paying for their lunches they headed to the back of the cafeteria.

They sought out a place where no one else was sitting so they could discuss what they had discovered during their morning pursuit. The Chief of Police made his way to their table as the detectives were deeply engrossed in their conversation.

"Hello, men!" he said heartily.

Paul Sheppard was a tall, muscle bound man in his mid fifties. His years as a police officer earned him many accommodations and service awards.

Known for his dedication to the department and his commitment to his men, Sheppard commanded the respect of almost everyone who ever had reason to work with him or for him. He sat down and flashed a devilish smile towards Jack.

"I understand you had lunch with our favorite reporter yesterday, Jack," he said, grinning slyly.

Jack rolled his eyes and sighed.

"What did she say now, sir?" he asked, not sure he really wanted to know.

The Chief laid his hand on Jack's shoulder. With a straight face, Sheppard leaned towards Jack and looked straight into his eyes. His voice took on a very serious tone.

"You two should really work on your relationship!"

The sparkle in the Chief's eyes made Dan laugh, and Jack couldn't help but laugh, too. Sheppard relayed the general details of his discussion with the reporter. It was the usual rhetoric: Jack wasn't moving fast enough, being cooperative enough, or keeping the press informed often enough. The aggressive reporter even hinted that she suspected Jack was hiding the truth about the case from the public.

The three men sat for an hour discussing the progress they had made in recent weeks. Sheppard's face grew somber upon hearing that Governor Langford could become a person of interest very shortly.

"When you are talking about a man like Langford," the Chief said earnestly, "you have to tread lightly. There are no second chances."

Jack and Dan both nodded, understanding all too well that they were heading deeper into already dangerous waters. Still, they had to follow the facts, even if they didn't like where the facts were leading them.

"Call my secretary when you get that third journal," Sheppard said. "Let's get together and come up with a strategy for interviewing Langford. He's an honest man, from what I know of him. But honest men make mistakes, too! And remember, there are facts, and then there's the whole story. I'm sure there's quite a bit of information you haven't uncovered yet."

Jack and Dan silently considered the wise words of caution from their superior.

"You've done a great job leading this investigation," he continued. "I have every confidence in the integrity of the work that you do."

His words lifted the spirits of the tired detectives. They had been traveling down a long road over the last several months and the end of the journey was not yet in sight.

After the Chief left, Jack and Dan tossed around ideas about how to divert Lisa Vick's attention away from the investigation. She was more interested in furthering her career than she was in reporting the truth. Jack was uneasy with the way she failed to verify her leads before printing them. He wanted no problems from Vick when it came to Governor Langford.

When they finished their lunches, Jack and Dan rode the elevator back to their offices in silence. Trying to comprehend the magnitude of the direction this case seemed to be going was exhausting. If any of this ends up being true, how many lives will be forever changed by a few indiscretions from so many years ago?

CHAPTER 13

When Jack finally returned to his office, Stephanie informed him that Miles Winston still had not returned his call.

"That's the good news, Jack," she said hesitantly.

Jack's eyes narrowed.

"And the bad news?" he asked, with irritation creeping into his voice.

"Well," she said, "the bad news is that his secretary said that Winston would not be available until sometime after next week because of the trial he is working on."

Stephanie could tell by the look in his eyes that Jack was not going to accept that response easily.

"Fine," he said curtly. "Would you put a call into Dan and ask him to meet me at the elevator? If Miles won't call me back, we'll just go visit him in person!"

"Of course," she replied as she picked up the phone.

Jack was beyond being annoyed. He turned on his heels and walked swiftly to the elevator to meet Dan. His gut was telling him Winston was stonewalling them, but he couldn't figure out why. Does he know what was in the third journal? And even if he does, why would it matter to him?

"Unless he has something to hide!" Jack said out loud to himself.

He looked around quickly to see if there was anyone listening to him talk to himself. Thankfully he was alone. Jack laughed to himself. He decided that he might need a few days off after they finish this investigation.

"So you got another brush off from Winston," Dan said as he walked up to his friend.

Jack nodded and smiled.

"Well," Jack said facetiously, "we'll have to make it convenient for him to spend some quality time with us since he's just *so* busy!"

Dan agreed.

"He's not going to appreciate this impromptu visit, you know," Dan said.

"That may be true," Jack replied. "However, this journal, which he failed to tell us about in the first place, is looking more and more like an important piece of evidence in our investigation. As far as I'm concerned, this is another unnecessary delay. I hope it isn't an intentional one. My patience is running pretty thin with Miles Winston right about now."

Dan could tell Jack had had enough. They made the drive to Winston's office in good time. As soon as they walked into the building, Dan pointed towards the directory on the wall near the elevators. A quick glance told the detectives that Miles Winston's office was on the seventh floor.

After a brief elevator ride the men walked down the hall towards the attorney's office suite. As Jack reached for the door, he looked down at his watch. Almost three o'clock. Hopefully Winston was not in court today.

The law office was elegantly decorated. Paintings from local artists adorned the walls, which were exquisitely wall papered with an unassuming floral pattern. A spray of brightly colored flowers prominently displayed in a lead crystal vase graced the far corner of the front counter.

The woman seated at the receptionist's desk looked up from her computer and promptly smiled. The name plate in front of her identified her as Robyn Lightwood.

"Hello!" she said brightly. "May I help you?"

Her brown eyes were deep and sincere, and the tone of her voice was warm and inviting. Jack estimated her to be about thirty years old. He returned her smile and extended his hand. She placed her hand in his and shook it gently.

"Hello, Robyn! My name is Jack Russell and this is my partner, Dan Meyer. We're with the Meadowbrook Police Department. I've been trying to reach Miles Winston by phone for quite a while now but he hasn't returned my calls. We were hoping to meet with him in person. Is he available?"

Robyn paused for only an instant, but both Jack and Dan noticed her obvious hesitation. She shifted slightly in her seat then gently shook her head.

"I'm very sorry, detectives. Mr. Winston is preparing for a court appearance next week and has requested not to be disturbed. I can take a message and have him return your call but it may be several days before he is able to get back to you."

Her tone was apologetic, but she was careful to avoid eye contact with either of the men. Jack was struggling to hide his frustration. He did not understand why Winston was avoiding this conversation, and his patience had been tried to its end.

"I've already left several messages for him," Jack said firmly. "He has yet to return any of my calls. We really need to speak with him. *Now.*"

Jack was not going to take no for an answer this time. He moved slightly towards an open doorway. It appeared to lead to the offices that housed the law partners and other employees of the firm.

"Please, detective – you really can't go back there!"

Robyn stood up abruptly and began to walk around the corner of the desk to intercept him.

"It's alright, Robyn," a deep voice declared.

Miles Winston loomed in the doorway, a slight frown flashing briefly on his thin lips.

"Please, detectives," he said graciously.

He stepped to the side and extended his arm to grant passage into the inner chambers of the law firm. After asking Robyn to hold his calls, Miles led Jack and Dan to his office.

Once inside, the attorney closed the door and invited the men to be seated in the black leather chairs in front of his desk. Miles walked behind his desk and sat down. He looked directly at Jack as he began to speak.

"I apologize for not getting back to you, Jack," he began, his voice steady and confident. "I'm preparing for court next week and the case I'm working on has consumed me, I'm afraid."

Jack and Dan both nodded in response to his dilemma.

"We understand completely, Miles," Jack said sincerely. "I apologize for the intrusion, but we have questions about the journals you gave us. We seem to be missing one that may contain crucial information into our investigation of the Swanson family murders."

Miles eyes softened at the reminder of the grim fate the family had suffered. Sadness rested squarely on his shoulders as he slowly shook his head.

"I can't help you, Jack," he responded wistfully. "The journals I gave you were the only ones we found when we went through the offices."

He paused briefly before continuing.

"If there is another one I don't know where it is. By now I'm sure you realize the sensitive nature of the information contained in those journals," Winston stated. "My greatest desire is to preserve what is left of their family legacy. The Swanson's meant so much to this community and to me personally. I don't want their reputations tarnished by gossip mongers who are only looking for their fifteen minutes of fame."

Jack agreed with him. The Swanson family deserved to be remembered as people who lived their lives with dignity and honor. When reporters or gossip columnists expose confidential issues about prominent people, their lives are often damaged or destroyed. Irresponsible journalists strip people of their private lives while they claw over them just to get a front page story and a byline.

"Miles, I understand what you are trying to do," Jack said passionately. "I even support it.

But there are some questions we need answers to and we need your help to get to the truth here."

Jack paused for a moment. He looked at Dan, who was watching the attorney closely. When he sensed that Miles was ready to hear what he had to say, Jack continued.

"Miles, did Melody have an affair?"

Jack looked directly into the attorney's pale blue eyes. Miles returned the detective's gaze without flinching. He paused for a moment, then leaned forward slightly in his chair.

"If she did, Jack," Miles began slowly, "I could not tell you because of attorney/client privilege. The estate is still open, and until it is settled, I am bound by that obligation to the family."

"This is a murder investigation, Miles!" Dan said earnestly. "Attorney/client privilege ends upon death. If Melody had an illegitimate child as a result of an affair with someone like, say the Governor of Virginia that could be motive!"

For a brief moment Jack thought he saw tears in the aging attorney's weary eyes. It was obvious that this was very personal to Miles. After all, Michael Swanson was not just a client to Miles. Grief was taking its tragic toll on Michael Swanson's friend.

"Gentlemen, my hands are tied. I want this case solved as much if not more than you do. My primary obligation, however, is to protect the family and the estate. I simply have nothing else to contribute to your investigation at this time."

It was clear that the attorney was not going to budge. For now, it was best to drop the matter until they had solid evidence to support their theories about an affair.

Lose the battle to win the war, Jack thought to himself.

"Of course, Miles," Jack said calmly. "We do appreciate your cooperation."

He stood up, silently announcing that the meeting was over. He reached out to Miles and shook his hand.

"Thank you for seeing us. I do apologize for the intrusion."

He and Dan walked towards the office door. Miles followed them out, making idle conversation as they walked back to the reception area. After saying goodbye, the two detectives left the law office and headed towards the elevator.

Neither spoke on the ride down to the main level. The Governor's mansion was going to be their next stop. The thought of that visit weighed heavily on both of them as they walked to Jack's car.

During the drive back to headquarters, they brainstormed about how to approach the situation. Alienating the Governor would be a fatal mistake, for the investigation and possibly for their careers.

They agreed that they needed to meet with the Chief to chart out a plan of action. Jack would make the call to the Chief's secretary to set it up for Monday. When they drove into the parking garage, Jack dropped Dan off at his car.

Jack climbed the stairs to his office. Stephanie was already gone for the weekend, so Jack scanned her desk for any sign of messages.

He didn't see any, so he proceeded to his office to make the call to the Chief.

When no one answered, Jack looked at his watch. Since it was after five, he would have to call back on Monday morning. He gathered notes from the case that he wanted to review over the weekend.

As he started to walk down the hallway to the elevator, he stopped and smiled. He pulled his worn brown leather wallet from his back pocket and fished out a wrinkled piece of paper.

Tonight, Jack thought, *might be a good night to get to know Sara Bronstein better!*

CHAPTER 14

The muffled chimes from the old grandfather clock in the living room quietly announced that it was three o'clock. Jack turned and peered through tired eyes at his alarm clock. Groaning, he rolled over and tried to fall back to sleep.

By almost four o'clock it was obvious that was not going to happen. He made his way to the kitchen for some cold water. The notes he had been reviewing the evening before were still sprawled out across the kitchen table.

Sara had been getting ready to go to work when he called her on Friday evening. Her shift ended at seven on Saturday morning. She suggested that they meet for dinner at the Italian restaurant near the hospital that evening. Sara could not remember the name of the quaint little hideaway, but Jack knew where it was.

She sounded excited, he thought to himself. He wasn't as nervous as he thought he would be – yet, anyway. As he leaned against the sink, he slowly swallowed the last bit of water from the bottle he grabbed from the refrigerator.

He placed the empty container on the counter and made a mental note to take it outside in the morning – the *real* morning. He walked over to the table and sat down to review more of the case files.

In past cases he had found it helpful to review the lives of the victims to determine if there was anyone who stood out as a possible suspect. Jack's previous reviews of the files on the family had only revealed that, like their parents, the Swanson sisters led lives that could withstand the closest scrutiny.

Still, Jack thought, *maybe something would stand out this time. There might be someone they did not know who envied them or resented them for their family's good fortune. This would not be the first time a total stranger killed someone wealthy or famous because of jealousy.*

He had reviewed police reports from a year before the murders in the hopes of finding a report of a stalker. No complaints had been filed by any member of the Swanson family.

Jack was trying not to be discouraged by his findings. After all, it would be easier to find a perpetrator who knew the family than it would be to find a random killer. In theory, anyway. The pages stared back at him as he turned his attention to the file on Melody Swanson.

If she did have an affair, it was so long ago that Jack was beginning to wonder if it had anything to do at all with the case. Why would someone wait so long to exact revenge, if that was the motive behind the slaughters?

And why would they go after *all* of the girls? Jack was beginning to think that the murders had nothing at all to do with Melody's alleged indiscretions. He was convinced the Swanson sisters were undoubtedly the target – but why?

Jack sighed. He had danced this dance in his head so many times before. He always seemed to end up in the same place. It was a little like having one foot nailed to the floor and walking in circles around it.

He plucked the files on the three girls from the piles of paper on his kitchen table.

After pushing the rest of the folders to the corner of the table, Jack opened the file that contained the details of the eldest Swanson sister's life.

Elizabeth Marie Swanson. At five feet four inches tall, with dark brown hair and deep brown eyes she looked remarkably like her mother. After she attended an Ivy League school on an academic scholarship, she worked for her father's software corporation upon graduation. By the time Beth was twenty-six she was the Vice President of Sales.

Beth shared her parent's passion for helping those less fortunate. She was involved in almost all of the same charities her parents were active in and still made time to serve in the soup kitchen at St. Bartholomew's Church.

Jack winced after he read that. He hadn't been back to church since Shelby died. Father Walter had called him dozens of times after the funeral, but Jack never returned his calls. He thought sadly about how much Shelby loved Father Walter.

He pushed aside his guilt and gazed back at the file in front of him. He searched through the pages outlining the details of Beth's work at the software company. Jack scoured the file hoping to find someone who had a conflict in any way with the Swanson's eldest daughter.

A secretary by the name of Jackie Hartzell had motive. After the employee failed to complete several projects Beth was forced to write her up for performance issues. Hartzell responded by running her keys down the sides of Beth's car. The vandalism occurred about eighteen months before the murders.

The crime was captured by the security cameras in the parking garage of the software corporation. Hartzell was arrested and fired on the spot. At a pre-trial hearing, the former employee agreed to make full restitution. When the repairs to her car were completed, Beth dropped the charges.

According to the investigator's interview with the former employee, Hartzell had been in Pennsylvania visiting an ailing parent at the time of the attack. Her alibi was verified by a rookie cop by the name of Austin James.

Jack knew Austin James. He was a young guy out of the police academy for a little over two years. His work was thorough and the report was detailed. Jack was confident it was accurate.

As he examined Hartzell's mug shot from the arrest, Jack doubted that she was capable of such a violent attack. Although he knew appearances could be deceiving, Jack also had an eye for the physical capabilities of potential suspects. Hartzell just did not seem to fit the bill. Even with an accomplice he just didn't believe she was capable of murder. Not this one, anyway.

Interactions with other employees proved to be insignificant. Interviews conducted with Beth's employees revealed that Beth was a popular manager who was respected and well liked by employees and other managers as well.

Jack turned his attention to Beth's personal relationships for the two years prior to her death. Although she dated frequently, Beth did not have a steady suitor. Three men were interviewed during the initial phase of the investigation.

Tom Rose, Michael Anthony and Paul Alan each knew Beth from their high school years at Thomas Johnson Preparatory Academy. Rose and Alan had been on the high school football team together and were both active in student government. Anthony had been captain of the wrestling team and editor of the school newspaper. The four of them had all been very close throughout their high school years.

All three of the men attended different colleges and secured jobs in the Meadowbrook area after they graduated. Their relationships with Beth were casual, more friendly than romantic. No history of conflict with either Beth or each other was uncovered during the interviews.

Only Anthony was in town when the murders took place. He was at a bachelor party in honor of his brother during the hours of the attack, a fact that was verified by at least thirty witnesses. None of her three male companions could think of any reason for someone to hurt Beth or any of her sisters.

Jack turned his attention to the hundreds of interviews with people Beth knew from church and from the numerous social and charitable activities she was active with. He had already highlighted anything that he found interesting during his prior reviews of the files. Nothing stood out as he reviewed the pages again.

The second folder he reviewed was the file on Stacey Ann Swanson. The Swanson's second daughter was as polished and refined as her elder sister. She had also attended an Ivy League university on a full academic scholarship.

When she graduated Stacey started her own graphic design company that grew steadily until the time of her death. Jack briefly considered the possibility of a jealous competitor but quickly ruled it out. A competitor would have had no reason to attack all three girls. Jack scanned each page slowly, hoping some detail would jump out at him.

Like Beth, Stacey had been popular and enjoyed participating in many of her parent's charity events. She favored her father in appearance with her blond hair and blue eyes. According to people who knew her well she shared her mother's deep sense of compassion.

He read over all of the interviews conducted with her employees, colleagues, social acquaintances and friends. Everyone seemed to share the same sense of disbelief that either she or any of her sisters could be the victims of such a violent crime. Jack found nothing in the prior interview notes to suggest that anyone had a motive to kill her.

Finally, he turned his attention to the notes on the Swanson's third daughter. Madeline Ruth Swanson was only twenty-one years old when she was slain. Hers was another example of a life well lived. Unfortunately, the boating accident robbed the young woman of her mind. Her killer stole the rest of her life.

Jack marveled at how much she had resembled her mother. Her serious brown eyes gazed back at him as he looked into the face of another young woman who had been taken too soon.

He closed his eyes and tried to forget how she looked as the medics wheeled her out of the house. She had survived the brutal ordeal only to die days later at the hospital. Jack wondered if that was just coincidence, or if there was a reason she had been left alive.

Madeline was to begin a career as a college professor, the youngest Milford University had ever hired. Unfortunately, she never had the opportunity after the boating accident that left her permanently brain damaged.

Jack could not imagine why anyone would want to kill her. She was so mentally incapacitated from her injuries that she no longer had any connection with her life prior to the accident.

Once again he was left with no solid leads. He found no motive, no opportunity and another dead end. Jack sighed as he placed the folder on top of the pile at the corner of the table. He was exhausted. The grandfather clock chimed eight times, reminding him that he could still get a few hours of sleep.

Forcing himself to block out the details of the investigation, Jack dragged himself to his bedroom and climbed back into his waiting bed. As his body gave into fatigue, he let his thoughts turn to his dinner with Sara later that evening. Jack smiled as he slipped off into blissful rest.

CHAPTER 15

Saturday. Stirring slightly, Jack tried to move but his body wasn't cooperating. He forced one eye open and moved around just enough to see the clock. Sleep stubbornly clouded his vision so the time was obscured.

Jack sighed. He knew he should get up soon. There were so many things he had been meaning to do around the house. If Shelby were here, she would never have let them slide like he had. She liked her house to be neat, always ready for a friend to stop in for a cup of coffee or a bite to eat. He cringed a little, thinking he should be a lot more like her.

He stretched and yawned as he rose from the bed. Dragging himself slowly to the bathroom, he glanced wearily back at the alarm clock. Almost three o'clock.

Three o'clock! Suddenly, Jack was wide awake. He was meeting Sara at the Italian place in four hours. A million thoughts went racing through his mind all at once.

Breathe, he thought to himself. *Just breathe.*

After a few deep breaths he was able to focus again. What really needed to be done before he met Sara?

Jack counted off four things that had to happen before seven o'clock: he needed to shave and shower, he had to find something to wear, he had to wash the car inside and out, and he really needed to get a hair cut.

No problem. There was a car wash right near his barber, and almost a block away was a shop where he could buy a new pair of casual pants. He would wear a white shirt with a tweed jacket and boots. Shelby always liked that look on him.

He shaved quickly and jumped into the shower. Jack usually liked to wake up slowly with a long, hot shower but he had given up that luxury today by over sleeping. It was a small price to pay. He had been exhausted.

Jack was glad he had to focus on the tasks at hand. That way he didn't have to think too much about tonight. Not thinking was good. He would not have a chance to think about how nervous he was. It had been many, many years since he had been out on a date. *A date!* Jack sighed.

He jumped into a pair of jeans and a sweatshirt and headed off to the barber. About twenty minutes later he was pulling into the busy parking lot. He mentally checked off his chores one by one as they were completed and found his car heading back home by six o'clock.

He walked quickly into the house with his package cradled neatly under his arm. Jack hastily donned the dark brown pants he had just purchased. Tucking in the tails of his off-white shirt, his eyes caught his new hair cut in the mirror.

"Looks like I just got a haircut," he said to his reflection.

Jack frowned. Upon closer inspection he noted a hint of grey trying to crowd its way into his dark brown hair. Oh well. Maybe the restaurant will be dark and Sara won't notice.

By the time he slipped on his tweed jacket and cowboy boots, it was nearly twenty minutes until seven. Perfect. He had just enough time to make it to the restaurant a few minutes early. After one more look in the mirror, he was off.

As he backed out of his driveway, he thought about how Sara's eyes seemed to capture the light at every angle. She had a pretty smile. Jack was sure Shelby would approve. If she were alive, he imagined that she and Sara would be friends. It made him a little sad to think that the only reason he was going to spend time with Sara was that Shelby was gone.

He pulled into the parking lot and looked around to see if Sara was there. He didn't see her dark blue sedan. He put his turn signal on and waited for an elderly man to back his truck out of the parking space. When the spot was finally open, Jack skillfully navigated his car into the space. He took one last look at himself in the rear view mirror.

She's just another person, he thought to himself as he rubbed his sweaty palms on his slacks. *Just another person.*

Sure she is.

He got out and walked towards the restaurant. It looked busy, but not over crowded. He noted several couples that appeared to be waiting already.

Shouldn't be too long of a wait though, he thought. *I should have made a reservation.*

As he stepped up onto the curb his gaze turned towards the entrance. Sara smiled brightly as their eyes met, her face glowing from the light reflected from the window. Jack couldn't help but smile back as he made his way to where she was standing.

"Hi, Jack!" she said, a little shyly, he thought.

It made him feel a little more at ease. She was wearing her hair down this evening. Blond curls teased her shoulders as she spoke. He liked that.

"Hi!" he replied, hoping he didn't sound over anxious. "I hope you haven't been waiting long."

"Oh, no," she assured him. "I just arrived myself. I put your name on the list. It shouldn't be long at all now."

She smiled up at him, and he felt his heart melting as he smiled back. Almost immediately the hostess appeared to escort them to their table. Without hesitation Jack placed his hand on the small of Sara's back as they followed the young woman to the back of the restaurant. He held her chair for her then sat down across from her.

Jack watched as Sara neatly placed her napkin across her lap. He liked how the deep blue sparkles in her dress shimmered in the light from the candles. Every time she smiled he felt more at ease. A tall, slender red head promptly appeared at their table. She smiled broadly as she introduced herself.

"Good evening," she said brightly. "My name is Anna and I'll be serving you this evening. Would you like to see a wine list?"

They settled on the house white wine. Anna took their dinner orders and left to get their wine and bread. Sara shifted slightly in the high backed chair. Jack could see she was a little nervous. He was relieved. At least he wasn't the only one.

"So, Sara, what brought you to Virginia?"

"Well, actually," she said, speaking slowly and a little softer now. "I was engaged once. My boyfriend was a Lieutenant in the Army."

"We don't have to talk about this, Sara," Jack said as he laid his hand gently on top of hers.

He saw the pain in her eyes and her body language told him that whatever happened still hurt. He regretted asking her the question.

"That's okay, Jack," Sara replied sadly. "It's part of my life. I want to tell you."

She took in a breath then looked in his eyes.

"He was sent to Desert Storm. He was only there for six months, but when he came back, everything had changed. *He* changed. He called off the wedding and I haven't heard from him since."

"I'm sorry, Sara. I really am."

Jack didn't know what else to say. Sara reached over and gently touched his arm. She looked intently into his eyes.

"It's alright, Jack," Sara said softly. "We all have pain, right? We just have to learn how to work through it and move on with our lives."

Jack nodded as he looked into her somber face. He couldn't help but think that they were both just casualties of different wars.

Anna arrived with their entrees and their conversation moved back to happier subjects as they devoured their delicious pasta and seafood dinner. Shortly after they finished Anna appeared to remove their empty plates. They declined her offer to show them dessert menus and settled for coffee instead. For another half an hour they talked and laughed as if they were old friends.

Finally, the waitress collected their empty cups and laid a black leather folder with the check near Jack. He placed money in the folder and he and Sara left the restaurant.

There was a slight chill in the air, but they hardly noticed anything except each other. Jack gently took Sara's hand in his and they walked slowly along the row of boutiques near the restaurant. They laughed and talked for a long time, neither wanting the evening to end.

Finally, they reached the last of the shops. Jack knew that Sara had an early shift at the hospital, so it was time to call it a night. They strolled slowly to her car, where they talked and laughed for another half an hour. Eventually, they knew it was time to say good night.

"I had so much fun tonight, Jack," Sara said gently.

She looked down, then glanced shyly back up at his smiling face.

"Me, too," Jack said.

He wanted to take her in his arms and kiss her. In his mind he could feel her body against him, his lips pressed on hers. But his heart wouldn't let him do it. Not now. Not yet.

He took her hand and gently kissed it. The look in her eyes said she was disappointed, but she graciously thanked him again for a wonderful evening. He promised to call her as he helped her into her car. They talked for a few more minutes. He waved as she finally she drove off into the darkness.

Jack walked back to his car slowly, recalling the details of the evening. He unlocked his car door and climbed in. After he started the engine he closed his eyes, letting the sweet memories sink in. The night hadn't been as difficult as he thought it would be. He found himself smiling the whole way home.

As he pulled into the garage, Jack concluded that the evening was a success. He was trying to decide when he would call her next. Dan and Jennifer were going to have a backyard party in a few weeks, but Jack did not want to wait that long.

When he walked into the living room, the grandfather clock gently chided him for staying out until one in the morning. He knew he should be exhausted but he was wide awake. Adrenaline was surging through his veins.

Jack looked around at the chores that he had been neglecting. He winced. It would take hours to clean this mess up. For the next three hours he cleaned until his energy finally ran out. He felt better knowing that his home was ready to receive visitors, whenever he was ready to extend the invitation.

Jack placed the cleaning supplies he had been using back in the closet. He tossed the filthy towels he used into the laundry basket, which he was certain was groaning under the mounds of dirty clothes. He sighed. Tomorrow is another day.

He made his way into the bedroom and sat on the bed by the night stand. Tenderly Jack picked up Shelby's picture.

"She's nice, honey," he said sadly to the beautiful face staring silently back at him.

He placed his fingers on his own lips and kissed them gently. Then he placed his fingers on her lips.

"I miss you, babe."

CHAPTER 16

Almost as soon as Jack sat down at his desk on Monday morning he was on the phone with Chief Sheppard's secretary. A pleasant, middle-aged woman, Judy Lane had been with the Chief for much of his career on the force.

"Good morning, Judy," Jack said cheerily. "How's the Chief's right arm today?"

Judy laughed. She held a tender spot in her heart for Jack. She and Shelby belonged to the Meadowbrook Garden Club for many years before Shelby passed away. Judy still missed her dear friend.

"And a good morning to you, detective!" she replied. "You're very chipper today. Are you up to something?"

Jack could hear the smile in her voice. He chuckled to himself as he pictured the gleam in her eyes and the smile on her lovely face. She was a gentle soul who loved to tease him, and he enjoyed teasing her right back.

"Why, Judy, whatever do you mean?" he protested innocently.

They both laughed. She was glad to hear the smile in his voice. After his wife died it had taken a long time for him to laugh again. *It's good to hear,* Judy thought to herself, *and a long time coming.*

"Dan and I need some time with the Chief today. What's he got open?"

Jack waited patiently for Judy's response.

"He has some time this afternoon, Jack. Will an hour be sufficient?"

"We might need a little more time, Judy. Can you fit us in for an hour and a half?"

Jack hated to ask, but he knew that they would need time to come up with a solid plan for approaching the Governor.

"I can move his one o'clock meeting to three o'clock. That will open up two hours. Will that do?"

"You're a gem, Judy!" Jack said.

He thanked her and smiled as he hung up. Jack called Dan and arranged to meet him in the conference room to review the Swanson crime scene photos again.

There were a handful of bystanders whose alibis still needed to be verified. Jack had requested that two rookie cops who had assisted during the initial weeks of the investigation be assigned to him to complete the task.

The young men had been extremely thorough when they conducted prior interviews. Jack respected that. He was confident they would be able to rule out these remaining spectators as suspects as well. The rookies were to report to him at nine. Jack was getting ready to walk over to the conference room when Dan popped his head into the office.

"Need a refill?" he asked, as he held up his coffee cup.

"Just got one," Jack replied.

He scooped up a handful of file folders, grabbed his steaming coffee mug and walked to the door. He and Dan talked about their meeting with the Chief as they walked down the hall, trying to find a way around investigating the Governor.

When they reached the conference room, they examined the boxes of photographs that were waiting for them. Dan rifled through the files to find the photographs they wanted to review with the rookies while Jack pulled out their initial reports.

As Jack and Dan were sorting through pictures, Austin James knocked on the conference room door. His partner, Shane Cook, stood next to him.

"Right on time," Jack said with a smile.

He had expected nothing less.

"Come on in, men."

Jack motioned for the young policemen to enter the room. He could tell the rookies were eager for the chance to work on the case again. It seemed personal to them, although Jack was not sure why.

"You remember Dan Meyer, right?" Jack asked, as he shook their hands.

They both nodded and shook Dan's hand. Jack motioned for them to sit down. He moved a few boxes out of the way and laid out folders for them to review.

The four men spent the next two hours looking at pictures of the spectators outside of the house the night of the murders. The police photographer had done an excellent job of capturing images of the crowd that grew larger as word of the murders spread rapidly throughout the community.

"As you know," Jack began, "there is a strong possibility that the perpetrator might have been among the spectators. Most of the people in the photographs have already been identified and ruled as suspects."

James and Cook did know. Establishing the identities and whereabouts of most of the onlookers was their first assignment when they were transferred to the homicide division. The interviews consumed countless hours during the first few weeks of the investigation. The rookies had been pulled off the case when a hit and run involving a diplomat's son required extra hands.

Only seven alibis remained to be verified. Jack opened a folder and removed a photograph which he laid on the table in front of James and Cook. They listened intently as one by one Jack and Dan discussed what they knew about each of the seven people.

"David Olsen heads up the crew of mechanics that maintains the fleet of vehicles owned and operated by the county. He's been there for over thirty years. Olsen is a large man, certainly strong enough to commit the murders, but he has no motive as far as we know."

Jack held the picture up so James and Cook could see it.

"He appeared at the scene in overalls stained with oil and grease. There are no signs of blood anywhere on his clothing in these pictures. The horrified expression on his face appears to be genuine, I believe."

The rookies nodded in agreement.

"The next person," Jack continued, "is Brooke Meininger, a personal trainer at the gym where the Swanson family belonged. At five feet ten inches tall, someone in her excellent physical condition could possibly have done it, especially considering that the victims were drugged."

"We know that Meininger was friends with Beth and Madeline since Elementary School," Dan said. "Prior inquiries into her relationship with the Swanson sisters did not uncover any history of conflict."

"I remember her," James said. "She was in shock and seemed genuinely upset. She didn't strike me as the type to do something like this."

"Perhaps not," Dan said. "Maybe she'll remember something about the family or about someone who might have had a problem with any of the sisters."

Jack nodded his head in agreement as he laid her picture to the side and picked up the next one.

"This woman is Sharon Hayes," he said. "She is a high school physics teacher who is pretty popular with all of her students. She has a reputation for being one of the best teachers in Meadowbrook."

"It's doubtful she has either the physical strength or the emotional capacity to have carried out the murders," he added. "From this photograph I'd say her grief appears to be sincere."

Again, the young police officers nodded. Dan slid a picture of a lone figure standing a short distance away from the rest of the crowd towards the rookies. The small, slight wisp of a man almost seemed oblivious to the onlookers a short distance from where he stood.

He was wearing blue jeans and a faded denim jacket over a green flannel shirt. A dark substance lightly stained the jacket and jeans as if something had splattered on them. The pictures weren't clear enough to reveal what the stains were from.

"This man," Dan said, "is Tim Woods. I'm guessing he's in his early twenties. He does odd jobs for several of the local residents, possibly including the Swanson's. He stays to himself, kind of a strange bird from what we understand. No one seems to know much about him."

"Woods told the policeman who initially interviewed him that he was home alone when the young women were killed. His alibi will be difficult to prove. Even so, his small stature would make it virtually impossible for him to have committed these heinous crimes."

"If the women were drugged, maybe he could have," Cook said thoughtfully. "But did he even know them?"

Jack smiled. He liked these young guys. He liked the way they thought things through.

"That's what you're going to find out," he replied, with a twinkle in his eyes.

Dan winked at Jack, trying to keep his smile hidden. Cook blushed. He hoped his embarrassment wasn't showing.

Of course that's what we're here for, he thought to himself. *Good going, rookie!*

The next photograph Jack showed them was a picture of a middle-aged couple standing next to a tree. They were huddled together with their arms around each other.

"Robert and Elise Duncan own the local dry cleaners," Dan said. "They had been dining at the Back Porch Ale House that evening, one of the more elegant restaurants in the area. They are well regarded in the community. The Swanson's sent their dry cleaning to them. As far as we know that's their only connection to the family."

"Robert Duncan had back surgery about six weeks prior to the murders," Dan continued. "He was still walking with a cane at the time of

114

the murders, which is documented in the crime scene photos. Elise is barely five feet tall. Even together they probably could not have pulled off such a brutal crime."

"The couple said they had been heading home when dozens of police cars and ambulances raced past them," Jack said. "They followed out of curiosity and joined the slew of onlookers outlining the rows of crime scene tape surrounding the Swanson's property. It's possible that with their connections in the community they may have heard something that could be helpful to the investigation."

Jack handed James the last picture from the folder.

"The final spectator whose alibi has not been verified is Steve Wilson," he said. "At six feet four inches, Wilson's size might have made him a person of interest had it not been for the stroke he suffered two years ago that left his right side weak. He also has no discernable motive."

"You'll need to verify his claim that he had been at the movies with his wife Caroline earlier that evening. He said his wife was asleep when he first heard the sirens."

The photograph taken at the scene showed Wilson standing by himself dressed in pajamas covered by a bath robe. Although he was surrounded by dozens of people, his wife was not among them.

"We'd like you to talk with each of these people and interview anyone who can verify their whereabouts from between six and eleven o'clock the night of the murders."

Jack gathered the photographs and notes and placed them into the file folder closest to him.

"These loose ends need to be tied up as quickly as possible," Dan added. "None of these people had any reason to want to harm the Swanson sisters as far as we know. Frankly, we don't believe you'll find anything here, but we want to be sure all of this information is verified. Any questions?" he asked as he placed the photographs in the file and extended the folder to Austin.

"No, sir," James replied.

"No sir," Cook chimed in, shaking his head.

James accepted the file folder from Jack. The rookies stood up and shook hands with the detectives and said their goodbyes, heading off to begin their investigation.

Jack and Dan began to discuss their meeting with the Chief. By the time they had prepared their agenda for the conference it was almost noon. The two detectives ducked down to the cafeteria to grab a quick bite to eat. Potentially naming the Governor of Virginia a person of interest in a murder investigation was not something to be done on an empty stomach.

CHAPTER 17

By one o'clock Jack and Dan were seated in the reception area of Chief Sheppard's office. The Chief was on the telephone, so Judy offered the men coffee, which they accepted gratefully. After a few minutes, Judy looked up from her computer and smiled.

"Chief Sheppard will see you now, gentlemen," she announced brightly.

They thanked her and entered the office of the Chief of Police, leaving their coffee cups behind. Awards and accommodations covered the walls of his office along with pictures of community events and his family. Paul Sheppard was a popular and well-respected civil servant, known as a devoted family man who cared deeply about Meadowbrook.

They greeted each other and the Chief waved his hand at the empty seats in front of his desk. The three men sat down and exchanged brief pleasantries as they made themselves comfortable.

"So," the Chief stated, "you're ready to meet with Governor Langford?"

His brow was furrowed as his tone grew serious.

"Let me hear what you've got."

For almost an hour, Jack and Dan recounted the results of their investigation into the relationship between the Swanson's and the Governor. They painstakingly reviewed the details of the journals and their suspicions of what might be contained in the journal that was still missing.

Jack related the timeline from the first time the Swanson's met Langford to the last time they were photographed together in public. He showed the Chief the connection to the entries made towards the end of the second journal.

The Chief listened somberly as Dan reluctantly conveyed the rumors from many years ago that had circulated through the floors of Meadowbrook General Hospital. Both detectives acknowledged that what they had were a lot of suspicions and not enough facts.

Even still, what they had uncovered so far seemed to point in the direction of the Governor's mansion. Talking to Langford seemed to be a logical next step. Chief Sheppard sighed as he solemnly shook his head from side to side.

"It isn't enough, men," he said. "There is no hard evidence. We can't march up there and make accusations based on innuendo and circumstantial evidence. I'm sure you know what a nightmare that would be."

The detectives nodded their heads in agreement. Jack leaned forward in his chair.

"We know that, sir," he said soberly, "and we aren't ready to make any accusations. But the Governor may have knowledge about the Swanson's that could help us determine who killed their daughters. If he had a close relationship with the family, he might know who would have wanted to hurt them."

"If he did have an affair with Melody Swanson, that could also be motive," Dan added. "We have to look at that possibility, even though the affair would have taken place so many years ago."

"That's right," Jack agreed. "Marital infidelity would definitely threaten the Governor's reputation and career even after all of these years. If it turns out that Megan Swanson was actually Langford's daughter and that became public knowledge, it could mean the end of his political career – and possibly his marriage. And that, sir, is definitely motive."

The Chief sat silently with his hands folded as he listened to the detectives lay out their reasons for wanting to meet with the Governor. He knew it was a necessary step, but he also knew it had to be handled with kid gloves. If anyone could do that well it was Jack Russell and Dan Meyer.

"As I see it," the Chief began, "we have two issues. The first is how to approach the Governor in a friendly, non-threatening way to find out what he knows about the Swanson's and to get a feel for his relationship with them."

"That's right," Jack said. "We'd also like to find out what Michael Swanson contributed to his campaigns. We know about his financial contributions, but we don't know if he aided the Governor in any other ways."

"And we need to delicately probe for details about his relationship with Melody," Dan added, "which is dangerous territory."

"Agreed," the Chief nodded and frowned. "I find it doubtful he will appreciate being associated with these murders. You're going to have to dance around these topics very lightly. He's a smart man. He might become defensive as soon as you start asking questions, especially if they did have an affair."

119

"We have to keep him on our side," Jack said gravely. "The last thing we want to do is alienate him."

"Certainly," the Chief agreed. "But I know Lawrence Langford. He's a fair man. He understands the work that needs to be done to solve crimes. Even if your questions touch a nerve, he's not the type to hold a grudge or retaliate. Let's give him the benefit of the doubt. Innocent until proven guilty, right?"

Jack and Dan nodded. The Chief was right. They had no hard evidence. All they had were a lot of questions. The only way to get the answers was to talk it out with the source. Hopefully, the Governor was the type of man the Chief said he was, the man the people of Virginia believed him to be.

"Wait a minute," Jack said. "What's the second issue?"

The Chief smiled and the twinkle he was famous for flashed in his eyes.

"Why, we have to find a way to distract your lady friend from the newspaper, of course!"

Jack blushed and shook his head in embarrassment as Dan and the Chief burst out laughing.

"Of course," Jack snickered. "My gal Lisa Vick!"

The skillful reporter was particularly proficient at tailing someone without being detected. If she discovered that Jack and Dan were headed to the Governor's mansion, she would be on them like bees on honey. Rumor had it she had an insider in police headquarters, although no one seemed to know who it was.

"Leave our reporter friend to me," the Chief said confidently. "I'll take care of her. Just tell Judy when you'll be meeting with the Governor and I'll do the rest."

The three men concluded their meeting with promises of getting together for golf in the near future. Jack and Dan thanked the Chief for his time and made their way out to the corridor.

"What do you think?" Dan asked.

"Well," Jack replied, "we didn't solve anything, but at least the Chief agrees that it's time to talk to the Governor. I agree with his 'tread lightly' approach. I wish we had more concrete information to work with, though."

Dan nodded reluctantly. He did not completely share Jack's confidence that meeting with Langford was the way to go. He trusted Jack's judgment, though, and the Chief's as well.

The two detectives returned to Jack's office and discussed what information they were hoping to obtain from the Governor, and how they would pose the questions. When they had an outline prepared, Jack picked up the phone to call the Governor's secretary.

"Governor Langford's office. This is Belinda speaking. How may I direct your call?"

The voice of the switchboard operator was young, friendly and confident. Jack liked that.

"I'd like to speak with the Governor, please," he answered, knowing full well he would be re-directed to the Governor's secretary.

"One moment, please."

After a series of clicks another voice came on the line. This time, the woman who answered sounded older and more professional.

"This is Miss Fenwick. How may I help you?"

"Miss Fenwick, this is Detective Jack Russell of the Meadowbrook Police Department. My partner and I would like to arrange a time to sit down with the Governor. Can you tell me when we might be able to do that?"

Jack listened intently as the woman briefly paused.

"Let me check the schedule for you, Detective. Will you hold, please?"

"Of course," Jack replied, curious at the hesitation he detected in her voice.

He wondered if she knew why he was calling, then promptly dismissed the thought. *How could she?* Jack thought to himself as he cast the idea aside. After listening to almost an entire symphony he was relieved when the woman finally returned to the line.

"Unfortunately, Detective Russell, the Governor's schedule is full this week. I can fit you in next Tuesday at three in the afternoon, if that works for you, but he only has thirty minutes available."

"That will be just fine, Miss Fenwick," Jack replied.

He wasn't sure it was enough time, but then again, he wasn't sure how their conversation was going to go, either. For now, thirty minutes would have to do. He thanked her and hung up. It was almost five o'clock. Jack rarely left the office before six, but today, he would make an exception. Just as he was

122

clearing his desk his secretary popped her head into the room.

"You have a call on line three," Stephanie said with a smile. "She says her name is Sara Bronstein. Is there anything else I can do for you before I go home?"

Stephanie noticed how quickly Jack sat up when he heard Sara Bronstein's name. She smiled to herself, hoping this was a personal call.

"Would you please call Judy and let her know that Dan and I have a meeting set up next Tuesday at three o'clock with the Governor?" Jack asked quickly.

He hoped that Stephanie hadn't noticed his excitement when she told him about Sara's waiting call. She had.

"Sure thing, Jack! Anything else?" she asked, waiting patiently for him to reply.

"That's all, thanks." Jack replied gruffly.

Stephanie smiled and said goodnight as she returned to her desk to make the call. Jack took a deep breath then calmly picked up the phone.

"Hello. This is Detective Russell," he said confidently. "How can I help you?"

CHAPTER 18

"Wow!" the delicate voice on the other end of the line exclaimed. "That sounded very professional!"

Jack laughed as he imagined Sara's smiling face.

"And how can I be of service to you this evening, Miss Bronstein?" he asked, hoping she couldn't tell that he was grinning from ear to ear.

"Well, Detective," she replied. "I was hoping to talk you into meeting me at Madelyn's for a bite to eat. You need to keep up your strength, you know!"

Jack laughed again.

"You sound like Jennifer!" he exclaimed. "What time did you have in mind?"

"Actually," she said, a little sheepishly. "How does right now work for you?"

"I believe I can work that into my schedule," he said, amused by her directness.

"Great! Then I haven't wasted the trip!"

Jack looked up just as she walked into his office, her cell phone still held up to her ear. He smiled and hung up as she closed her phone and put it in her purse.

"I hope you don't mind," Sara said, apologetically. "But I was right around the corner running some errands and I remembered that Jennifer said you eat here by yourself almost every night. That can't be good for you!"

Jack made a mental note to thank Jennifer someday as he stood up and walked around his desk. He removed his jacket from the back of the door.

"You're right! Let's get out of here!" he said with a smile.

Jack slung his jacket over his shoulder. They walked down the hall chatting light-heartedly. Madelyn's was just a short walk from the station. In no time at all they were seated and looking at menus. A familiar face appeared at the table to take their drink orders.

"And how are you tonight, Detective?" the waitress chirped brightly.

Sonya was a favorite among the regular patrons of Madelyn's. She was sharp and knew most of her customers by name and profession after the first time she waited on them.

"I'm great, Sonya, and how are you?"

Jack could see the waitress was curious about the woman sitting across from him. She hadn't seen him with a woman since his wife died.

"Busy as always!" she replied, smiling brightly.

"Sonya, this is my friend Sara."

Jack turned his hand towards his dinner companion. Sonya reached over and shook Sara's hand.

"Welcome!" she said graciously. "You're a nurse, right? I remember you from the last blood drive."

"I am," Sara replied. "I'm surprised you remember me. There are always so many people at the hospital blood drives!"

"Well," Sonya said, her face flushed with embarrassment. "I got a little lightheaded and almost fainted. I tend to remember people who keep me from falling flat on my face!"

The three laughed and Sonya took their drink orders. In just a few moments she returned and placed glasses of iced tea in front of the couple. After they made their dinner selections Sonya disappeared into the kitchen.

"She's very nice," Sara said, leaning her head slightly.

"She's one of the best things about coming here!" Jack said. "Well, her and the wings, of course!"

They laughed and settled into a conversation about their respective days. Sonya returned with their steak dinners and refilled their glasses with sweet tea. As she walked away she greeted another familiar face.

"Hello, Lisa! How've you been?"

Lisa Vick just waved as she walked past the waitress and headed directly for Jack's table. Before he knew it the reporter's tall frame was looming above him, leaving him no way to escape. Jack tried not to show his annoyance, but he was irritated. This was just like Lisa Vick to interrupt his personal life with her pursuit of professional advancement.

"Why, Detective Russell," she said sweetly. "What a coincidence running into you here! I hear you have a meeting with the Governor next week!"

Lisa smiled triumphantly as she stood directly next to the unhappy detective.

"Miss Vick," Jack responded, wisely refraining from calling her the name that was running through his mind. "It's a great night for a good dinner, isn't it?"

He was hoping she would just move on but, true to her nature, she remained solidly planted where she was. Jack was livid. How could she possibly know about the meeting? Not even an hour had passed since he made the appointment.

Jack was trying to decide how to get rid of her when Sonya appeared like a white knight from the crowd that had begun to fill the restaurant. The waitress politely excused herself as she gently nudged the reporter aside and placed an extra order of bread and butter on the table.

Sonya then began to tell Jack and Sara how sorry she was that they had run out of their first dinner requests. She insisted that she wanted to make it up to them by offering the couple free desserts.

Vick waited impatiently for the waitress to leave, but the shrewd journalist found herself being forced further and further away from their table by the moving flow of people heading towards the bar. She eventually gave up and disappeared into a sea of unfamiliar faces.

"That was masterful!" Jack exclaimed, clapping his hands. "I owe you!"

Sonya just laughed.

"I saw the look on your face when she came over," she said. "It was the least I could do! Sorry, but I can't *really* give you free desserts!"

She winked as she moved on to her next table. Sara looked at him curiously.

"So I'm guessing that woman is not a friend?" she asked, puzzled.

Jack explained who Lisa Vick was and described her brash style of reporting, especially where he was concerned. Sara's face grew serious.

"So *that's* Lisa Vick!" she exclaimed. "I've read her articles. She really crossed over the line a number of times. It's a shame a professional newspaper encourages that kind of irresponsible reporting!"

Jack took some comfort in the way Sara defended him. The darts Vick had thrown at him in the past had been piercing. Right now, though, he was angry that she had once again become privy to information that should have been kept confidential. He was even more irritated by the interruption of his time with Sara. Jack waved his hand and smiled, trying to make light of it.

"Well, she's gone for now so we can relax and enjoy our dinner!" he said, trying to sound unruffled by Vick's interruption.

Sara agreed. The couple enjoyed their meal while they talked and laughed together for the next hour. Finally, Sonya left their bill on the table and bade the couple goodnight. Jack reached for the check but Sara snatched it away before he could pick it up.

"Oh, no!" she insisted. "I invited you! I want to pay!"

She looked so serious that Jack laughed.

"Well, then, Sara. I thank you. I enjoyed our time together."

He laid his hand over hers. She smiled back. Jack could see a hint of a blush as she looked away. He had to admit that it felt good to flirt again. He thought Sara might agree.

After the bill was settled they left the restaurant hand in hand. They walked slowly to the garage where Sara's car was parked, talking and laughing along the way.

When Sara was safely on her way home, Jack walked to the level that his own car was parked on. He had kissed her hand again when they said goodnight, but this time, he didn't see disappointment in her face.

"She understands," Jack said out loud to himself.

He sighed as he wondered if life was meant to be as hard as it could be at times. He was just about to unlock his car door when a familiar voice called out his name.

"Jack Russell! It's been a very long time! How have you been, my friend?"

Jack swung around and looked straight into the smiling eyes of Father Walter Edward Benedict, the priest from Saint Bartholomew's Church.

CHAPTER 19

Father Walter Edward Benedict was a kind, soft spoken man with a reputation for his poignant messages and loving spirit. His quick wit often ignited the sparkle in his piercing blue eyes.

Jack first met Father Walter when he was investigating a homicide that had taken place in the alley a few blocks from the church. A man fitting the description of one of the parishioners from Saint Bartholomew's was seen fleeing the scene. Jack interviewed Father Walter to get background information on the suspect.

Jack and Shelby began dating shortly after the case was solved. The couple became very close to Father Walter while they helped served food to the homeless alongside other members of the parish.

When they became engaged the couple insisted that Father Walter perform their wedding mass, which he was delighted to do. Many of their guests declared that theirs was the most eloquent marriage ceremony they had ever experienced.

A touch of sadness tugged at Jack's heart as he looked into the face of this gentle man of God. He shifted his feet slightly and smiled.

"Father! How are you?" Jack exclaimed as he reached out to grip Father Walter's extended hand.

Father Walter pulled the detective in and hugged him like a son, holding him tightly for a few short moments.

"I am well, Jack my boy! And how are you?"

Jack sheepishly looked down as he moved away from Father Walter's embrace. He hadn't returned any of Father Walter's numerous telephone calls after the funeral. He brushed away the guilt and forced a smile.

"I've been well, Father, very well! What brings you out tonight?"

Jack had been taken by surprise at running into him. He hoped it wasn't obvious. If Father Walter noticed Jack's discomfort he did not acknowledge it. He talked to Jack as if it had only been a few days since their last conversation instead of several years.

"Do you remember Jan O'Brien, Jack?" Father Walter asked.

Jack nodded. Jan was a little older than he was. She had been caring for her wheelchair bound husband for many years. Jack remembered the smile on her face as she made her way into the sanctuary with him, navigating the chair as if it was an expensive vehicle carrying precious cargo.

"Frederick finally passed away last week. We were spending time this evening pondering the mysteries of God's ways. She's a woman of great faith, that one. Her trust in God is her rock."

Jack cringed at the mention of God. He had heard it all before, even believed it once, but it wasn't anything he was sure of now. Faith, trust, God.... He couldn't put it all together anymore.

What kind of a God would take away someone as amazing and loving as Shelby and leave murderers and rapists behind? Thinking about it made him crazy. Jack had finally

131

stopped trying to make sense of it all. It was too overwhelming to comprehend.

"I'm sorry to hear about his passing, Father," Jack answered, hoping he sounded sincere rather than cynical.

Father Walter nodded as he gazed intently into Jack's troubled eyes. He sensed Jack's confusion, but he also knew that Jack was not ready to open up yet, even after all of the time that had passed since Shelby died.

"We've missed you in church, son," he said gently.

Jack blushed and shifted again.

"I know, Father," Jack responded awkwardly. "I've been working on a rather important case and it has me tied up almost every day of the week."

It was true. Jack was becoming obsessed. Rare was the day that passed by when he wasn't working on the investigation for at least a few hours either at the office or at home.

"Hmmmm," the priest responded soberly, nodding his head. "That would be the Swanson case, I imagine?"

"Yes," Jack replied. "It's been a tough one."

Father Walter nodded again. He looked intently at Jack, wondering how much to tell him right now.

"We should talk about it sometime, Jack. You have the key, you know."

Jack thought about what he said.

"What do you mean?" he asked curiously.

He couldn't help but wonder what Father Walter was referring to. What was the key? Did he know about Melody Swanson and the Governor?

"Why don't you come by my office sometime and we'll chat for a while?"

The words sounded like a question but Jack knew it was more of a command. He agreed to call the church office and make an appointment in the very near future. As he heard himself say the words Jack wondered how he was going to get out of it.

"It was great to see you, Father," Jack said sincerely as he shook his hand.

"You too, my son," Father Walter replied. "I look forward to our visit."

The men turned and began to walk towards their cars. Father Walter swung around and watched for a moment as Jack walked away, his shoulders sagging.

"Jack," he called out.

Jack spun around at the sound of his name.

"Do you know the difference between faith and trust?"

The expression on his face told the priest that Jack was puzzled by the question.

"Faith, Jack, is believing that God can do anything He says He can."

He tried to look into Jack's eyes but the detective looked away. Father Walter continued his explanation.

"Trust is staying committed to God even if you don't get what you asked Him for, even when it looks and feels like He isn't there. Do you understand the difference, Jack?"

Jack didn't know how to respond. He simply shrugged his shoulders and waved his hand as he turned back to walk to his car. Father Walter turned and slowly moved towards his own car, his heart heavily burdened for his friend. Seeing the cloud of confusion Jack was under pained him greatly.

Father Walter returned to the parish hoping that Jack would somehow be able to release the heavy load that was crushing him. He prayed that God would help him find what he was looking for, and soon.

Jack dug his car keys out of his pocket as thoughts of Shelby began flowing through his mind, bringing with them a string of emotions he did not want to face. Tears flirted with his eyelids as he opened his car door.

"Focus," he chided himself furiously. "Just focus!"

He thought about what Father Walter had said about having the key as he drove the entire way home. What was the key? The affair? The Governor?

More questions, he thought to himself, irritated because of his confusion. *That's just what I need. More questions!*

As he parked his car in the garage, Jack decided to put it all out of his mind for the night. It was still early. Okay, maybe not so early, but he might be able to catch the end of the ball game.

He picked up his mail from the mailbox and walked through the front door into the living room. Darkness shrouded the weary detective as he chased away thoughts of the Swanson sisters and Father Walter.

Silence. Not even the grandfather clock greeted him as he flipped on the light switch. He laid the letters he had carried in on the end table and plopped onto the sofa. The remote beckoned to him from the floor, which was where he had left it the last time he watched television. He picked it up and began flipping through the channels.

The game had already ended but if he watched the news he might be able to catch the highlights. Aimlessly he pushed the buttons until he found a sports channel. He watched the highlights from the game as well as sports news from around the world.

Somewhere between a tennis match and a cycling competition his body gave in to exhaustion. Tempestuous dreams began to taunt him as he fell into a deep sleep. Visions of boats being chastised by angry waves chased restfulness far away from his tired frame.

Large raindrops shaped like skeleton keys began to pound the boats, causing dents and holes in the vessels that would eventually force them to sink to the bottom of the sea. In his dream Jack was grabbing at the keys, trying to stop them from causing further destruction.

"I have the key!" he cried out over and over again, trying to catch them before they made contact.

The keys evaded his reach and assaulted the boats again and again until finally obvious doom was upon him. One last key came hurling towards him, only this time he caught it and held it up like a prize. To his amazement it was the key that was left for him at the front desk of the police station, the one with the numbers 737 on it. He woke up with a start, his body shaking frantically and soaking wet with sweat.

"I have the key!"

CHAPTER 20

Jack was filled with excitement as he rushed to get ready for work. Still, he was a little frustrated. He should have known that the key was related to the Swanson case. He wanted to get to the office early to dig it out of the mountain of work he had been setting aside until 'later'.

Guess it's 'later', Jack thought sheepishly as he backed out of his driveway. Procrastination caught up with him once again. Driving to the police station in the wee hours of the morning had its advantages. With no traffic to contend with Jack arrived at headquarters faster than usual. He parked his car and walked briskly into the station.

Jack greeted the sergeant with a wave as he rushed past the front desk. The elevator was running particularly slowly this morning, but Jack was undeterred. His focus was on the key. If Father Walter knew what that key opened it would be worth the pain of meeting with him.

He would take Dan along. That might keep the conversation away from things Jack didn't want to talk about. It wasn't as if Jack had been deliberately avoiding the priest, after all. Okay. He *had* been. Jack sighed.

As he rounded the corner to his office, Jack felt his heart pounding, beating rapidly in his chest. He was almost trembling as he fumbled with his keys to unlock his office door.

"Could this be it?" he wondered out loud. "Could this be the break we've been looking for?"

He flipped on the light and walked to his desk. He waded through mounds of documents searching for the envelope that contained the tarnished key.

"Yes!" he exclaimed when he finally found the brown envelope.

He pulled the key out and looked at the number 737 written in black marker. Was it for a locker somewhere, like maybe a bus or train station? It didn't match the locks of local safety deposit boxes or post office boxes, but what about a gym locker somewhere? And how did Father Walter know about the key? Did he know about the affair – if there was one?

Jack shook his head as the questions kept coming. Hopefully they would have some answers after he and Dan met with the aging priest. A glance at his watch reminded Jack that the precinct gym would be opening soon. He placed the key in his desk drawer and locked it.

He removed his gym bag from the hook on the back of his office door and ran down the stairs to the locker room. Lately early morning workouts had become a chore for Jack. Today, however, he was pretty sure he had energy to spare.

By the time Jack returned to his office Dan had already stopped in and left a fruit pastry and a cup of fresh, steaming coffee on his desk. About a dozen packages of sugar were stacked neatly beside the tall cup.

Jack grinned as he thought about Dan's wife Jennifer. He wondered if she knew how much sugar her husband consumed in a single day. Jack picked up the phone and was dialing his number just as Dan poked his head into the office.

"Morning!" he said boldly in his usual cheerful manner. "You're here early. What's new?"

Dan plopped his large frame into one of the chairs and waited patiently for Jack to respond. He noticed that Jack did not look as weary as he had for the last several weeks.

Jack dropped the receiver back into its cradle as he related the details of his conversation with Father Walter. His excitement escalated as he divulged the connection between the key and the priest. When he told Dan that the priest wanted to meet with him to discuss the case, Dan immediately began to laugh.

"The old man finally found a way to get you to call him back, did he?"

Dan laughed even more as Jack shook his head and smiled.

"Well, my friend," Jack shot back, his cheeks flushing slightly. "*You're* going with me! I'm going to try to set up a meeting with him today."

Dan laughed again. Deep down, he was glad they would have to see the priest. Jack had been avoiding him for too long. Dan shared Jack's enthusiasm at the possibility of a new lead. Maybe Father Walter would provide them with information that would break this case wide open.

After agreeing to keep his schedule open for later in the day Dan headed back to his own office. Jack would call Father Walter after the church office opened at nine.

Jack struggled to focus as he began to prepare notes for their meeting with Governor Langford. Thoughts of his encounter with Lisa Vick the night before came rambling into his mind.

How did she find out about the meeting so soon after he made the appointment? She had to have a source from inside headquarters – but who could it be? If he hadn't had such a great time with Sara, Jack decided, he would be really ticked off. Instead, he found himself only mildly irritated.

He smiled to himself as his thoughts wandered back to the night before. They had enjoyed a pleasant evening together. Time seemed to stand still when Jack was with her. He thought about Sara's easy smile, and her delicate, beautiful face.

Sara was a much needed and very lovely distraction. He found himself looking forward to seeing her this weekend at the cookout at Dan and Jennifer's house.

He struggled to get his mind back on the case. He knew they would need to be prepared for just about anything when they met with the Governor. Jack picked up his notes and tried to formulate questions that would not appear to be threatening.

He sighed as he laid the papers back down. He was fairly certain Langford would already be defensive just because they wanted to meet with him. Did the politician have something to hide? Or is it possible he wasn't involved at all?

Jack ran his fingers through his hair. He looked up at the wall clock, and noted that it was a few minutes after nine. Time to call the church.

He thumbed through the black leather book that he stored business contacts in, searching for Father Walter's card. When he found it, Jack drew a deep breathe. He wondered if he was really ready for this.

Jack picked up the phone and dialed the number to the church office. A very cheerful voice greeted him immediately.

"Good morning! Saint Bartholomew's Church. This is Angela. May I help you?"

Jack could hear the smile in her voice. Angela King had been the church secretary for as long as he could remember. A pretty woman in her early thirties, she was married with one little girl. The child must be nine or ten by now.

"Good morning, Angela. This is Detective Jack -"

"Jack Russell!" she gushed. "It's so nice to hear your voice! Father Walter told me to expect your call. Let me get him for you!"

Jack was speechless. Angela had caught him off guard, which was pretty hard to do. He worked on regaining his composure while he waited for Father Walter to pick up the phone.

The only sound was the ticking of the wall clock as the seconds passed. He was starting to feel a little nervous when he heard the sound of Father Walter's voice.

"Good morning, Jack!"

Jack smiled as he pictured the friendly priest with the smiling eyes.

Father Walter is in good spirits this morning, he thought to himself.

"Good morning Father. How are you today?"

"Fine, son, just fine. And you?" the priest inquired.

Jack swallowed hard and began to shift in his chair. He just needed to make an appointment. That was all. For now, anyway.

"I'm well, Father, thank you," Jack replied. "I was just following up on our conversation from last night. I'd like to come in and see you. Do you happen to have any time available this afternoon?"

"Well, now, Jack, let me see," he said, pausing for a brief moment.

Jack smiled to himself. He could almost see the priest flipping through the pages of his calendar.

"Why don't you come to my office at around three o'clock?" Father Walter finally asked.

Jack agreed. He wondered if he should mention that he was going to bring Dan along then decided against it. Almost as if the priest had read Jack's mind his tone softened.

"Come alone, Jack, won't you? We have other things to talk about, you know."

A cold shiver ran down Jack's body. He found himself agreeing when he wanted to say *"absolutely not!"* Father Walter had that effect on people, getting them to do things they really did not want to do. Not in a bad way, certainly. But Jack wasn't sure he was ready for what the priest really wanted to discuss.

They said their goodbyes and the call was over. Jack felt heaviness creeping into his shoulders as he placed the receiver back into its cradle. He shook his head slightly as he thought about what Father Walter might have to say.

Losing Shelby was like losing part of himself. The only way he could stop thinking about her after she died was to medicate himself with work. The first few years had been the worst. Fortunately, or not, homicides never seem to end, so he had plenty of distractions to carry him through those dark times.

Lately, though, especially after meeting Sara, he had begun to realize that there was something in his way. It was as if a wall was blocking him from stepping into the next phase of his life, shutting off any chance for happiness. Maybe Father Walter was right. Maybe they did need to talk.

Jack called Dan to let him know that he was going alone. He unlocked his desk and removed the envelope holding the key so he could take it with him when he went to the church. Walking through the park always seemed to help to clear his mind, so he decided to take a breather before the meeting.

He placed the envelope in his pocket and slipped his jacket on as he walked out of his office. After touching base with his secretary, he left headquarters and walked briskly to the park.

The smell of grilled chicken and hot dogs filled the air. He could feel the embrace of the bright morning sun as he walked towards the pond where people flocked to launch their toy boats.

Jack soon arrived at the bench that he and Shelby used to share when they came here together. He sat down on 'his' side, leaving plenty of room for his absent bride. He could not help but think about how much he missed being here with her.

Tenderly he ran his hand over the smooth wood, imagining her sitting next to him, smiling at him, laughing with him. She used to love watching the children sail their boats in this pond. Shelby was the one who had shown him this amazing place. It had become their private haven.

He spent the morning lost in thoughts of their life together. Tears burned in his eyes as memories flooded his mind. He brushed at them furiously with a swipe of his hand. No time for tears now. She was gone. Time to move on. Time to let her go.

Finally Jack stood up and looked at his watch. Almost two o'clock. Where had the day gone? He began the walk back to headquarters to get his car for the drive to Saint Bartholomew's. The hot dog vendor he frequently visited waved as he walked by.

Jack smiled and mechanically waved back. He was numb to the activity around him. Sadness seemed to cling to him, tugging at him like a child with an urgent request. Even his favorite hot dog couldn't entice him today. Something deep in his soul had robbed him of hunger, too.

After a short walk he arrived at the parking garage. He tried to shake the melancholy off as he unlocked the door to his car. Meeting with Father Walter would be difficult enough. He couldn't let the priest see him like this. It would just be too painful.

Jack slid in behind the wheel and slid his key into the ignition. He drew a deep breath and backed out of his space. Apprehensively he turned out of the lot and began the quick journey to the church. Silently he hoped today would be the day they would finally discover the truth.

CHAPTER 21

As Jack pulled into the church parking lot, he thought about how the church looked exactly the same as it had the last time he was here. The sun had been shining that day, too, almost as if it were saying goodbye to a precious friend.

The funeral was beautiful. Dan and Jennifer took care of all of the arrangements. Jack had been too devastated to do it himself. Even though he knew that Shelby was dying months before she passed, no amount of time could have prepared him to lose the love of his life.

As he walked towards the church, he pushed aside the memories of that day and tried to focus on his meeting with Father Walter. Jack ran down the list of questions he had for the priest. Hopefully, he would be out of here in less than an hour.

The doors that lead to the church offices were propped open. Jack walked through the entrance and down the corridor, his footsteps echoing loudly as he made his way down the empty hallway.

As he approached the receptionist's office, he found himself walking at a slower pace. Jack swallowed hard as he noticed the sweat creeping onto the palms of his hands. He wiped his hands on the sides of his slacks, cleared his throat and boldly walked through the silver framed doors into Angela King's office.

The dark-haired woman stood up immediately and greeted him with a warm smile. Jack extended his hand to her as he said hello but she rushed around her desk and threw her arms around his neck.

"It's so good to see you again, Jack," she said.

Jack felt her sincerity as he returned her embrace. Suddenly he felt comfortable, like he had returned home after being away for a very long time. Angela led him to a chair and prompted him to sit. She offered him water or coffee but he politely declined. He didn't want to have any distractions while he was here. He just needed to get information from the priest.

She returned to her desk and called Father Walter to let him know Jack had arrived. Almost immediately the priest appeared at the door, beckoning Jack to follow him.

Jack felt a little like he had been summoned to the principal's office as they walked down the hallway in silence. Father Walter glanced over at Jack from time to time, a soft, warm smile on his lips. His blue eyes glistened in the light that streamed through the windows. Finally they reached the sanctuary. Father Walter sensed Jack's hesitation as he held the door open for him.

"It's alright, my boy," he said softly as he motioned to Jack to enter.

A flood of memories from the funeral came rushing back as Jack stepped into the empty worship center. Shelby had loved this place. He closed his eyes as he pictured the shiny, white casket where his angel rested at the front of the sanctuary. Sunlight pierced through the stained glass windows that day, too, just like it did today. He could almost smell the red and white roses that covered the top of the casket.

Bright, beautiful flowers surrounded the tables that were covered with pictures of a smiling, happy Shelby. Hundreds of people filed sadly by as they said goodbye to the beautiful woman who had once been so alive.

Jack could see it all again as clearly as if it was happening right now. Father Walter's strong hand on his shoulder brought him back to the present. Jack hadn't realized that he was shaking. He hoped the priest hadn't, either.

He cleared his throat as he followed Father Walter to his office behind the front of the sanctuary. The office was exactly as he had remembered it. There were two windows on the wall that faced the prayer garden, one of Father Walter's favorite places.

Book shelves lined the walls, filled with volumes of literature on almost any biblical topic imaginable. Jack wondered if anyone had ever read all of them.

Father Walter walked behind his desk to his high backed black leather chair. He waved his hand in the direction of the two chairs in front of his desk. Jack walked over to them and sat down on the one directly across from the priest.

His eyes fell upon a worn, black leather Bible that lay open on the desk, and the rosary lying nearby. He couldn't remember the last time he had even read the Bible, much less prayed. He shrugged off the guilt and concentrated on the questions he needed answers to.

"Well," Father Walter began gently. "It has been a very long time."

He looked intently at Jack, waiting for the detective to speak. Jack shifted slightly and pulled his notebook out of his jacket pocket.

"Yes, it has," he replied, a nervous smile on his lips.

Father Walter watched him closely as he pulled the key from his pocket and turned it over and over in his hands.

"What do you know about this key, Father?"

Jack peered into the priest's eyes, hoping to see some type of reaction to the question. Instead, he was mildly surprised by Father Walter's composure.

"I left it for you, Jack, but I can't tell you what it goes to, I'm afraid."

The priest seemed calm, unmoved by Jack's question. He couldn't tell if it was the priest's professional demeanor or if he truly had no idea what the key opened.

"Where did it come from?" Jack asked a little gruffly, feeling irritation creeping into his tone.

"Melody Swanson gave it to me, Jack," the priest replied, looking weary and a little sad. "Many years ago, a few years after Megan was born."

"Why would she give it to you without telling you what it opened?"

He directed the question at Father Walter, but Jack was really only thinking out loud. He was confused. What point was there in giving the priest a key and not telling him what it was for?

"Now, Jack, you know that, as a priest, I am bound to keep the confidence of my parishioners. I can only tell you what I know that won't violate that trust."

The priest looked apologetically at the tired detective. He suspected the key was important, but he didn't know why. The conversation he had with Melody when she gave it to him would go with him to the grave.

"All I can tell you is that Melody asked me to hold onto the key. She said if I ever thought it was necessary that I should pass it on so that the truth could be known."

"So she suspected she would die and her girls would be murdered? That doesn't make any sense!"

Jack shook his head in unbelief. He was more confused now than before.

"The person whose initials are on the key may have the answers you are searching for," the priest replied gently.

Father Walter watched as Jack turned the brass key over and over in his hand. The thick sound of silence consumed the room. At first Jack was puzzled. He looked down at the key. 737. 737.

"Wait a minute," Jack exclaimed. "These aren't numbers – *they're initials!* Of *course!*"

He turned the key at a different angle.

LEL. Lawrence Elliott Langford!

He was practically jumping in his seat as he realized what this meant. The governor *was* involved with Melody Swanson. He didn't know how, but they were definitely connected. But was he connected to the murders?

"Father, I need you to tell me everything you know about the relationship between Melody Swanson and the Governor."

Jack looked hard at the tired man sitting across from him. He felt awkward pressuring the kind man, but it had to be done. He needed to get to the truth.

"Jack, you know that I can not divulge the nature of my conversations with my parishioners. What I can tell you is that Melody advised me that, if for any reason it became necessary, this key should be presented to the owner and he would reveal its meaning."

The expression on Father Walter's face softened as he spoke. A touch of sorrow flickered in his eyes.

"I don't believe Melody ever thought this would be necessary."

The priest bowed his head slightly, as if he were uttering a silent prayer. Jack knew that no amount of cajoling would break the priest. He knew the priest to be a man of his word. Besides, his gut was telling him that Father Walter had shared everything he knew about the key.

At least he knew for certain that there was a connection to the Governor. That was something. That was a *big* something.

"Father Walter," Jack said. "One more question."

"Yes, Jack?" the priest answered softly.

"Why didn't you tell me about this key when the girls were first killed?"

Jack hated to ask, but he needed to know. The key might have saved them a lot of leg work. He waited silently as the priest shifted slightly in his seat.

"I wasn't sure it was related, Jack. I'm still not. But I could never forgive myself if I unwittingly allowed the person who took the lives of those wonderful girls to go free."

He stopped and looked at Jack fondly. He knew how much the lonely widower had been struggling since he lost his bride. He leaned over the desk and placed his hand over Jack's.

"You've been searching for the truth for a long time, Jack," he said gently. "Sometimes the freedom that we gain from knowing the truth is only discovered during the journey we make to find it."

The two men fell silent for a moment, both lost in their own thoughts. As much as he wanted to talk with Jack about Shelby, Father Walter sensed that Jack had been through enough just returning to the church. As they said their goodbyes, Father Walter hugged Jack tightly.

"Call me anytime, Jack, anytime at all. We miss you around here!"

Father Walter patted him on the back as they walked back through the sanctuary, now illuminated only by the prayer candles that flickered in memory of lost loved ones.

Jack paused.

"I think I'll stay for a little while, if that's okay," he said, avoiding eye contact with the priest.

Father Walter said a silent prayer of thanks.

"Of course, Jack. Take all the time you need. I'm here if you need me."

He smiled as he made his way back to his room on the other side of the church grounds. Jack stood quietly and watched the candles flicker. He thought about how much time they had spent here lighting candles and praying for healing that never came. He lit a candle for Shelby and sat down in the front row to watch it dance in the darkness.

Tears filled his eyes, but this time he didn't brush them away. He bowed his head as they crept slowly down his cheeks, spilling onto his jacket. He felt betrayed.

"Why did you take her from me, God?" he asked in his anguish. "Why did she have to suffer like that? How am I supposed to go on without her?"

Instead of denying the many questions he had silently been screaming at God all of these years, Jack let them come, one by one. For hours he sat there, challenging God to respond, wondering if God even heard him as he cried out. Finally, he had no strength left to fight. He was exhausted. And yet, he felt oddly at peace.

"I'm sorry, God," Jack whispered through his tears. "I just don't understand."

Jack stood up and wiped the tears from his face. His eyes stung as he walked to his car. Slowly he drove home, exhaustion taunting him as he struggled to stay alert.

The grandfather clock was chiming as if it were welcoming him home when Jack opened the front door. Ten o'clock. Jack walked straight to the bedroom and collapsed onto the bed. Fatigue quickly consumed him as he fell into a deep, troubled sleep.

CHAPTER 22

The clanging of the windup alarm clock rudely aroused him from a deep slumber. Ten o'clock at night. Time to get up and get ready for work. Slowly he sat up and rubbed his eyes. He reached out into the darkness in the direction of the small night stand near his bed.

Finally his hand touched the matches he needed to light the candle. With one smooth swipe the match was lit and a tiny flicker of light from the wax pillar invaded the darkness. He made his way to the desk and switched on the tiny desk lamp. The room was still dark, but he liked it that way. His gaze landed on his masterpiece, his life story, his legacy. For a brief moment he felt complete.

He glanced into the mirror that hung on the wall not far from the desk. Gingerly he ran his fingers through his tousled blond hair. After brushing his teeth, he swiped a cold, damp washcloth across his face.

He briefly flirted with the idea of shaving, but decided against it. The small framed man donned a brown flannel shirt and dirty blue jeans. He pulled on a pair of dirty white socks and promptly covered them with work boots.

Sighing, he walked to the small refrigerator. After a few seconds he pulled out a milk carton and placed it on the little table. He shook the lone box of cereal that had been on top of the refrigerator. There wasn't much but it would have to do. He poured a small amount of cereal into a pink plastic bowl.

After he splashed some milk over the flakes he put the carton back into the tiny ice box and picked up a spoon. Slowly, he munched down his meager breakfast. When he was done he rinsed his bowl and spoon and laid them on a towel next to the sink in his tiny room.

He walked over to the candle and blew it out, then made his way back to the lamp. With a quick flip of the switch he was surrounded once again by total blackness. It was time for his day to begin.

Cautiously he opened the door to the hallway. He listened for several minutes until he was satisfied that no one was wandering around the halls outside of his humble home.

As he stepped out into the lonely corridor he pulled the door shut behind him and turned the knob twice to be sure it was locked. Slowly he made his way through the hospital to the time clock next to the administrative offices. After punching in he headed towards the janitor's closet located in the next hallway.

Working at night had afforded him opportunities to explore areas of the hospital that were too busy at other times. Under the cover of night he slipped easily into and out of offices and rooms full of medical records without drawing unwanted attention to himself.

Mama told him how his real family didn't want him. He had decided at that moment that, one day, he would find the people who had cast him aside like an unwanted pet. He would hunt them down. And he would make them pay. Just like they did in the books he read.

As he pulled the bucket out from the closet, he smiled to himself, the smile of wicked satisfaction. Moving the mop back and forth across the floor, he thought about the hours he had spent reading old records.

He had volunteered to work extra shifts during the days just so he could watch the ladies in the file room as they worked. When they needed to hunt down old records, he listened intently as they discussed where they would look for them.

In only a few short months he had learned all about finding old medical charts. Still, even under the shroud of night with no one else around it had taken a very long time to locate his birth records. Mama would be so proud.

When he finally found them he felt as though he had discovered a valuable artifact worth millions of dollars. That feeling paled in comparison to the thrill of vindication he had experienced as he exacted his revenge on the family that had so coldly scorned him.

Selfishness has a price, he thought to himself as he methodically pushed his mop over the floor with smooth, even strokes.

Mama always said it wasn't nice to be selfish. And they had paid the ultimate price. One cold bullet at a time. Pop. Pop. Pop. Pop. He could still feel the cold steel against his palm as he pulled the trigger over and over. Dozens of bullets were required to do the job well. That's what Mama always said. If you have a job to do, then do it well. And he did. Just like Mama said.

He snickered to himself as he thought about the look in their eyes. They acted so innocent, like they had no idea who he was, or what they had done to him. Priceless. The hall echoed with the sounds of the sloshing of his mop. He smiled maliciously as he worked his way down the hallway. Slosh. Slosh. Pop. Pop.

Justice, he thought, smiling to himself. *Sweet, sweet justice.*

CHAPTER 23

The sound of a garbage truck rumbling from somewhere down the street forced Jack out of a sound sleep. He groaned and pulled the covers over his head. In no time at all he drifted back into the dream that had been so rudely interrupted.

A short hour later his alarm clock rang out, demanding that he get out of bed. He hit the snooze button and rolled over. When the clock screamed at him a second time Jack decided it was no use. He might as well get up and face the day.

Swinging his legs over the side of his bed he sat up slowly, wiping exhaustion from his face. Jack stood up and made his way into the bathroom. He turned the shower on and let the water run for a few moments before stepping in. The pulsating stream thumped mercilessly on his tired muscles.

His mind wandered to his conversation with Father Walter. Spending time at the church had been a good thing, he decided. The emptiness he had been feeling was still there, but Jack couldn't help but notice that he felt lighter somehow. The old priest was right. Jack *was* on a journey. Who knew how long it was going to last?

As the shampoo stung his eyes Jack's thoughts turned to the key. He was anxious to tell Dan what he had learned. He was no longer apprehensive about their trip to the Governor's mansion. It was time to find out what Lawrence Elliott Langford was hiding.

The razor hummed softly as he shaved off the morning stubble that invaded his face while he slept. He smiled as he remembered how Shelby would use his razor on her legs, which made the blades dull and pretty much useless. She would pretend to be hurt when he asked her about it. Her eyes used to twinkle as she proclaimed her innocence. Jack smiled again and shook his head. How he missed those days.

After dressing quickly he combed his hair and brushed his teeth. The smell of fresh coffee beckoned to him as he made his way to the kitchen. He did not know who invented automatic coffee makers, but Jack was eternally grateful to whoever it was.

There are just some things a man needs, he thought to himself, *and fresh brewed coffee in the morning is one of them!*

He lifted the glass pot and poured the steaming brown liquid into his waiting coffee mug. He returned the pot to its perch and opened the refrigerator. After pulling out the milk carton and pouring a few drops into his cup he placed the almost empty container back on the shelf.

Jack pulled out a handful of fresh strawberries and closed the door. He made a mental note to add milk to the virtual grocery list. As he sat down at the kitchen table his eyes moved to the empty place across from him, Shelby's place. She was a morning person, unlike Jack. By now, she would have already run three miles, showered and had breakfast waiting for him.

He drank the last swallow of coffee and wondered why she was on his mind so much today. Maybe it was being at the church again, seeing Father Walter after all this time. Shelby always felt at home there. He remembered when he used to feel that way, too. But that was a long, long time ago.

Jack placed his empty mug in the sink and tossed the strawberry hulls into the trash can. He washed his hands and tossed the towel onto the counter. He leaned against the sink as he listened to his voice mail from the day before.

According to a message from his secretary, Austin James seemed very excited about something he and Shane Cook had uncovered during their interviews. The rookie cop and his partner wanted to meet with Dan and Jack right away. Stephanie set up a meeting for the four of them at nine o'clock this morning.

As he made his way to the car he tried to focus on the meeting ahead of him. The rookies had jumped at the opportunity to take part in the investigation again. Jack was looking forward to hearing about their progress.

The trip to the office was a little slower than usual due to a conference in town near the police station. Those events always made traffic a nightmare and parking even worse. Thankfully he had a designated space in the garage. All he had to do was get there, which was easier said than done on a day like today.

After what seemed like hours Jack finally pulled into his parking space. He briskly walked into the building and bolted towards the elevator. Jack glanced at his watch and winced. The traffic delayed him longer than he realized. It was nearly eight o'clock, an hour later than he usually arrived at work. He had hoped to have some extra time to prepare for Tuesday's meeting with Langford.

As he walked into his office, Stephanie glanced up and greeted him with a bright smile. Jack loved her pleasant disposition. He smiled back and thanked her as he took the handful of messages she held out to him. He was thumbing through them when Dan appeared at his doorway.

"Good morning, Jack!" the beaming detective said cheerfully. "How was your meeting with Father Walter?"

Dan sat down in the chair across from Jack and waited eagerly to hear the details.

"Well, Dan," Jack began, "for starters, I was way off base with the key. It *is* related to this case. I still don't know what it goes to – but I did find out where it came from!"

"Who does it belong to?" Dan asked, not sure he was going to like the answer.

He wasn't happy when Jack told him that Father Walter had left the key for him. Dan was concerned about what that might mean for the kindly man. He didn't want the priest to be accused of withholding evidence or obstructing the investigation.

"Melody Swanson gave it to Father Walter after her fourth baby was born!" Jack exclaimed. "The markings on the key aren't numbers. *They are the Governor's initials!* Our meeting with him on Tuesday is going to be enlightening, to say the least!"

He spent the next several minutes summing up the background of the key that Father Walter had relayed to him the night before. Dan whistled softly as he took in Jack's words. This was big, *really* big. And the consequences could be far reaching, possibly even devastating.

"Does the Chief know yet?" Dan asked.

"No," Jack shook his head. "I haven't had a chance to call him. I thought I would wait until after we meet with Austin and Shane so I can bring him up to speed on everything at the same time."

Dan sat silently for a moment, trying to absorb the magnitude of this new information. He wasn't sure what he wanted the outcome to be. This could be very, very bad news for somebody.

"Well, Tuesday will be the day then," he finally said. "I guess that's when we'll find out what it's all about."

"I hope that's a good thing, Jack," Dan added pensively. "Honestly, I'm concerned about where this is leading us. If the Governor is involved, the scandal around this thing will be explosive!"

Jack nodded his head. He completely agreed with his partner. The two detectives earnestly discussed their concerns about where the case was headed for over an hour. Solving these murders had been their only priority for months now. It would be a relief when the case was finally closed, but to what end?

Finally, Stephanie popped her head in Jack's office and announced that Austin James and Shane Cook had arrived. She had directed the officers to the conference room where they were anxiously waiting to meet with Jack and Dan.

Jack thanked her, grateful for a break from this disturbing conversation. The two detectives silently walked to the conference room, trying to digest the magnitude of what might lay ahead for the most powerful man in Virginia.

CHAPTER 24

Austin James and Shane Cook stood up and greeted the senior officers when they entered the conference room. Their excitement was obvious and almost contagious. Jack smiled as Austin started to blurt out a flood of information before they were even seated.

"Whoa, there!" he said, holding up his hands as he winked at Dan.

They all laughed, and Austin blushed. The men sat down and got comfortable before he began again.

"I - I - I'm sorry, sir," he stuttered nervously. "I think, well, *we* think we might have a suspect!"

The room fell silent. Jack was beginning to understand their excitement. He only hoped their enthusiasm hadn't influenced their judgment. They needed solid evidence to back up their theories.

"Okay, son," he said gently. "Now take it slowly from the top. Let's hear what you've got."

Jack stole a look at his partner and saw from the expression on his face that Dan was as curious as he was. He turned his full attention to Austin as the young man began to speak.

"Well, sir," he began, speaking at a slower pace this time. "We checked out the alibis from everyone on the list that you gave us."

Austin waved his hands as he reviewed the highlights of each witness statement he and his partner had obtained. He pushed the files to the side one at a time as he spoke until only one folder remained.

"We interviewed each of the witnesses and did a thorough background check on each of them as well," Austin said. "Whenever possible we matched their stories with anyone who could verify them. Every single one of them checked out."

"Except one," Shane injected.

"That's right," Austin continued as he glanced towards Shane.

"This is him," he said, his cheeks flushed with excitement. "*This* one could be the guy we've been looking for!"

He pushed the remaining folder towards Jack and Dan. Although they didn't let on, they were both doubtful when they saw the name on the tab. The file belonged to Tim Woods, the strange young man who hops from odd job to odd job all over Meadowbrook.

Jack paused for a moment then slowly sat back in his chair as he looked at the rookies. Austin and Shane obviously thought they had something. He folded his hands and laid them on his lap.

"Okay," he said thoughtfully. "*Why* do you think he might be a person of interest?"

"Wait 'til you hear this, sir," Shane blurted out. "I know it might seem far fetched, but you've *gotta* hear what we found out!"

Jack could not help but smile at Shane's enthusiasm. He tried to look serious again as he listened to what they had to say.

"Well, Detective Russell," Austin began solemnly. "First of all, he was the *only* one who was nervous at all when we tried to talk to him. He couldn't sit still, he wouldn't look us in the eyes – and he stumbled over his words like he didn't want to say them!"

"That might just mean he was nervous," Dan said. "People usually get nervous when they are questioned by the police."

"True," Shane responded. "But listen to this – he answered our questions with questions! When Austin asked where he lived, he asked why it mattered. When I asked if he knew the Swanson family, he asked if everyone who knew them was being questioned."

"That's right!" Austin exclaimed. "He wouldn't even verify if he had been at the crime scene that night. When I showed him the photos we had of him he asked if we could prove they were originals or if someone had touched them up!"

"He sounds like a real wise guy," Dan remarked, shaking his head.

"That's not even the best part!" Shane exclaimed, his eyes gleaming with excitement. "The best part," Shane continued, "was what we discovered when we were trying to do the background check on him!"

Jack was extremely curious now. The rookies had his full attention. He sat up and listened intently as Austin and Shane listed detail after detail that made Woods seem more and more suspicious with each revelation.

"This guy has never filed a tax return. He claims he isn't employed, that he just lives off of money he makes from doing odd jobs around town. When we asked where he lives, he wouldn't give us the street address, only a post office box. He claims he doesn't drive. The

Department of Motor Vehicles has no record of him having a license or owning a car."

Shane took a deep breath and began again.

"We finally got him to give us a street address, but when we went there, it was a huge piece of land - owned by the state – with a mailbox in the middle of nowhere. The mailbox had the address he gave us painted on it. The post office box he gave us was a fake, too!"

After a few moments of silence, Dan sat up and turned towards Shane.

"I agree that some of this is disturbing. I'm just not getting what it is you think makes him a suspect. He's physically smaller than most of the women that were interviewed. That would have made it difficult for him to lift the victims, especially since they would have been dead weight after being drugged."

He looked over at Jack, who nodded slightly in agreement.

"Well," Austin said emphatically. "*Here's* why we think that."

He pushed the picture of the man at the crime scene towards the detective. They looked at it intently for a few seconds, then back at Austin.

"*And*?" Jack asked curiously.

Austin pointed to the man's small frame.

"And when I shook his hand, he almost broke my fingers!"

Austin's eyes were wide open and his expression was dead serious.

"He looks small and meek, but he is anything but!" Shane chimed in. "I haven't felt a gripe like that since my dad shook my hand when I came back from boot camp!"

Dan chuckled to himself at the expressions on their faces. He thought about Shane's father. The man was a decorated war hero who didn't make it back from his last tour in Iraq. Dan imagined the soldier's death had been hard on his son, who seemed a lot like his father in many respects.

Jack sat looking at the photo, thinking about this small man committing these brutal murders. If what these officers uncovered is true, then maybe they did need to investigate Tim Woods further.

"And what would be the motive if he did do this?" he asked.

"That's the one piece we're missing, sir," Austin said. "Tim Woods is practically a ghost. We did manage to talk to about a dozen people who have hired him to do odd jobs in the past but no one seems to know anything about him. He does what he's asked and then disappears again."

Shane nodded his head in agreement.

"That's right," Shane added. "He gets his jobs by word of mouth. People tell him when they know of someone looking for help. No one has any way of reaching him other than by running into him on the street."

"He probably is worth looking into closer," Jack said thoughtfully.

Dan nodded.

"We still need more information if we're going to look at him as a suspect, though" Dan added.

"That's right," Jack said. "Keep digging and see if you can find out anything else about Tim Woods. The information you've gathered here so far has been a big help. You've done a great job and we appreciate the effort you guys have put into it. I will be sure to mention to Chief Sheppard how much your leg work helped us during the course of this investigation."

"Thank you, sir!" Austin said gratefully.

"Yes sir," Shane said. "Thank you. We appreciate it."

The rookies left to continue their work. The two senior detectives sat for a while longer deciding on how to proceed.

"It's great to have someone to focus on, and I know it looks like there is something not right about this guy," Dan said, shaking his head. "But I'm not sure his issues have anything to do with this case. Does Woods even have any connection to the family?"

"Honestly, I don't know, Dan," Jack replied. "He sure looks suspicious, though. And if he's as physically strong as they seem to think he is then maybe he *could* have done it. We need to rule him out, at any rate. If it was him, that lets the Governor off the hook."

As they looked through the notes complied by Austin and Shane Jack's eyes fell on the date of birth listed on Wood's credit report. For some reason it struck a chord with him but he couldn't imagine why.

It's probably nothing, he thought to himself.

He considered mentioning it to Dan but let it go when Dan started talking about the cookout this weekend. *This weekend! The cookout!* Jack had nearly forgotten about it. Sara would be there. Jack smiled at the thought.

Dan gave him the pertinent details and reminded him to bring along his swimming trunks and a towel now that their pool was open for the summer. Finally, the men returned to their respective offices to wrap up for the weekend.

While he was tying up the loose ends of his day, Jack couldn't get Tim Woods out of his mind. Could this small, unusual character really be the vicious killer that has eluded them for so long?

Maybe all roads don't lead to the Governor's mansion, Jack thought to himself as he picked up the phone to finish his calls.

CHAPTER 25

Sunshine was streaming through the curtains when Jack's eyes finally opened. Saturday. He reached for the clock radio. Squinting, he finally made out the numbers. Almost nine o'clock. He rarely slept this late, even on weekends.

Jack climbed wearily out of bed, yawning as he walked into the bathroom to turn on the shower. He stretched his arms a little as he waited for the water to warm up. When he stepped under the blasting spray, he breathed a grateful sigh.

Seeing Sara had been in the back of his mind all week. He was excited. He no longer felt guilty about *wanting* to see her. Maybe he was ready to move on after all.

Once he was showered and dressed, Jack walked to the front door to get the morning paper. He could not remember the last time he had actually read the entire newspaper. Lately he had begun to miss his old routine.

Jack put a bagel in the toaster and poured himself a cup of coffee. He took the cream cheese from the refrigerator and grabbed a knife from the silverware drawer. Finally, the bagel bounced up, toasted to a light brown crisp.

He glanced at the local headlines as he layered cream cheese on the rings of toasted dough. *Unbelievable.* Lisa Vick snagged another front page story. She mercilessly ripped apart a local politician for his position on a recreation program. Jack shook his head with disgust. At least this time it wasn't about him.

His thoughts turned to the brash reporter as he polished off his breakfast. Where did she get her information? Was there a mole in headquarters? He had barely made the appointment to see Langford when he saw her at Madelyn's. She knew about the meeting less than an hour after it was arranged.

Jack was troubled at the thought that someone close to him could not be trusted. With the way she lurks in the shadows waiting to pounce all over unverified facts, a nuisance like Vick could jeopardize the entire investigation.

As he finished his coffee, Jack started to run down a mental list of anyone he had ever seen with the journalist. There was Chief Sheppard, but he disliked Lisa Vick as much as Jack and most of the detectives did. He had also seen her talking to the desk sergeants, but they were not privy to the details of criminal investigations.

His thoughts were interrupted by the shrill sound of his cell phone. He smiled when he saw Jennifer's name on the display.

"Well, good morning, gorgeous," Jack said cheerfully into the receiver.

"Good morning to you, too, pumpkin," Dan replied sarcastically. "Do you always flirt with my wife that way?" he asked, chuckling as he imagined the color of his friend's face.

After he stopped laughing, Dan asked Jack if he would mind picking up Sara and bringing her to their house for the picnic.

"Jennifer thought since we have *so* many people who are coming it would be nice to have one less car in the driveway," Dan said slyly.

Jack could almost hear the smirk that he suspected was plastered on Dan's face.

"*Right*," Jack responded with a mildly sarcastic tone in his voice. "One less car will make such a *big* difference. Your wife is a master manipulator. You know that, don't you?"

Dan laughed, and Jack smiled as he agreed to their request. The truth was he didn't mind at all. When they ended their conversation, Jack dialed Sara's number. One ring. Two rings. Jack glanced at his watch. Almost eleven o'clock.

"Where could she be?" Jack wondered.

Somewhat impatiently he listened to the third and fourth rings. Finally, Sara picked up the phone. She sounded a little winded.

"Hello?" she gasped.

He could tell she was struggling to catch her breath.

"Are you okay?" Jack asked. "You sound like you've been running!"

"Well," she answered in between gulps of air. "I was outside cutting the grass. The lawn mower stalled for the thirty-seventh time when I heard the phone ring. Of course, as I was running into the house to answer it I tripped over a planter!"

"I'm sorry," he said as he tried not to laugh. "Are you alright?"

Sara started to giggle and the sound of it made him smile. He could picture her eyes twinkling as she began to speak.

"Oh, I'm fine!" she said. "There's nothing like a little yard work to get your heart rate up!"

She laughed again and he couldn't stop himself from laughing with her.

"So," Sara said, "what are you up to on this gorgeous day?"

"Well," Jack replied. "Dan and Jennifer are a little concerned over the number of cars that will be at their house today. Would it be okay if we ride together? I can pick you up at three o'clock if that works for you."

"Okay," she agreed. "That will be wonderful. My house is the one with lawn mower parts strewn all over the front yard!"

Jack chuckled softly. He empathized with the exasperation he knew she was feeling.

"If it would help you, I could come over now and see what the problem is," he said sympathetically.

He hoped he didn't sound too anxious.

"Oh, great!" she replied. "Bring a hammer. We can beat it to death!"

They laughed again, and Jack assured her help was on the way. A few moments later he jumped in the car with the tools he thought he might need and backed out of his driveway. His mind wandered as he thought about Sara. Before he knew it he was already driving by the side entrance of the hospital.

As he glanced at the building Jack noticed a small framed man shuffling towards the steps leading down to the side doors. He recognized Tim Woods from the photos in the police files. Jack slowed down and watched with great interest as the man looked furtively around before entering the building.

He was certain this man was Woods. It seemed unusual that he was entering the hospital through a side door instead of through the main entrance. The rookies were right to question his actions. They *definitely* need to find out more about this guy.

A few minutes later Jack arrived at Winchester Street. He turned right and drove until he saw Sara sitting on her porch. Her body language screamed of frustration. He couldn't help but smile as he made the turn into her driveway.

Sara's face brightened when she saw Jack. She jumped up to greet him. When he stepped out of the car he noticed her meticulously kept yard. Flowers were nestled in their neat little beds. The water from a fountain in the pond near the house gurgled happily as it flowed over smooth stones. Jack gave Sara a quick hug.

"Your yard is beautiful! Of course," he teased, "it wouldn't hurt to cut your grass more often!"

"You are *not* a nice man!" she yelped as she punched him playfully in the arm.

He feigned injury as she marched him over to the obstinate garden machine. After almost an hour of removing parts, cleaning them, and replacing them, Jack stood up and slowly began to wipe his hands on a towel she had given him.

"Sara," he announced soberly. "I've found the problem!"

Her face grew serious as she looked at Jack, who was now covered in grease.

"What is it, Jack?" she asked solemnly.

She was hoping he wouldn't tell her that the mower could not be fixed. After all, it was only a few years old. Jack sighed and rubbed his brow.

"Sara," he said with a somber expression on his face, "your lawn mower is broken!"

He laughed hysterically as she punched him in the arm again.

"You are *mean*, Jack Russell! Just plain *mean*!" she exclaimed.

He laughed again and announced that the mower was as good as new. Sara smiled and thanked him profusely. She offered him a glass of iced tea, but after a quick glance at his watch he declined.

"I'd better go so I can get cleaned up," he said. "I still have to buy the angel food cake with strawberries and ice cream I promised to take to the cookout!"

Sara hooked her arm through his as they walked to his car, talking and laughing on the way. Jack was pleased at how easily conversation came between them now. It was nice.

"I'll be back by three or so to pick you up, okay?" he asked.

"That will be fine," she replied. "I'll be ready and waiting!"

His kissed her on the forehead before he got into his car. Sara waved as he drove off. He had less than two hours to get cleaned up and buy the cake and fruit.

Jack didn't remember the drive home, but he arrived safely. And the smile that was on his face when he left Sara's was still there when he walked into his house.

This is a great day, he thought to himself. *This is a really great day!*

CHAPTER 26

True to his word, by the time Jack made it back to Sara's house, it was nearly three o'clock. Sara's contribution to the cookout was corn on the cob. She had covered the ears with butter and neatly wrapped them in foil so they could go right on the grill. He helped her load the trays into his car and began the short drive to Dan and Jennifer's.

The Meyer's were a gracious couple who loved spending time with their family and friends. They were known for their elaborate parties. Jack was certain today would be no exception. Jennifer and Shelby had spent hours together planning and preparing for various celebrations. Jack sighed as he thought about how much he missed those times.

Today, however, was a new day. Jack was determined to focus his attention completely on the petite blond sitting next to him. She was chatting happily about how much she enjoyed working with Jennifer.

"I'm so glad I found a job here," Sara was saying. "We had so much fun in nursing school. I didn't realize how much I missed that until I moved to Meadowbrook. I knew it would be great to work with her again."

She smiled sweetly at Jack, who smiled back as he wove around the Saturday afternoon shopping traffic. He made his way through the congestion and they finally pulled into Dan and Jennifer's driveway. They were early, but both Jack and Sara had agreed to help get things ready for the rest of the guests. Jennifer came out of the house waving.

"You're here! Thank you for coming so early!" she said graciously.

She gave Sara a quick hug and turned her attention to Jack. Winking at Sara, her eyes sparkled as she wrapped her arms around his waist.

"Hello, handsome!" she said. "I hear you were flirting with my husband this morning!"

Jack's jaw dropped, and Jennifer began to laugh, pleased that she had caused his strong face to turn such a beautiful shade of crimson in less than a second. The perplexed look on Sara's face made Jennifer laugh even more.

In between giggles she explained about Dan's phone call to Jack earlier in the morning. Jack's face turned three different shades of red before Dan came out of the house to rescue him.

"Now, Jennifer, leave him alone. He's got important work to do!"

Dan smiled broadly as his friend seized the opportunity to make his escape from the laughing women. Dan walked to the back of the car to help Jack retrieve the food from the trunk. Once everything was inside, Sara and Jennifer attended to the last minute menu details. Dan motioned to Jack to follow him to the back yard, where the grill was ready and waiting.

Dan had the mass production of hamburgers and hot dogs down to a science. When they arrived at the grills, Dan looked at Jack very seriously.

"Today, Jack," he said soberly, "you have only two responsibilities. First, you are in charge of making sure the raw meat keeps coming. That's one of the secrets to a successful cookout. Second, and, in my opinion, most important, you have the task of keeping my beer mug full. A chef could become parched pretty quickly behind a hot grill without proper hydration!"

"As long as we have our priorities in order," Jack replied with a smile.

He laughed at his friend's interpretation of what was important. They worked as a team to get the meat on the grill so it would be hot and ready when the other guests arrived. Soon the men were surrounded by Dan and Jennifer's two youngest children.

"Hi, Uncle Jack! That smells great!" Scott exclaimed.

The sandy haired boy gave Jack a high five as he looked with longing at the steaming grills. At eleven years old the Meyer's middle child was already showing signs of impressive physical prowess. He was hoping to try out for the Middle School football team this year, much to Jennifer's chagrin.

"Hey, Scottie!" Jack replied with a big grin. "You're getting strong!" he said as he rubbed his hand.

Scott smiled broadly as he puffed out his chest. Out of the corner of his eye Jack noticed a delicate figure inching her way slowly towards the grill.

"Are they ready yet, Daddy?" Dottie asked, her eyes wide with anticipation.

Dan laughed at the serious expression on the face of his seven year old baby girl.

"Soon, honey," Dan replied. "Very soon!"

"Hi, Squirt!" Jack said as he patted her strawberry blond curls.

She smiled up at him adoringly.

"Hi, Uncle Jack," she responded shyly.

"Come on, you two," Liz said with great authority as she walked up to the grills.

The oldest Meyer daughter was remarkably like her mother, even at the tender age of thirteen.

"Now come away from there before you get burned! You know the rules! I'm sorry, Daddy," she said apologetically in her most grown up voice. "The children just don't understand that they shouldn't bother you when you are grilling!"

Liz ushered her brother and sister away from the hot grills and into the house to help their mother and Sara with last minute preparations. Jack and Dan looked at each other with smiling eyes as they took it all in.

"They're growing up fast," Jack remarked.

"I know! It's all going by too fast for me!" Dan exclaimed. "This year Liz goes to her Middle School Prom!"

Jack laughed.

"Well," he replied with a glimmer in his eyes, "just make sure you show her date your gun!"

The friends laughed as they finished grilling the last of the burgers. Before long, the neighborhood was filled with the sounds of laughter and music. The delicious aroma of freshly grilled meat and vegetables floated through the summer air. The rest of their friends began to arrive just as Jennifer and Sara finished displaying the food.

Tables lined the back walls of the house, covered with salads, fruit and vegetable trays, pasta dishes, plates filled with stacks of hamburgers and hot dogs, and rows of cakes and cookies. Ice cold beverages were in coolers at the end of the food line. The spectacular cuisine seemed to beckon to the partygoers as they made their way through the array of tempting dishes.

Jack and Sara eventually made their way through the buffet line and found a table near the pool. As they took their seats, their heads turned towards the sound of a booming voice that was announcing that the DJ had arrived and would be taking requests shortly.

The man behind the voice was Paul Sheppard, the Chief of Police, with his wife Laura, who was beaming as she stood by his side. Jack caught Paul's eye and motioned for him to join them. The Chief waved back and the couple moved through the crowd to where Jack and Sara were seated.

Judy Lane and her husband Jim, another detective on the Meadowbrook police force arrived soon after. Dan and Jennifer joined them when the rest of the guests had been served.

The four couples chatted easily with one another as they devoured the delicious meal in front of them. Several second trips were made through the food line, until everyone was pleasantly full. After dinner, conversation turned to what the life of a police officer is really like.

"You must be so proud of your husband," Sara said to Laura. "Jack tells me Paul is one of the finest police officers he has ever worked with!"

"Why, Jack," Laura said as she turned to look at him. "What a nice thing to say! Are you looking for another promotion?"

Jack blushed. They all laughed good-naturedly.

"I *am* proud of him, Sara," Laura said seriously. "He's not just a great policeman. He's a great husband and my best friend, too!"

Sara thought she was glowing like a schoolgirl as Laura looked at Paul.

"How long have you been married?" Sara asked.

"Over thirty years. It's been a great life together with my bride!" Paul said, rubbing his wife's shoulder tenderly.

"I couldn't do this job without her support!" he continued.

The Chief lovingly took Laura's hand into his own.

"Laura is a role model for all of us wives," Jennifer said with admiration. "She knows what it's like to face the uncertainty we all deal with. When our husbands leave the safety of our homes for another day on the job we never know what that day might bring."

Laura blushed.

"Why, thank you, Jennifer," she said graciously. "You're very kind. It isn't easy, I know. Paul's been shot twice in the line of duty. Both times, it was only by God's grace that I was not left a widow. It's a frightening reality of how dangerous police work truly can be. But Paul is determined to keep Meadowbrook one of the safest places in the state. And I support him in that."

"We do, too," Jim Lane said, lifting his beer towards the Chief.

Everyone at the table joined in the toast. When they were done, Dan and Jennifer stood up.

"Please excuse us," Dan said cheerfully. "We need to check on our other guests."

The couple left the company of their good friends and headed towards another table. The others began to mingle as well, catching up with old friends and meeting new ones.

By six o'clock, the Meyer children had ushered their friends into the pool where they splashed each other and had fun playing volleyball and water basketball. Jack and Sara finally returned to their seats, laughing as they tried to help each other remember the names of the dozens of people they had just met.

As the evening drew later, the DJ began to play songs that were more conducive to dancing. Jack watched a little nervously as couples started moving towards the grassy area near the sound equipment. He hadn't done this in a very long time. Hoping that it was like riding a bike, he rose from his seat and extended a hand to Sara.

"May I have this dance, Madam?" he asked with a slight, exaggerated bow.

"Of course you may, sir!" she exclaimed.

She stood up and responded with a slight courtesy as she placed her hand in his. He led her to the grassy dance floor and took her in his arms. As they began to move with the music, almost immediately it seemed as if they had been dancing together for years. No words were spoken as they floated on the grass. Their eyes were fixed on each other, oblivious to the bodies moving around them.

Dan and Jennifer were standing near the DJ's table when Jennifer caught a glimpse of Jack and Sara. She nudged Dan and motioned with her head towards the dance area. They looked at each other and grinned.

"Finally!" she exclaimed softly, nodding her head.

She wiped a tear away from her eye.

"You did good here, baby," Dan said gently, as he wrapped his arms around her waist.

Jennifer smiled up at him and leaned her head on his chest.

"After all these two have been through," she said softly, "they deserve to be happy again."

Silently she wished this night would never end.

CHAPTER 27

Scotch had become his new best friend since Michael Swanson died. The ice cubes clinked merrily into the glass as Miles Winston released them from his hand. Sadly, he wished he felt anything remotely like 'merry'. The caramel liquid rolled slowly over the frozen chunks as he tilted the glass bottle. They seemed to be calling out to him, taunting him.

Nothing is the same now, the aging attorney thought to himself. He sat silently in the dark, wishing he could go back in time, maybe change the events of the past. But it was out of his hands now. Who knew where the chips would lie when they finally fell?

As an attorney, it was part of his job to protect the privacy of his clients at all costs. When he was younger, Miles relished the task. At one time he even welcomed the sense of power he held knowing things about people that had the potential to change their lives forever - *if* those things were made known.

Now, as he considered the consequences of those kinds of secrets, he hated what he had done, had been forced to do, all because of something called attorney/client privilege. Who thought up that crap anyway? When did it become 'just' to hide truth? He always thought the justice system was about making things right.

It isn't, he thought sadly as he held his glass up to the light sneaking in from the street. *If you have enough money you can buy a different truth. When did that become 'right'?*

As he stared out his office window, he wondered how different things might have been if Michael had never died. What if the family had stayed home that month, instead of going to their beach house? What if they hadn't gone fishing that awful day?

Miles was starting to notice that his glass was becoming empty faster and faster in recent weeks, but he didn't care anymore. He had plenty of scotch – and he needed plenty of comfort. It seemed to be a perfectly amicable arrangement. Anything to dull the pain.

"How did I get to this place?" he wondered out loud.

Sighing, he picked up the bottle and poured himself another round. The ice cubes were gone now, but he didn't bother to get more. His throat was numb. He wouldn't notice if the scotch was warm or cold anyway. The liquor flowed easily out of the tumbler and down his throat.

He slammed the empty glass down hard on his desk. Fiercely he stood up and walked over to the safe on the wall behind the picture of the state capitol. He flipped through the combination and yanked open the door. Inside the deep, dark cavern rested the documents, the evidence of a fateful decision made years ago.

He pulled the bundle of papers from the darkness and carried it to his desk. There were scores of medical reports, confidentiality agreements and other documents signed by Michael, the doctors, the medical staff, and of course, Miles.

Miles laid the sheets out in order and began to scrutinize the legal documents and the medical records staring back at him. Do these records mean anything at all? Is it possible that this has something to do with why a family who was so dearly loved by an entire community is gone?

Michael had never consulted Melody about the decision he had made. After all, given the circumstances she could not possibly have understood how Michael felt about the baby. She never knew why Michael feared raising a disabled child. *As it all turned out,* Miles thought, *it was for the best. Regretfully, it was for the best.*

But should someone else have been consulted? Is there someone out there who knew about this and wanted to cover it up? Or maybe they want to expose it now, after all this time. Is that why the girls were killed? Is it possible that after all of these years, someone was still trying punish Michael or Melody for one questionable indiscretion?

Guilt over his own actions tore at Miles as he tried furiously to drown his anguish. After all, Michael said he wanted it 'taken care of', and Melody wasn't to know about it. He wasn't specific, although Miles was pretty sure he meant 'terminated'. Had he made a mistake in how he handled his part?

Miles wished he knew everything, but it had been best for no one to know all of the details. Plausible deniability, it was called. If everyone knew only a small piece, no one could be held completely accountable. *Any way you slice it,* he thought angrily, *he's still dead. They are all still dead!*

He sat back in his black leather chair and closed his eyes. Miles had a decision to make. If only he had found all of the journals, it might have been easier to tell the detectives about the documents he had preserved for all of these years. Not knowing what information the missing journal contained made it too risky to let the police review these papers right now.

Still, the investigation has gone on far too long as it is, Miles thought. He had finally resigned himself to the fact that the toll it was taking on him could drive him to an early grave. Perhaps this information could shed some light on – well, something. Miles wasn't sure if it meant anything at all, but he did know one thing: keeping it hidden was slowly killing him.

"No secret is worth all this," he mourned softly.

He wanted it to be over, *needed* for it to be over so he could grieve for his friend and move on with his own life.

Am I being selfish? he thought, loathing the heaviness in his heart.

Miles sighed deeply and leaned forward, resting his arms on the cold, hard desk. He laid his forehead on his hands, breathing slowly, desperately hoping for peace. None came.

"What have we done, Michael?" he asked wearily of the silent, empty room. "What have we done?"

CHAPTER 28

Monday morning found Jack with a smile still plastered on his face as he pulled into the parking garage. He was feeling lighter these days, happy even. It was both strange and exciting at the same time. His thoughts kept taking him back to Saturday night.

When they finished helping Dan and Jennifer clean up after the cookout, Jack drove Sara back to her house. They sat and talked on her porch swing until dawn, wrapped in each other's arms, and watched as the sun rose warmly in the morning sky.

Finally, Jack knew he had to leave so Sara could rest before heading to the hospital for her three o'clock shift. When they said good night, or, rather, good morning, he gathered her gently in his arms, pulled her chin up to his, and slowly and tenderly kissed her. It seemed to last for an eternity, and that was just fine with him.

He wanted to do cartwheels to his car, but smiled to himself as he wisely chose to walk instead. He felt slightly ridiculous at the thought, but he didn't care. He wondered if Sara felt the same way. The sound of a horn off in the distance brought him back to the parking lot.

Today Jack was going to focus on the report they had received from the rookies last week. After seeing Tim Woods skulking around the hospital on Saturday, he was now completely convinced that Woods deserved closer scrutiny. Jack was going to meet with the hospital administrator to see if they could track down who it was that Woods was visiting. It might be nothing, but he didn't want to overlook any possibilities here.

When he popped his head into Dan's office, he saw coffee, about two dozen packs of sugar and a fruit pastry lying on his desk, but no Dan. Jack broke off a piece of the Danish and was just about to make a clean getaway when Dan came flying in the door.

"Stealing my breakfast, are you?" Dan asked suspiciously as he watched Jack lick his strawberry covered fingers.

Jack shrugged sheepishly and smiled.

"Thought you might want to go to the hospital with me today," Jack said.

"Why? Are you sick from eating stolen food?" Dan retorted.

"Oh, no. Nothing like that," Jack grinned. "We need to find out what Tim Woods was doing there on Saturday."

They sat down and Jack began to describe watching the young man acting oddly outside the hospital on Saturday afternoon. Jack and Dan kicked around some theories, but could not really determine if Woods was a viable suspect or not. They knew the rookies felt sure he could be. The only way to be positive was to either rule him out completely or find enough evidence to build a case against him.

They made arrangements to leave for the hospital by nine, which gave them each enough time to check their phone messages. As the detectives were about to get on the elevator, Dan watched Lisa Vick walk into Paul Sheppard's office.

"What's that about?" he asked Jack as he jerked his head in the direction of the Chief's office.

Jack hurriedly stepped on the elevator and motioned for Dan to step in so he could shut the door.

"I don't care," Jack said flatly, "as long as she isn't here to see me!"

They chuckled as they made their way to the garage. Dan drove so Jack could review his notes and photos of Woods. He was hoping the hospital administrator did not try to claim confidentiality on this one.

"As far as anyone knows," Jack observed, "Tim Woods might as well have been raised by wolves. His social security number is phony, and so are his ID's and address."

"Someone has to know something about this guy," Dan replied. "Maybe the patient he visited on Saturday will be able to shed some light about him."

Jack nodded. Once Dan parked the car in the hospital lot, it was a short jaunt to the office where they were to meet with Dylan Kiser, who has served as the Administrator at Meadowbrook General Hospital for nearly thirty years. Jack knew that he had also been a very close friend of Michael Swanson.

Once the men were seated in his office, Jack began the painful task of explaining that they were there as part of the Swanson murder investigation. Kiser's shoulders dropped slightly as sadness crept into his eyes.

"Of course," he said quietly. "What can I do to help you?"

"We are looking at this gentleman as a potential person of interest in this case," Jack replied.

Jack slid a photo of Woods across the desk to Kiser's open hand. He stared at the picture for a few seconds and a puzzled look flashed across his face.

"I saw him enter the hospital on Saturday through a side door, and he was acting a little suspiciously," Jack explained. "Do you have any idea who he is and who he might have been here to see?"

"Yes," Kiser said slowly. "I believe I do know him, but I'm not sure he was visiting anyone here. As a matter of fact, I believe he works here!"

Jack and Dan looked at each other, surprised to hear that Woods had a job at all, *and* that it was at the hospital.

"What exactly does Tim Woods do here?" Dan asked.

"Tim Woods?" Kiser looked even more puzzled. "The gentleman I have in mind is Tim Wilson. I feel sure this is him. He's been a night janitor here for many years now. Let me get my Human Resource Director on the line. She will be able to clear this up."

With a quick phone call, Kiser arranged for the Human Resource Director to bring Tim Wilson's personnel file, including the photo for his hospital identification badge, to his office.

"I believe Wilson works the third shift," Kiser said. "He has never caused any trouble that I'm aware of. From what I understand he's a loner who also never participates in any hospital functions unless attendance is required."

"I daresay," Kiser stated matter-of-factly. "I wouldn't know who he was if I hadn't needed someone to mop up a spill in the cafeteria one morning. I came in during the wee hours that day and found that someone had spilled coffee all over the floor. The man came right away when he was paged. Didn't say much, just cleaned up and went back to where he came from."

There was a sharp knock on the door. A small framed woman with large glasses partially concealed under a mass of bright red hair entered his office.

"Here you are sir," she said quickly as she handed Kiser the folder. "This is all there is."

"Do you know Tim Wilson, Miss?" Jack asked.

"Please forgive me, detectives," Kiser interrupted. "This is Kim Darling, our Human Resources Director."

"Nice to meet you, Ma'am," Jack said. "I'm Detective Jack Russell and this is Detective Dan Meyer."

Dan smiled and nodded as Miss Darling nodded back.

"Nice to meet you both," she responded politely. "I do know Tim Wilson. Well, a little, I guess. I have to talk to him once in a while when issues come up like needing new badges or keys, things like that."

"Did you do a background check on him before he was hired?" Dan inquired.

"I wasn't here when he was hired, sir," the mousy woman explained. "I've only worked here for a year. Anything that was done when he was hired is in his folder."

After asking a few more questions, it was obvious to the detectives that Miss Darling was not going to be able to provide them with much more information. Jack turned to Kiser.

"Is it possible for us to get a copy of this file?"

"Absolutely!" Kiser responded. "Miss Darling, would you take care of that please?"

She nodded and disappeared with the file. When she returned, she laid a small stack of papers in front of Jack.

"Thank you, Miss Darling. If we think of anything else, we will give you a call."

She nodded and returned to her office. As the men were getting ready to leave, Kiser lifted his right hand in the air as if he were making a pledge.

"Please, Detectives," he said, with sadness in his voice.

"Find the monster that did this. Our hearts were broken when Michael died. And then his family……. My wife was crushed by the whole thing. Such good people. Who could have done such a terrible thing?"

The detectives reassured him that they were looking into every possible lead and hoped to find the answer soon. Kiser thanked them and told them to call if they needed anything else. Jack and Dan left the hospital and began the drive back to headquarters. Jack dialed Austin's cell phone. The rookie answered on the first ring.

"Austin," Jack said. "We have an interesting development concerning Tim Woods!"

Jack had Austin's full attention as soon as he said the strange man's name. Austin grew more and more excited as he listened to Jack describe the meeting the detectives had just come from. When Jack was done talking, Austin was quick to jump in.

"Do you want us to dig up information on Tim Wilson now, sir?" the young man asked eagerly.

"Absolutely," Jack replied. "This could be a significant break for us, so we need you to be thorough. Gather as much information on Tim Wilson as you can find. Let's find out who this guy really is."

"We will sir," the rookie said earnestly. "I will call Shane and we will get on this right away. Can we get a copy of his personnel folder sent to our phones?"

"I will have my secretary take care of that as soon as we get back to the station," Jack replied. When he hung up, Jack smiled at Dan.

"These guys are good," he said.

Dan nodded, smiling as he thought about the enthusiasm the young police officers had for the job. Jack and Dan began to compare the facts documented in the personnel folder to what they already knew about Tim Woods.

"There is no background check in this file," Dan noted. "They don't have any documents on him at all. How did he slip through the cracks?"

"It's hard to say," Jack replied. "It's almost as if someone was pushing him through, or helping him cover up something. If they are the same person why did Woods change his name? What does this guy have to hide?"

Dan paused as the detectives considered this new development in the case.

"The rookies did good," Dan remarked thoughtfully, interrupting the silence.

"They did," Jack agreed. "It might just be time to send them undercover. Do you think?"

"I *do* think!" Dan said. "It will be a great opportunity for them. They might as well get some of the credit. They've sure earned it!"

"Now," Jack said slowly as he looked intently at his partner. "If only tomorrow with the Governor is as productive as today has been so far....."

CHAPTER 29

When Jack and Dan arrived at headquarters on Tuesday morning, they were greeted by none other than Lisa Vick. The impatient reporter was leaning on the wall outside of Jack's office, with a triumphant smile on her face.

"Good morning, Jack!" she exclaimed. "What time is our meeting with the Governor today?"

Jack tried not to let his disdain for her show as he feigned ignorance.

"Meeting?" he asked innocently. "What meeting?"

"I know you are hiding something, Jack," Vick declared, staring straight into his eyes, "and it's something big. You'd better think twice if you think you're going to pull something over on me!"

"Why, Miss Vick," a booming voice declared. "You aren't threatening one of my detectives, are you now? And after we had such a nice chat yesterday!"

Paul Sheppard stared hard at the reporter who seemed to be growing smaller by the second.

"Of course not, Chief!" she exclaimed. "Jack and I are just good buddies sharing some lighthearted banter – isn't that right, Jack?"

She turned and waved her hand in Jack's direction, but he had seized the opportunity to slip away. Sheepishly she looked at Sheppard and shrugged her shoulders.

"I'm sure it was," Sheppard said evenly. "Come with me. I have several matters to discuss with you regarding coverage for some upcoming events."

He held her elbow firmly as he guided her down the hall to his office. Sheppard smiled to himself, knowing that Jack and Dan would be long gone before he would be done with her. She might have known about the appointment with the Governor, but she didn't know it had been rescheduled for ten o'clock.

Jack and Dan both agreed that preparing for the meeting with the Governor had been unpleasant, to say the least. After all, how do you ask '*Did you have an affair with Melody Swanson and is her fourth daughter your child?*' in a way that can be construed as anything but offensive?

They spent hours organizing their notes so that they did not have to ask those particular questions. Not today, anyway. They had decided that their focus would be completely on Langford's relationship with Michael Swanson and any other common relationships.

Dan was going to gently try to slip in a question or two about Melody while Jack watched for the Governor's reaction. The whole way to the Governor's Mansion they rehearsed the sequence.

As she escorted the men to Langford's office, Miss Fenwick, the Governor's secretary, chatted pleasantly about the mansion and the grounds.

"The recent renovations have really given life back to the building, don't you agree?" she asked as she ushered them into the conference room.

The men were quick to agree. An aide quickly appeared with coffee and bagels. Jack thanked Miss Fenwick and she left to inform the Governor that the detectives had arrived.

Neither Jack nor Dan had ever met Langford face to face before. His reputation was that of being a gracious, honest and no-nonsense man who was a straight shooter. Jack hoped it was all true. He was always a little disheartened when a person who should be a solid role model fell from grace.

The detectives rose when Governor Langford entered the room. Smiling, he shook their hands and welcomed them to the Mansion. He motioned for them to be seated.

"Now," Langford said. "What can I do for you today?"

Jack paused, and then began his monologue on Michael Swanson. He explained that they were following leads to determine if the deaths of his daughters had anything to do with Swanson's financial dealings. The Governor listened patiently. When Jack finished, Langford nodded his head.

"I see," he said. "So, exactly how can *I* help?"

"Well, sir," Dan interjected. "It would help us to know about your relationship with Michael Swanson. How long did you know him?"

The Governor paused for a moment. He looked at each man squarely in the eyes before he spoke.

He is obviously choosing his words carefully, Jack thought to himself.

"I did not know Michael Swanson well at all," the Governor stated. "He did help me with my campaign years ago but to be honest, our relationship was more about fundraising than friendship. He was a very generous man to many causes, for sure, my campaign being one of them."

"Actually," he continued, "it was his wife I was more closely involved with, because of the baby, of course. That *is* why you're here, isn't it?"

Jack and Dan looked at each other, trying to disguise their surprise at his candid question. Langford noticed their discomfort immediately and quickly spoke up to put them at ease.

"Of course, I'm sure you understand that this is a very sensitive subject," he said earnestly. "It has been a well-guarded secret for many years, and hopefully we can keep it that way."

He looked at both of the detectives as if asking for their confidence. Jack returned the Governor's gaze steadily, trying to determine what the Governor was alluding to. Was he telling them he had an affair with Melody? That the child was his? Or perhaps that he knew of someone else who had stepped out with her? Cautiously, Jack tried to ease his concern.

"I hope we can, sir," Jack said, choosing his words guardedly. "But that's going to depend on how this impacts the investigation."

The Governor looked confused for a moment.

"How would their handicapped son impact your investigation?" he asked.

"Don't you mean their daughter, sir?" Dan responded, with a puzzled look.

The Governor sat back in his chair. He sighed, and his face softened. Jack and Dan waited for him to continue, wondering what was coming next.

"Then you don't know about the boy, do you?" he asked gently.

From the blank looks on their faces, Langford knew they did not.

CHAPTER 30

The Governor paused for a few moments before continuing on. After taking a small sip from the water glass sitting in front of him, he quietly began to speak.

"I met Melody through her husband," he said. "They were both delightful, but she had a spark that just filled a room. After a few months of working with Diana on my campaign, Melody confided in my wife that she was having another baby."

"Unfortunately," he continued, "the doctors had to tell them that the baby, *if* Melody carried it to term, would not live long after birth. If it did manage to survive, the child would be severely handicapped. It was also possible that Melody could die."

"They were heart broken, of course," Langford said. "Michael wanted her to have an abortion, but Melody insisted that this child was a gift from God. She was determined to go through with the pregnancy with or without Michael's support. For most of the pregnancy it was without."

The Governor paused for another sip of water, and then continued on.

"My wife stood by her as she got closer and closer to the delivery date," Langford continued. "Unfortunately, Melody went into labor far too early. She had a little girl. And then she had a little boy. Twins. The doctor never heard a second heart beat during her examinations, and only saw one baby on the sonograms."

Jack and Dan looked at each other in disbelief. They were completely stunned. Nothing in any record they had ever researched on this family prepared them for this revelation. Langford continued his story.

"The girl was small but relatively healthy. The boy was sickly and the doctors expected him to die soon after he was born. By then, Michael had come around and accepted his daughter. But he turned his back on the boy – wouldn't allow any measures to be taken to prolong his life. He told his wife the boy had died. Melody was deeply grieved, but so grateful for her daughter that she was able to accept her son's death."

"Wait a minute," Jack said. "When did the baby actually die?"

"That's just it," the Governor said sadly. "He didn't. We found out later that Michael did not want the boy. He signed over their parental rights to an attorney immediately after he found out the baby was sickly."

Langford paused, his lips pursed. After a moment he went on.

"Swanson forbade anyone to mention their son to Melody for any reason," the Governor continued. "Michael even restricted who she had contact with for a long time after Melody returned home with their daughter."

Langford cleared his throat.

"My wife was devastated when she found out that the child wasn't being properly cared for," he continued sadly. "She knew Melody would have never allowed that to happen. So, we made - *arrangements* – for the boy to be moved to another hospital. He was treated as an abandoned baby, a Baby Boy Doe, if you will."

"You and your wife made these arrangements?" Dan asked.

"Yes," the Governor responded. "With the assistance of our attorney, Miles Winston."

Jack looked at Dan, then back at Langford.

"Miles Winston knows about this?" Jack asked tersely.

"Of course," the Governor replied. "He did the legal paperwork. Michael signed all parental rights for the child over to Miles. I'm sure Michael thought the baby would never live. But that boy was a fighter. My wife and I paid for his medical care, and after about eight months he was strong enough to leave the hospital. He was very small. The doctors said he would always have physical and mental challenges, of course, but he was growing stronger every day. When we found someone to adopt him, Miles did the paperwork for that as well."

Silence fell on the room as the detectives tried to process this shocking development. Finally, Jack decided to ask the Governor outright about his relationship with Melody Swanson.

"Governor Langford," Jack said matter-of-factly. "Did you have an affair with Melody Swanson?"

To Jack's amazement, the Governor's eyes softened. For a moment, Jack thought he looked sad.

"Is that rumor still floating around the halls of Meadowbrook General?"

Langford shook his head slowly.

"No, we never had an affair. I believe that started when I drove Melody to the hospital to deliver her babies. She went into labor at our headquarters while she was helping me with my campaign. It was the least I could do for her!"

Jack shook his head as he considered the damage that could have been done if Lisa Vick had spouted off in her newspaper about Melody Swanson having an affair. He was still trying to process the conversation when Dan asked Langford about the baby boy.

"Who adopted their son, Governor? Do you know?"

"I do, as a matter of fact," he replied promptly. "We had a maid working for us during that time. Her daughter and son-in-law had been trying to conceive for years. Around the time of the delivery they found out that they would not be able to have children of their own. They were willing to adopt the little one in spite of his mental and physical handicaps. We had Miles Winston draw up the paper work and we paid the adoption fees."

"Did you ever tell the Swanson's?" Jack asked.

The Governor shook his head.

"Melody thought the baby was dead," he said sadly, "and Michael signed away their rights to the child. We didn't think it was something they needed or wanted to know. I hope we did the right thing."

"Unfortunately," Langford continued, "many years later I heard the adoptive parents were killed in an automobile accident. I believe her mother took the boy in to raise him. We've lost touch, though. It's been many years."

The Governor looked sorrowful as he recounted the story.

"What were their names, sir?" Dan asked.

"Our maid was Mattie Hanson," he replied. "I believe her daughter and son-in-law's last name was Woods."

"Woods!" Dan looked at Jack with astonishment. "Tim Woods!"

The Governor stared at the detectives, unsure of what they were saying. Jack did not want to divulge any further details of the case, so he thanked the Governor and asked if he would meet with them again if necessary.

"Of course," he assured them. "Anything I can do to help. I hope we can keep this quiet. There is no need to make this information public knowledge, is there?"

"We will do our best sir, but we can't promise that. We have to see where the investigation goes."

Jack started to walk towards the door, but paused. He turned back towards the Governor and held out his hand. In it was the key with the letters LEL.

"Do you know what this goes to, Governor Langford?" Jack asked.

He noticed a look of recognition and slight surprise on Langford's strong face.

"Maybe," he replied thoughtfully.

Langford turned and walked towards a walk-in wall safe. He stepped inside and returned with a metal box the size of an encyclopedia.

"Melody gave this box to my wife a number of years ago," Langford said. "She told

206

her the only reason Diana should let anyone have it would be if they had the key. My wife asked me to keep it in a safe place. Quite honestly, I had forgotten about it!"

He placed the box on the table and Jack slid the key in the chamber. With a quick turn of the key they heard a dull 'click'. The lid of the box popped open. Inside the metal case was the missing journal.

Jack picked it up and flipped through it, scanning the notations. He was certain it had quite a story to tell. He thanked the Governor for meeting with them. The two detectives left the mansion with the journal and a lot more questions than they had when they arrived.

One thing they were certain of was that Langford was not involved in the murders of the Swanson sisters. Jack and Dan agreed that the most important task at hand now was to locate Tim Woods, or Tim Wilson, and find out what he knew about the Swanson family and the murders. Was he the missing twin?

CHAPTER 31

On the drive back from their meeting with Langford, Jack and Dan reviewed what they had learned from the Governor with great amazement.

"That was some secret they kept all of those years," Dan said. "Why do you think Miles Winston didn't tell us?"

"I'm not sure," Jack said testily. "I'm certain *he* believes it falls somewhere along the lines of attorney/client privilege. As far as *I'm* concerned hiding that kind of information borders on hindering a murder investigation."

"Still," Dan mused. "We don't know for sure if this missing twin has anything to do with the murders. I mean, *if* he's still alive, and *if* he's still in the area, the kid probably doesn't know who he really is."

Jack nodded his head slightly. What his partner said made sense.

"And," Dan continued, "even if it turns out to be Woods or Wilson, whatever his name is, why would he kill the girls? What reason would he have had to hurt them?"

"I really don't know, Dan," Jack said. "I do know I'm going to have Miles come down to headquarters and explain himself. At least we have the missing journal now. That should help fill in some of the blanks."

Jack shook his head as he thought about it all.

"Can you imagine keeping all these secrets from each other? It's like the right hand didn't know what the left hand was doing."

Jack paused, letting it all sink in.

"You know, I don't understand why Swanson didn't want his son. If the child was going to die anyway, why didn't he just go through the motions for Melody's sake? It's not like they didn't have the resources to care for a sick baby."

"But Jack," Dan said somberly. "The baby may not have died. He might still be out there somewhere."

Jack shook his head again.

"I just don't get it. Was what Swanson did even legal? Wouldn't Melody have had to sign away her parental rights, too?" Jack asked, perplexed by Swanson's actions.

Dan just shrugged. The men rode in silence for a few minutes, still trying to process what they had discovered during their meeting with the Governor. Finally they arrived back at headquarters.

They stopped in the Chief's office to update him on their meeting with Langford. He listened intently as Jack and Dan relayed the details of their conversation. Chief Sheppard sat in stunned silence for a few minutes, letting their report sink in.

"I'm at a loss for words," the senior officer finally declared slowly. "Who could have ever predicted something like this?"

"Now more than ever, sir," Dan said earnestly, "we believe Tim Wilson is a person of interest. We need to find out more about him to see if we can tie him to the Swanson's."

"That's right," Jack chimed in. "He might very well be the missing twin. *And* our perpetrator."

The Chief folded his hands in his lap. He stared thoughtfully at the wall past where Jack and Dan were sitting for a moment before he responded.

"That does seem to be the most logical course of action at this point," he stated without emotion. "Who do you have to put on this?"

"Austin James and Shane Cook are already looking into him. We expect to hear from them anytime now," Jack replied.

"Excellent. They've done good work on this case," Sheppard acknowledged. "Let me know when you get an update on their investigation into Wilson."

Jack and Dan agreed to keep the Chief informed of their progress. As they walked to Jack's office, his cell phone rang. He looked at the caller ID – the caller was Austin James.

"Sir," Austin said breathlessly. "You won't believe what we've uncovered about Tim Wilson!"

"Where are you now?" Jack asked. "Is Shane with you?"

"Yes sir," Austin replied.

"How soon can you get here?" Jack asked.

"We're about half an hour away, sir," Austin answered.

"Okay," Jack said. "Get here as fast as you can. We'll be waiting for you in my office."

The rookie agreed and the line went dead.

"The rookies are on their way, Dan," he said to his partner. "Austin seems pretty excited. Let's hope they found out something useful."

"I think it's time for a stakeout," Dan declared.

Jack nodded.

"Let's see what the rookies have to say," he said. "Maybe we'll have them pose as undercover orderlies to get close to Wilson."

When Austin and Shane walked into his office, Jack knew they were fired up. Excitement lit up their faces. He was sure they thought they were on the trail of something big. Patiently he and Dan listened as the men went over every detail.

"Tim Woods apparently began to use the name Tim Wilson several years ago. His parents died in a car accident when he was ten. Woods was being raised by his grandmother for several years after that happened. Then she died around his sixteenth birthday. Sometime after her death we suspect he began to use Wilson as his last name."

Austin looked steadily at Jack and Dan. Jack nodded.

"Did you find out how his grandmother died?" he asked.

"We found a police report that said she fell down some stairs in the building where they lived. No one was with her when her body was discovered. Apparently she was lying at the bottom of the steps for a few hours before another tenant found her. The medical examiner listed the cause of death as accidental. There was no mention of her grandson in the police report."

"Okay," Jack nodded approvingly. "Go on."

"As far as we can tell, there were no other relatives. We reviewed his records at Maplewood Academy for Special Children. Tim was enrolled there during elementary school and part of middle school. His grandmother withdrew him shortly after he started eighth grade. Apparently the kid was starting to get into trouble and the teachers and aides couldn't handle him anymore. They felt his needs would be better served somewhere else."

"The principle at the school, Miss Wasko, said that Woods was very highly functioning," Austin continued. "He was extremely intelligent but was also emotionally very immature. Apparently he had no understanding of basic social skills. His anger issues made him difficult to be around and the younger children were terrified of him."

Austin paused briefly, flipping the page in his notebook.

"So where did he go after that?" Dan asked.

"We have no idea," Austin said frankly. "We checked with all the private and public schools in the area. Tim Woods just fell off the grid."

"We also interviewed several of the grandmother's neighbors," Shane added. "Most of them didn't know either Mrs. Hanson or her grandson very well. They don't remember seeing the boy for a while before his grandmother died. Mr. Richard Donaldson who lived on the same floor in their building thought her grandson might have been institutionalized, but he didn't know for sure."

"That's right," Austin chimed in. "He said the young man had become very aggressive. He often heard him shouting at Mrs. Hanson."

"Was there a Mr. Hanson in the picture?" Dan inquired.

"No," Shane said, shaking his head. "According to Mr. Donaldson, the grandfather had never been around for the eleven or so years he knew Mrs. Hanson."

"Hmmm. Did you check the hospitals?"

Jack watched patiently as Shane thumbed through his notes.

"We did," Shane replied. "We checked all hospitals within a fifty mile radius for the last eight years. There is no record of Tim Woods or Tim Wilson ever being treated at or admitted to any of them, even the private Psych hospital in Buffington."

"That's right," Austin nodded his head. "However, we did find out some interesting information on Tim *Wilson*!"

Austin shifted in his seat and sat up as if he were ready to make an important announcement.

"Tim Wilson does not seem to have existed until he got a part time job doing odd jobs at Meadowbrook General about four years ago – around the same time Tim Woods disappeared," Austin proclaimed. "Eventually Wilson worked his way into a full time janitorial position there. He is now twenty years old according to the information in his employment folder – if that is accurate."

"Interesting," Jack noted as he briefly scanned the copy of Wilson's file. "The birthday listed here is the same as Megan Swanson's."

"The address he gave to the hospital belongs to a local thrift store that Wilson often visits," Austin continued. "We interviewed the owner. She said he has the maturity of an adolescent and has a vivid imagination. She said he's also very bright. He goes there often and frequently brings in clothes to donate. She has no idea where the clothes come from. She also doesn't understand why he would use their address as his own. She doesn't know where he lives."

Austin paused for a moment. Shane spoke up.

"We weren't able to locate Wilson at the thrift store or at the hospital this morning, but we did find out that he is on the schedule this evening starting at eleven. Do you want us to go to the hospital tonight to interview him?"

"Well," Jack said, half smiling as he looked at Dan out of the corner of his eye. "How would you guys feel about doing some undercover work at the hospital?"

He almost laughed as the young men practically fell out of their seats with excitement.

"Yes, sir!" Austin exclaimed loudly.

Shane nodded enthusiastically in full agreement with his friend. Jack and Dan spent the next hour outlining their plan.

"You will both pose as new hospital orderlies working the third shift. You're going to cause a small water spill about an hour before your shift is over."

Dan looked at the young men to see if they understood. They both nodded.

"After that, one of you will page a janitor to mop it up. Wilson is the only janitor on duty, so he will be the one who responds to your page. When he is done, we want you to discretely follow him until after he finishes his duties for the night. Then we want you to follow him when he leaves the hospital."

"That's right," Jack said. "Hopefully, you will find out where Wilson is living."

"Should we try to talk to him, Detective Russell?" Shane inquired.

"No," Jack replied. "Not yet. First we want to know where he goes after his shift ends. If you try to talk to him the first time he sees you around the hospital, he might get spooked."

"That's right," Dan said, nodding in agreement. "He's pretty much a loner. He might get suspicious if someone he has never seen before starts chumming up to him."

The rookies nodded their heads.

"Now, we'll be waiting in one of the conference rooms upstairs at the end of the shift," Jack explained. "That's just in case Wilson gets suspicious for any reason and something goes wrong. Tonight is strictly about gathering information. Once you follow him and find out where he lives, we will look into the possibility of getting a warrant to search his home."

The rookies nodded. Armed with their instructions, the young officers headed to the hospital to meet with Miss Darling for ID badges and uniforms for the operation. They were excited at the chance to be part of this action.

Jack placed a call to Dylan Kiser and requested access to the birth records for Melody's last delivery. Kiser assured Jack that the night supervisor of the Medical Records Department would be on hand to help the detectives obtain any information they needed.

It was nearly five o'clock by the time arrangements were completed for the undercover operation. Jack and Dan each headed home for some sleep before they had to report for the stakeout. They both hoped tonight would reveal more about the man who called himself Tim Wilson.

CHAPTER 32

The candles flickered silently, their tiny finger-like reflections dancing joyfully on the cinder blocks. He didn't feel joyful tonight. Tonight he was angry. Angry, but he didn't know why.

Mama was gone. *She and daddy have been gone for a very long time now,* he thought to himself. Nana said they weren't coming back, but Mama wouldn't do that. She would come back, he was sure of it. And when she did, she would be proud of him. After all, he did a good job. Just like she taught him to. Mama was coming back, alright.

He walked over to his masterpiece. He couldn't wait for Mama to see it. She would be proud of him, of how he figured it all out. She had taught him to read and write, even though no one ever thought he would. And she helped him to learn how to take care of himself, too.

Mama told him he could learn to do anything he wanted to. And so he did. He learned how to put money in his little baseball bank, and he learned how to buy candy and toys and other important stuff with his quarters and dimes and nickels.

Even after Mama went away he still took the bus and went to special school just like she showed him to. The teachers told him they were sorry about Mama and Daddy. He told them Mama and Daddy are fine. They just went away for a little while. The teachers looked sad.

Mama once told him it didn't matter if his real family didn't want him, because she and Daddy did. And that made it okay. Until his friend at school said he was dumb and no one wanted him and *that's* why Mama and Daddy went away.

And that made him mad. And that was when his friend fell out of the tree they were climbing and the teachers said he couldn't come back to school anymore. Funny. He didn't miss that friend.

He went to live with Nana when Mama and Daddy went away. But Nana didn't really understand him. She didn't think he was smart like Mama did. Nana wasn't Mama, and that made him sad.

One day Nana said he had to live by himself. She found this little room for him to sleep in. And she showed him how to find trays that people left in the hallway with perfectly good food on them. He asked Nana when Mama was coming back, and she said Mama wasn't coming back. And that made him mad.

And that was when Nana fell down those stairs. But it wasn't his fault. Not really. She shouldn't have said Mama wasn't coming back. He told her over and over not to say it, but she wouldn't listen. It isn't nice to lie. Mama said so.

So he had to push Nana to make her stop. And she did. And that's when the men came and carried her away. He waved at Nana when they put her in the big truck with the pretty flashing lights. But she didn't wave back. That made him sad. He wondered if Nana would come back when Mama came home.

"Mama," he said, whining with the voice of a young child. "Come home, please! I want to show you what I've done!"

Gently, he touched the worn photograph of his parents he had taped to the wall. He leaned in closer, and for a brief moment placed his lips on his mother's paper cheek.

"I love you, Mama," he said tenderly. "Come back soon."

CHAPTER 33

Jack and Dan arrived at Meadowbrook General at almost nine o'clock. They met with the hospital administrator to go over the plan for the night. Kiser then walked the detectives to the temporary command center he had set up for the operation.

Once they were settled in their hideaway, Jack called the night supervisor of the Medical Records Department. He was greeted by a jovial voice that sounded young and energetic.

"Medical Records Department. This is Christina Edgars," the voice declared. "How can I help you?"

"Good evening, Miss Edgars," Jack said. "This is Detective Jack Russell of the Meadowbrook Police Department. Mr. Kiser suggested that I call you about some medical records I need."

"Yes, sir!" she answered enthusiastically. "Mr. Kiser told me you would be calling tonight. I have exactly what you asked for. I'm a little tied up at the moment but as soon as I'm free I will bring them right up for you."

"I appreciate your help," Jack said.

Almost as soon as he hung up his cell phone began to ring. The caller was one of the undercover officers positioned outside the hospital.

"What can I do for you, Dave?" Jack asked.

"Jack," he replied, "I don't quite know how to tell you this. It's almost ten minutes after eleven. Tim Wilson's shift was supposed to start at eleven o'clock. No one stationed outside the hospital saw the subject enter the building. Do you know if he showed up for work?"

Jack was surprised by this information.

"Let me call the hospital administrator, Dave," Jack replied.

A quick call to Kiser confirmed that the employee had punched in at almost eleven o'clock exactly. Jack called Dave back and informed him that Wilson had indeed arrived in time for his shift.

"I wonder how long Wilson was at the hospital before his shift started," Dave mused. "I guarantee you we've been covering every possible entrance since around nine o'clock this evening!"

"I know you have, Dave," Jack reassured the frustrated officer. "This guy is pretty clever. Maybe the bigger question is how he went unnoticed by so many trained eyes. He's smarter than we've been giving him credit for."

When Jack told Dan about Wilson slipping by the outside surveillance team, Dan shook his head.

"This guy is not at all what he seems," he observed.

Jack agreed. They waited for Christina Edgars to deliver the records Jack had requested. Dan started reading the journal they had retrieved during their visit with the Governor. Soon he let out a long, slow whistle. Jack promptly looked up from the papers in front of him.

"What did you find?" he asked.

"As it turns out," Dan said, "Melody had taken an overdose of tranquilizers and was rushed to the emergency room. That's when they found out she was pregnant. Do you think she blamed herself for their birth defects?"

Jack remembered reading in other reports that Melody had used antidepressants and tranquilizers in the past. In fact, she died of an overdose. The coroner ruled it an accidental death.

"Maybe," Jack answered. "Does it sound like it was an accident or was she trying to commit suicide?"

Dan looked over at his friend and shook his head.

"I don't think so. She sounds remorseful. She hasn't mentioned any deep despair. It doesn't even sound like she was all that depressed. And so far, she hasn't mentioned anything about wanting to hurt herself."

"It didn't sound that way in her other journals, either," Jack replied. "She sure had a lot to live for. Maybe she was just feeling overwhelmed. Three young kids, a high profile life, an unplanned pregnancy - that had to be tough. She seemed kind of emotionally fragile to me."

Dan nodded.

"I see what you mean. I'll keep going and see what else is here."

Both men returned to their reading. A short time later they were startled by a loud knock. Jack got up and opened the door to expose a short, athletic looking young gal with long brown hair. She was staggering under the weight of three boxes that Jack could only assume were the records he had requested earlier.

"Wow! These boxes are heavy!" she said as she dumped them on the table.

"Thank you for bringing them to us," Jack said politely.

"I'm Christina Edgars, the Supervisor in Medical Records," she gushed. "Well, the Night Supervisor anyway!"

She blushed a little as she made the distinction.

"I'm Jack Russell. This is my partner, Dan Meyer."

"Oh, I know who you are, Mr. Meyer!" Christina exclaimed enthusiastically as she rushed to shake Dan's hand. "I saw the picture of you and your kids on your wife's desk upstairs! She loves the flowers you send her, by the way! All the other nurses get jealous when you do that!"

Dan looked at Jack as if he were begging for help. His partner was quick to oblige.

"Thank you again, Miss Edgars," Jack said firmly. "We appreciate your prompt response."

"No problem! That's what I'm here for."

She turned to leave then swung back around with a curious look on her face.

"There's one thing, though," she said, sounding mystified.

"The records looked like someone had gone through them after they were stored away. They were all over the place, not filed back correctly at all. And many of the duplicate copies are missing. I can't imagine why anyone would want to look at records almost two decades old! Well, except the police, of course!"

With that, she bounced out of the room, allowing the door to slam shut loudly behind her. Jack rolled his eyes.

"Good thing no one knows about us being here, right?" he said sarcastically.

Dan just laughed. They set aside the materials they had been reading to focus on the cartons of medical records. Each man took a box and began to sift through the medical jargon contained in the various reports. After nearly five hours, they were able to put together a timeline dating from Melody's visit to the ER all the way through her final discharge after the twins were born.

"Dan," Jack said curiously. "Have you noticed that the male twin is not mentioned again after the delivery? There aren't any chart notes, and no lab results or other test results. There doesn't seem to be any mention of him at all."

"I know," Dan said. "I find this very disturbing. Falsifying medical records is a crime. I understand now that Michael chose to give up his son, but I don't understand why the records just stopped. There is no mention of him being transferred to another hospital, either. Surely there has to be documentation of him somewhere."

Jack silently chided himself for not getting the name of the hospital where the baby was transferred to during their meeting with Langford. He would call the Governor in the morning to get that information.

"Someone was trying to cover up this baby," Jack said with a hint of sadness in his voice.

Dan nodded in agreement.

"Maybe it was too much for Swanson to admit he couldn't handle having a disabled child," Dan suggested.

"Maybe," Jack replied. "But why would he try to eliminate his records? Was he trying to make it seem like the boy never existed?"

"Who knows?" Dan answered. "Do you think they sent them to the other hospital? The one the Governor arranged for him to be treated at?"

Dan cocked his head slightly to one side, considering the possibility of his own words.

"I don't know," Jack replied. "But I think they would still keep a record here. Something isn't right about this."

"Wait a minute!" Dan said. "That woman just said it looked like someone had been rifling through these records. Do they keep logs of everyone who accesses a patient's chart?"

"One way to find out," Jack replied as he picked up the phone.

A quick call to Christina Edgars confirmed that yes, they do keep a log, but no, there has been no recent activity. The last person who signed the log was the nurse who did the discharge nearly twenty years ago.

As Jack replaced the receiver in the cradle, he wondered who would want to look at these records now. And why? What could they possibly be hoping to find? His thoughts were interrupted by a booming voice over the loudspeaker.

"Janitor to 3B. Janitor to 3B."

Jack glanced at his watch. Six o'clock on the dot. The rookies followed instructions well. He and Dan placed the records back in their boxes and called dispatch to send a car to pick them up later in the morning. Now was the time to be on guard in case Wilson became suspicious of Austin and Shane. They waited patiently for the young officers to contact them. Finally, nearly two hours later, Austin called Jack.

"Sir," he said slowly, "we aren't sure what's going on here."

Jack could hear the confusion in his voice.

"What happened?" Jack asked. "Where is Wilson? Did you lose him?"

"No sir," Austin replied with great confidence. "We know right where he is. That's what's so weird. He punched out, and we followed him deep into the basement. He used his keys to go into a room marked 'Hazardous Materials' and never came out. He's still in there. Shane's guarding the door."

"Okay, son," Jack said. "Stay where you are and keep your eyes on that door. I'll get in touch with Kiser to find out what's in that room."

He relayed the situation to Dan, who agreed that it was unusual for the employee to be in a place like that when he isn't on the clock. Jack put a call into Kiser, who immediately made his way to the conference room. When Kiser arrived a few minutes later he was accompanied by an older man wearing a maintenance uniform. The worker had a copy of the lower level blueprints in his dirty hands.

"Detectives," Kiser said. "This is Mr. Biglow, Tim Wilson's immediate supervisor. He has the floor plans from the lower section of the hospital."

After exchanging greetings Mr. Biglow laid the blueprints on the table.

"This is the floor plan of the basement of the hospital," Biglow explained. "The room your men saw Wilson go into is one of about two dozen rooms that were closed off nearly a decade ago. All of the extra rooms were emptied out and cleaned when that wing was shut down. Most of them are now being used for storage. There is only one way in and one way out of each room. Wilson has no reason to be in that room or in that part of the hospital as far as I know."

"Is it possible," Dan wondered out loud, "that Wilson stays there? I mean, that would explain some things, for sure!"

The men considered what Dan proposed.

"You could be right," Biglow said slowly. "There's a side door that isn't always locked down there. The maintenance staff uses it to haul out medical waste and other trash. He could slip in and out without being noticed pretty easily."

Jack quickly called Austin, who relayed that Wilson still had not come out.

"That's alright," Jack said to the anxious rookie. "You guys just stay put until I send someone to relieve you."

"We will, sir," Austin confirmed.

Jack turned to Dan.

"Dan," he said thoughtfully. "Would you make arrangements for relief officers to cover the room so Austin and Shane can be briefed on the next phase of the operation?"

"Sure thing," Dan replied.

He picked up the phone to make the call. Jack walked over the where the administrator was seated. Kiser looked up.

"Mr. Kiser," Jack began. "I'd like your permission to search all of the rooms in that corridor when Wilson leaves the hospital. That area is technically hospital property. We don't need a search warrant for anything of Tim Wilson's that is being stored in there. As long as you agree to let us perform the search, we won't need a warrant for the hospital, either."

Kiser nodded his head.

"Absolutely, detective," he said, waving his hand. "As I said before, anything you need!"

Jack thanked the administrator and the maintenance supervisor for their cooperation. Before Biglow left to respond to a page, Jack advised him that he would want to speak to him in more detail about Tim Wilson at a later time. The supervisor nodded in response to Jack's request.

By the time the rookies arrived at the conference room, Kiser had arranged for bagels and coffee for all of the officers. Once the food arrived Kiser returned to his office. Six men sat around the table as Jack and Dan explained how the search would be conducted.

"We have an additional four officers on alert and waiting outside the hospital," Jack explained. "Once Wilson leaves the hospital grounds, Austin and Shane will follow him. Now, we don't know exactly when he will be leaving, so we could all be waiting for a very long time."

The men all nodded, acknowledging the instructions.

"Jack and I will lead the search of the rooms with assistance from all of you. We are looking for information about Wilson as well as for anything that might connect him to the Swanson family or to the murders."

Dan looked around the room, searching for anyone who might have a question. There did not appear to be any.

"With luck on our side," Jack assured the officers, "today might be the day we capture a killer!"

Dan reviewed the rooms that needed to be searched with the teams and mapped out which room each pair of officers was assigned to. While they waited for Wilson to make a move, Jack contacted the Governor to ask about the hospital that treated the Swanson infant after he was born. Langford made a few calls, and within the hour the hospital had the records delivered to Meadowbrook General.

Late in the afternoon Wilson opened his door and peered out into the dark hallway. He listened for sounds of foot traffic, but was greeted by silence instead. Once he stepped out of his sanctuary, he gingerly turned the deadbolt with his key.

Quietly he made his way through several corridors to the hallway leading to the outside. He slipped out, leaving the door the slightest bit ajar, just to be certain he could get back in without being noticed.

Austin and Shane were excited. Finally, the hunt was on!

CHAPTER 34

The search teams descended on the downstairs corridor like clockwork as soon as Wilson was far enough away from the building. Two men were assigned to a room. Their orders were clear and they moved swiftly.

Kiser provided them with keys to all the locked doors. He accompanied Jack and Dan to the door of the room Wilson had been holed up in. When Dan tried to unlock it, the key wouldn't turn.

"That's strange," he mumbled to himself.

A second attempt proved fruitless as well.

"Allow me," Kiser said. "I have a master key that should do the trick. Maybe he changed the lock."

He pulled out a ring with a massive number of keys on it. Kiser found the one he needed and slid the worn metal into the waiting chamber. The deadbolt slid aside easily.

"Here we go!" exclaimed Jack as Kiser pushed open the door.

Dan felt along the wall for a light switch. When his fingers brushed against a metal chain he pulled it a few times, but darkness prevailed.

"Must be burned out," he grumbled as he reached for his flashlight.

Jack turned his on as well and the three men stepped into the tiny area. As the lights floated throughout the room, not one of them uttered a sound.

The musty stench of dirty laundry and spoiled food quickly engulfed them. Kiser muttered something about getting lights and disappeared. Jack and Dan walked slowly from the right to the left of the eight foot by ten foot room, taking note of the few belongings Wilson squeezed into this limited space.

A twin bed was pushed against the wall. Next to it was a small desk with a few candles and a tiny lamp. A broken chair was pushed up against it. Above the desk a tiny window allowed only a hint of light to trickle in.

A few boxes of clothes rested on top of piles of what looked like old newspapers stacked up neatly off to the sides of the room. Other boxes contained basic essentials such as toiletries, food staples and towels, all hospital issued. A garbage can next to a small sink looked as if it should have been emptied weeks ago. A small refrigerator completed the inventory of this hidden refuge.

Once they began to shine their flashlights on the walls, they noticed what looked like pictures plastered all over them. They stepped closer to get a better look.

"What is this on here?" Jack asked. "Can you tell?"

"It looks like some kind of collage," Dan replied. "But the pictures are all covered with paint!"

Jack leaned his face close into the wall to smell the substance that outlined many of the pictures.

"Dan," he said soberly. "I think this might be blood! We're going to have to send samples to the crime lab to see who it belongs to!"

"Here," Kiser's raspy voice echoed behind them in the tiny space.

He handed Dan a light bulb, which the detective quickly screwed into the socket on the wall next to the door. He pulled the metal chain and light immediately flooded the room.

The three men gasped as their eyes took in the walls of horror. Jack's gaze was drawn immediately to large bright red letters scrawled at the top of the wall near the window. SWEET, SWEET JUSTICE! He was sickened at the sight of it all.

Hundreds of photographs and articles about Michael and Melody Swanson and their children were cut out from old newspapers. They had been placed erratically over nearly every open space of the cinder blocks.

Words and phrases like 'LIARS', 'DO YOU KNOW ME?', and 'SWEET JUSTICE RIGHT MAMA' were scrawled randomly over some of the photos and articles. The handwriting appeared to be that of a child's. Pictures of what used to be a happy family were disfigured with wax and blood.

Rage poured out over every inch of concrete wall. The morbid display was made complete by photos that looked as though they had been stabbed over and over with a flat sharp object and spattered with blood.

Stunned, Kiser left the room. Dan and Jack began to walk around the small area, hoping to find something that would make sense of it all. Jack found one picture in a paper frame that had been spared the brutal assault. The faded photograph of a young couple was taped to the wall next to the bed.

"Look at this," he said, pointing towards the photo.

"Might be his parents," Dan observed.

Jack nodded in agreement. The men were almost numb as they walked around the room over and over. They were now confident the rookies had been right. This was the man they had been searching for. Dan pointed to the wall near the refrigerator.

"Looks like those photographs were professionally done," he remarked. "Could they have been taken from the Swanson home?"

"I'm not sure," Jack replied. "I didn't think anything was stolen from the house when the girls were killed. Did he ever do any work for them?"

Dan shook his head.

"I don't know. We can have the rookies check it out. We'll have them find out if that's a photo of his parents, too," he said, gesturing towards the unmarked picture.

Once the police photographer arrived the detectives stepped out of the room to let him take photos. They waited silently in the hallway until he collected the evidence he needed. When the photographer was finished, Jack and Dan went back in to search for a gun. Jack walked to the bed and lifted the mattress. Dan shook his head, indicating it wasn't there. He pulled out a stack of papers that looked like copies of medical records and showed them to Jack.

"Looks like he found out who he is," Jack remarked, shaking his head.

"Yeah, it does," Dan agreed. "I wonder how long he's known."

Jack just shrugged. Dan knelt down on the floor. The beam of his flashlight revealed notebooks and loose papers tossed carelessly around the floor under the bed. Dozens of old books were stacked erratically behind them, almost along the entire length of the bed. He reached under and pulled out one of the binders. He groaned as he flipped through the pages.

"Jack, check this out!" Dan exclaimed. "This looks like some kind of a diary!"

Jack walked to where Dan was kneeling and peered over his shoulder. The writing was almost illegible, but he could make out some of the words.

"Does that say what I think it says?" Jack asked Dan, his stomach beginning to turn.

"Shoot them and make them pay!" Dan said. "I think that's what it says!"

Both detectives shook their heads in unbelief. Dan labeled an evidence bag and placed the notebook inside. It would be sent to the crime lab to be documented and analyzed along with everything else from the room.

Jack walked over to the small desk and pulled open the drawer. A composition book was tossed carelessly on top of a pair of scissors, pens, pencils, a role of tape and a glue stick. He lifted the book out to see if there was anything else in the drawer. Tucked away carefully in the far back corner was a small pen knife. Forensics would determine if it was related to any criminal activity.

Their preliminary search of the room gave them probable cause to bring Wilson in for questioning. They were certain his arrest was imminent, but neither Jack nor Dan felt any sense of satisfaction by this turn of events.

With heavy hearts the detectives called in crime scene investigators to finish processing

Wilson's den of rage. They were relieved when they learned that the other officers did not find anything related to the case in the rooms they searched. One room like this was more than enough.

CHAPTER 35

Jack was concerned that no gun was recovered during their initial sweep of the suspect's room. The CSI's did discover nearly a dozen boxes of bullets. The ammunition had been carefully concealed behind the many stacks of books that were under his bed. The bullets were the same caliber as those used in the murders.

James and Cook had been able to confirm that neither Wilson nor his grandmother nor adoptive parents had guns registered in their names. When the weapon was eventually recovered they would be able to determine who its owner was and hopefully how Wilson happened to come into possession of it.

Jack glanced at his watch. It had nearly been three hours since the rookies followed Wilson out of the hospital. Jack was starting to grow concerned, but Dan reminded him that they had warned them not to get too close. If Wilson began to act suspiciously or started to return to the hospital they were to call Jack immediately.

"No news is good news, for now anyway," Dan said. "They have good instincts. I'm confident they will be fine."

Jack agreed. The rookies had common sense and followed instructions well. He and Dan made their way back to the conference room with the other officers to discuss the strategy for apprehending Wilson when he returned to the hospital.

"It's too dangerous to confront Wilson outside the walls of the hospital," Jack said.

"There are always civilians around and there are no guarantees. The risk that a bystander could be injured or killed is just too great. Instead, I think we should seal off the immediate area near where Wilson was staying, just in case he slips in another entrance for any reason. We don't want him being tipped off by the sight of uniforms in that area."

Everyone agreed. Jack continued.

"I want to cover all possible scenarios for Wilson's return to the hospital. I feel sure he will most likely re-enter through the side door he left from but I want to be prepared either way. Let's post troops on both ends of the corridor."

"You men," Jack said, pointing towards four of the extra officers, "will hang back in the doorways of the storage rooms until Wilson steps just inside the building. That corridor is far away from any staff, patients or visitors, and it's condensed enough to allow for a swift take down. It's also dark in that area so he won't notice that the doors to the other rooms are open. We need to wait for the door to lock behind him before apprehending him."

The men nodded.

"Jack," one of the officers said. "What about the gun? If it isn't in the room he probably has it on him."

"That's true," Jack responded. "We need to be aware that he may be armed. I think that we will probably take him down before he even has a chance to draw his weapon."

The men agreed on the plan and the officers proceeded to their assigned areas to wait for word of Wilson's arrival at the hospital. Jack and Dan walked through the corridors making sure everyone was exactly where they wanted them to be. Once they were satisfied, they headed back to the conference room to wait for Austin's call alerting them to Wilson's impending return.

Kiser was waiting for them when they arrived at their temporary command center. A small-framed elderly woman was with him. She was obviously very nervous.

"Mr. Kiser," Jack said curiously. "Can I help you?"

The administrator was not able to mask his distress.

"Detective Russell, this is Mrs. Isabelle Winterman. She was Human Resource Director a few years ago when Wilson was hired. She might have information that may be of help to you in your investigation."

Jack turned his attention to the elderly woman standing next to Kiser.

"I'm please to meet you, Ma'am," he said, reaching out to shake her frail, trembling, white-gloved hand.

"I'm pleased to meet you, too, sir," she replied, her shrill voice shaking.

She glanced over at Kiser.

"I hope I didn't do anything wrong, Mr. Kiser. I really do!"

Puzzled, Jack looked at Kiser, who was obviously anguished. He took Mrs. Winterman by the arm and gently walked her over to a chair.

"Please, Ma'am," he said softly. "Sit down. Can I get you anything?"

"No, no, I don't think so. Oh, this is just awful. This is simply awful!"

"It's all right," the administrator said gently. "You couldn't have known. Just tell the detective what you know about Tim Wilson, okay? He needs to know. It will be all right."

"Yes," Jack said as he turned his full attention to the matronly woman. "Please just tell me everything you know."

"Well," she began. "I knew Tim's grandmother for a long time before she died. She was so happy when her daughter and her son-in-law found a baby to adopt! It was hard, of course, with him being disabled and all. They said he'd never be smarter than an eight year old, but he fooled them all, yes he did! But then they were killed. It was awful – just awful!"

She glanced at Mr. Kiser, who motioned for her to continue.

"After that, Tim moved in with his grandmother. At first it looked like everything would be okay. He seemed like he was doing fine. At least I thought he was. Then this one day, Mattie – that's his grandmother – Mattie told me Tim was getting to be a handful."

Mrs. Winterman paused to catch her breath. After a quick moment she continued.

"Mattie didn't like to leave the boy alone while she worked. She asked me if it would be okay if he could stay over at the hospital while she worked her night shift here. She was a housekeeper here for a long time, just part time, of course. It was a second job for her."

Jack sighed. He tried to hide his impatience as he encouraged Mrs. Winterman to continue with her story.

"Well, I thought, 'Why not?' after she worked so hard, you know. And that poor child

239

had no parents now. It was hard for them! So I gave her a key to the room downstairs. He was just going to stay there when Mattie worked at night, you know. But when she died, that poor young boy had no one! Well, I just had to help him!"

She paused momentarily. Nervously, the elderly matron glanced at Mr. Kiser.

"Please continue, Mrs. Winterman," he prodded gently.

She nodded and shifted a little in her seat. She swallowed hard, and then continued her tale.

"Well, I asked Tim if he wanted to stay here, and he said yes. The rooms weren't being used, and he was such a good boy. He even helped clean up a bit so Mr. Biglow gave him a part time job. I helped Tim open a bank account and balanced his check book for him. He was doing so well on his own. I knew his Mama would be proud. He wanted her to be proud you know. How he missed his Mama!"

"Then," she continued, "Mr. Biglow gave him a full time job and, well, he's just been a wonderful employee. I'm sorry I let him stay here, Mr. Kiser, but he had no where else to go! I hope it was all right. He was such a good boy!"

Jack paused for a moment to give Mrs. Winterman a chance to regain her composure.

"Ma'am," he said. "We have reason to believe that Tim Wilson's name is actually Tim Woods. Do you know anything about him changing his name?"

She sighed, and then looked up at him over her thin wire framed glasses.

"Well, that's my fault. I suppose. You see, Mattie never told me his last name. He doesn't write very well, you know – he's handicapped and all – so when he filled out his application I thought it said 'Wilson'."

"Well, wouldn't you know after I had everything all done and he got his name badge, well, that was when he said his last name was Woods? I told him I could fix it but he said no, that was all right. He liked the name Tim Wilson! And so I said it could just be our little secret! He liked having a special secret! Just like the spies and detectives in the books he was always reading!"

Jack listened to the rest of her story, and thanked her for coming in. Dan walked up just as Mrs. Winterman finished speaking. After Kiser escorted the matronly woman out of the conference room Jack filled Dan in on what she had just told him. Dan shook his head.

"Well," he said. "That explains how he ended up here. But where did he get the gun?"

CHAPTER 36

After he left the hospital, Wilson walked quickly through the streets of Meadowbrook, stopping only long enough to wait for the street lights to give him permission to cross. Austin and Shane kept back far enough so they could easily duck into one of the shops along the way if their target became suspicious.

Wilson never looked back as he charged down the main street. Eventually he reached his final destination. Conlin's Bookstore and Coffee Shoppe was a popular local hangout for many of Meadowbrook's residents. Austin and Shane had both spent many hours there themselves.

They waited for Wilson to go inside, then peered through the windows to see where he went. Shane caught a glimpse of him walking up the stairs to the second level. The young officers cautiously made their way inside.

Austin took the same stairs Wilson used. Shane made his way to the opposite end of the first floor and walked up the back staircase. They positioned themselves at opposite ends of the upstairs level so they could keep an eye on Wilson while covering both sets of stairs.

Wilson settled in front of the young reader's mystery section. He sat at a small wooden table and pulled a crumpled bag from his jacket pocket. Methodically he opened it and removed an apple, a piece of cheese, and a sandwich of some kind.

He laid them in an orderly fashion on a paper towel that he pulled out of his other pocket, along with some kind of a juice box.

Austin couldn't help but think he was watching a kindergartner prepare for snack time.

This guy is one strange dude! he thought to himself.

When Wilson was done with his late afternoon feast, he wiped his face and hands with the paper towel. He then proceeded to gather his trash and wipe off the table.

On his way to the bookshelves he dropped the garbage into a small waste receptacle nearby. He studied the rows of paperbacks in front of him. Shane noticed a bright colored poster above the units. The Statue of Liberty stood proudly underneath the words 'SWEET, SWEET JUSTICE', proclaiming them loudly in large, bold letters.

After making his selection, he sat down at his table and slowly opened the book. The officers were both too far away to see what Wilson was reading. Almost three hours passed before Wilson abruptly stood up and returned his book to the shelf he had taken it from.

He promptly walked to the same staircase he came up earlier and made the trip back down. Before leaving the store he laid a handful of change on the counter where a clerk helped him count out what he needed for a cherry lollipop.

He carefully peeled off the wrapper and dropped it in the trash can. A few seconds later, Wilson opened the door and began his journey back to the hospital, enjoying his sugary treat along the way.

The men followed him as he trekked back in the direction of Meadowbrook General. Austin paused long enough to call Jack, who assured him the tactical units were all in place.

He reminded Austin and Shane to stay back when Wilson got close to the building.

Wilson made the trip back in no time at all, it seemed. When he arrived at the hospital he walked down the steps that led to the side entrance. He pulled the door open very slowly, just in case it squeaked.

Wilson listened intently for signs of anyone in the halls. When he was satisfied no one else was around, Wilson stepped inside the shadowy corridor and closed the door quietly behind him.

Almost immediately he was blinded by bright lights. A loud voice cried out, *"TIM WILSON, THIS IS THE POLICE! STOP WHERE YOU ARE!"*

For a moment Wilson froze in place like a deer in headlights. Swarms of large men in uniforms were rushing at him. He turned to run back outside but the door had locked automatically when he closed it. He was trapped! Agitated and afraid, he pulled out a small caliber pistol from his pocket and began waving it wildly in the air.

"GUN!"

Jack instinctively dove at the unstable subject, trying to take him down before he could fire. In his panic Wilson began to shoot. The officers fired back. A hail storm of bullets flew through the air. Wilson dropped immediately to the ground, his eyes wide open, his lips moving slowly, the cherry lollipop dangling from his mouth.

"HOLD YOUR FIRE!"

Silence resonated throughout the hallway. One officer handcuffed Wilson while another one called for paramedics. Dan checked around to make sure everyone was okay. It looked like they came through this unwanted confrontation unscathed. Dan saw Jack standing not far from where Wilson was laying on the ground. He had a strange look on his face.

"Jack! You okay?" Dan called out as he walked towards his partner.

"I think so, Dan," Jack replied weakly, wondering why the room was suddenly turning black.

He wouldn't remember slamming his head on the concrete when he dropped to the floor.

CHAPTER 37

The warm sun beat down on him as he listened to the sound of water slapping against the sandy beach. Jack watched the dolphins playfully leaping in the waves far from shore. Out of nowhere a beach ball dropped down right in front of him.

"Hey, mister!" he heard a little voice yell. "Can you throw my ball back, please?"

"Sure, kid!" he yelled back.

He tried to lean over to pick it up, but he couldn't move. It was almost as if he was paralyzed.

"What's going on?" Jack thought to himself, mildly annoyed.

Again he attempted to stretch his body, but it wouldn't budge.

"Jack!"

He heard a voice calling to him, but he couldn't see who it was. He moaned softly, trying to respond. Nothing coherent came out of his mouth.

"It's okay, Jack. Try not to move. It won't hurt as much if you lie still."

He opened his eyes slowly. Everything was out of focus. He blinked over and over, trying to see through the shadowy blur. When he tried to turn his head towards the voice, a sharp pain pierced his skull.

"No, Jack," the voice said gently. "Try not to move. Just lie still"

"Where am I?" he asked weakly, trying to understand what was happening.

"You're in the hospital. You've been here since yesterday. Do you remember being shot?"

"Shot? No. That can't be right. I'm on the beach."

The voice giggled.

"Well, good for you. That's *way* better than being in a hospital!"

He drifted back into a deep, deep sleep.

The next morning, Jack woke to the aroma of hospital coffee and scrambled eggs. He opened his eyes and looked around the room. His gaze fell upon the petite form wrapped in a crisp white blanket and curled up on the high backed chair. Her face was hidden under long blond waves, but Jack recognized the charm bracelet on her wrist.

"Sara," he called out hoarsely with all the energy he could muster.

She stirred slightly.

"Sara," he called again.

This time she sat up.

"Jack!" she cried out, with tears biting at her eyes. "Are you all right? You had me so scared!"

Sara rushed to the side of his bed and cradled his hand in hers. Gently she rested her head on his shoulder. Jack couldn't remember ever seeing anything more beautiful.

"Well, good morning, Jack!" Jennifer said brightly as she stepped into the room.

She moved to the window and opened the blinds to let daylight rush past them.

"How was the beach?" she asked with a grin.

"That's nice," Jack responded weakly, vaguely remembering something about dolphins and a beach ball. "Make fun of the patient!"

She flashed him a big smile and winked at her friend. Sara stepped aside so Jennifer could check his vital signs. The pain medicines were helping, but Jack was still extremely sore. She moved gingerly so as not to cause him any more discomfort than necessary.

"Well," she announced confidently when she was finished. "You're healthy as a horse. Except for a concussion and those gaping holes in your chest. Other than that, you're the poster boy for good health!"

"Why, thank you, nurse!" he exclaimed with a touch of sarcasm. "Now how about some of that coffee?"

"Sorry, hon," Jennifer said regretfully. "It's broth for you today. Your stomach can't handle much more than that right now!"

Jack let out a deep sigh. Sara smiled down at him.

"Don't worry," she said tenderly as she brushed the hair away from his forehead.

"As soon as we get you home, I will make you anything you want. Besides," she whispered. "I've had the coffee and eggs here. Believe me, you want the broth!"

Jack smiled. She was probably right.

"Detective Russell!" a strong, booming voice declared. "You are one lucky man!"

Jack looked up to see Dr. Michael Lundgren, Chief of the General Surgery Department at Meadowbrook General Hospital standing in the doorway, smiling broadly.

"I know, sir," Jack responded gratefully. "I just don't remember why!"

"He's right, Jack" Jennifer said seriously. "Two rounds of friendly fire managed to find their way under the side of your vest when the bullets started to fly. They bounced around in your chest like pool balls after a solid break! Dr. Lundgren and his team operated for nearly two hours to remove the fragments."

Jack groaned.

"That explains it," he said weakly.

Dr. Lundgren walked across the room and stood silently at the end of Jack's bed. He removed the chart that was hanging from a silver hook attached to the bed rail and quickly read through the notes. Eventually the physician looked over his glasses at Jack and smiled.

"How are you feeling, Jack?" the fifty-something physician inquired gently.

"Pretty sore," Jack replied honestly. "And my head is pounding. I almost don't want to move it, that's how much it hurts."

"You took a bad hit to the head," Dr. Lundgren said gravely. "You will need some time to recover, but eventually you will be good as new. I hear you have some excellent nurses available to take care of you!"

The fatherly man winked at Sara and Jennifer. The nurses were smiling as they left the room so the doctor could talk privately with his patient. After examining Jack's surgical wounds, the doctor turned his attention to the golf ball sized lump on the back of Jack's head.

When he was finished, Dr. Lundgren smiled and patted Jack's arm. He motioned for Sara and Jennifer to come back into the room.

"We're going run a few more tests once the swelling on the back of your head goes down," the surgeon announced. "Dr. McKenna will be in later to look at that lump. I will check in on you again tomorrow morning. In the meantime, don't give these nurses any trouble!"

"I don't think I could if I wanted to," Jack admitted with a slight grin.

Jennifer and Sara smiled. Dr. Lundgren chuckled and motioned for Jennifer to follow him. The pair left the room to discuss Jack's progress and the doctor's orders. A few minutes later Chief Sheppard and Dan strolled in. After greeting them and thanking the men for coming, Sara excused herself so they could talk.

"Jack, how are you feeling?" the Chief asked.

The concern showing in his eyes was genuine, Jack knew. He appreciated the way the Chief looked out for his men.

"Well, sir, I feel a little like I've been shot!" Jack replied, only half joking.

"You gave us a scare, that's for sure!" the Chief responded. "The doctor says you'll be off your feet for a while. You lost a lot of blood."

"How's your head?" Dan asked.

Jack could see that his partner was worried, too.

"Well, I've got a pretty big knot and the headache to go with it. But I don't know how that happened!" Jack said, sounding confused.

"I do!" Dan exclaimed. "You went down in less than half a second. The guys all the way down at the other end of the hallway heard your head hit the floor!"

"I don't remember," Jack said, shaking his head slowly. "The last thing I remember is seeing Wilson's gun."

Jack tried to sit up but a wave of nausea and dizziness washed over him. The color drained from his face and he slumped towards the edge of the bed.

"Easy, Jack," Dan said as he rushed to help his friend steady himself. "Don't try to move. You need to stay as still as you can."

After Jack was settled again, he asked Dan to fill him in on a few of the details after Wilson was shot. Dan hesitated for only a moment before shaking his head. He knew his friend was exhausted and needed to rest.

"Let's get you out of here before we worry about that," he said.

The Chief agreed.

"There will be plenty of time for that when you get back to work," Chief Sheppard added. "Right now, your only job is to take it easy and get well."

Dan moved the hospital tray closer to Jack so the ice chips in the pitcher were within his reach. He and the Chief quickly said their goodbyes and left the hospital. After the two men were gone, Jack thought about Sheppard's parting words.

"Now I want you to get some rest and try not to overdo it," Sheppard had commanded.

The way Jack felt at the moment he was positive that would not be a problem.

CHAPTER 38

A flurry of visitors poured in and out of Jack's room throughout the next five days as he recovered from his injuries. Cards and flower arrangements adorned his window sill. A colorful fruit basket rested on his night stand next to the magazines and newspapers his friends brought to help him pass the time.

Friday. Today was the day Dr. Lundgren had talked about sending Jack home. Impatiently he flipped through the TV channels while he waited for the doctor to appear. Over the clamor of a game show Jack heard a knock on the door. He looked up to see the smiling face of Father Walter from St. Bartholomew's.

"Jack!" the priest exclaimed. "How are you feeling, my boy?"

Jack smiled back, actually happy to see the elderly man.

"Father!" Jack replied. "I'm doing much better! Thank you for coming."

"You certainly look much better than you did a few days ago," Father Walter said. "You gave us all quite a scare."

"I know, Father," Jack said. "I appreciate all the cards and flowers. Several people from the church have stopped in. It was so good to see them."

Jack was amazed that he actually meant those words. He smiled to himself. It felt good to have Father Walter by his side again.

"Well, we all miss you, Jack," the priest said, his blue eyes catching the light from the sun that was gleaming through the blinds.

The two men talked like the old friends they were for about half an hour until Dr. Lundgren came in.

"Father Walter," Dr. Lundgren said pleasantly. "How nice to see you!"

"Ahhh," the priest replied. "Dr. Mike! It's always nice to see one of God's healers at work!"

Dr. Lundgren grinned and turned his attention to Jack.

"And how is our patient today, Father?" he asked.

"I believe he is ready to go home, if I interpret his body language correctly!"

Father Walter winked at the doctor as Jack nodded his head.

"That you certainly do, Father," Jack said enthusiastically. "That you certainly do!"

They laughed and Dr. Lundgren moved to Jack's side to examine him. After a moment he looked at Jack and began to speak, his words low and serious.

"I am going to let you go home today, Jack," the doctor began. "But only under the condition that you follow every single one of my orders. You took quite a blow to the head and you still need some time to recover. Agreed?"

Jack nodded.

"Agreed," he said.

"The lump on your head is finally gone," Dr. Lundgren continued, "which is good, of course, and the brain scan and the MRI both look good as well. I'm concerned about the dizziness you're still experiencing. That tells me the concussion is not completely resolved."

He looked hard at Jack, who was listening intently.

"You're going to need to continue to clean around your stitches and change the dressings twice a day. Call my office to make an appointment for Monday or Tuesday and we'll take them out for you."

Dr. Lundgren paused. Jack agreed. He was relieved that he was finally going home.

"I appreciate all you've done," he said gratefully to the doctor.

"It was my pleasure," the doctor replied. "Perhaps the next time I see you when this is over with it will be for a round of golf."

"That's a great idea!" Jack replied.

The men shook hands and Dr. Lundgren left to write up his orders.

"Well, Jack," Father Walter said as he clapped his hands together. "This *is* good news! Can I give you a ride home?"

"Thank you, Father Walter," Jack said appreciatively, "but someone is coming for me. She should be here anytime now."

Jack slowly swung his legs over the side of the bed. He had learned that if he took his time getting up he could avoid the dizziness and nausea that accompanied swift movements. Thankfully that was slowly passing as his head injury healed.

"Then I shall leave you to prepare for your triumphant return home."

Father Walter rose from the chair he was seated in and smiled at Jack.

"It was good to see you, Jack. Take care of yourself and don't be a stranger!"

Father Walter shook his friend's hand.

"I won't, Father," Jack said. "I promise. Thank you again for stopping by."

When the priest was gone Jack walked over to the tiny hospital closet. He removed the clothes Dan brought for him yesterday and carried them into the bathroom. After a brisk shower he dressed quickly. He knew he needed to hurry, as much as he could at any rate. Jack wanted to be ready to leave when Sara arrived. Jennifer bounced into his room just as he was combing his hair.

"You clean up pretty good," she said, grinning from ear to ear. "We're going to miss you around here."

"Well," Jack replied. "Please don't be offended by this but I'm not going to miss this place at all. I've decided that it's much better being on the visitor side of a hospital bed!"

Jennifer smiled.

"I know what you mean," she agreed. "Is Sara on her way?"

Jack nodded.

"I believe so. She said she would be here by ten o'clock."

Almost as if on cue Sara poked her head in the door.

"Taxi's here!" she announced cheerfully.

Jack turned and smiled. He was happy to be leaving the hospital. He was especially happy to be leaving with Sara. Jennifer reviewed Dr. Lundgren's orders with both of them. When she was done, Jack signed them and she gave him a copy to take home.

"Thank you for everything," Jack said to Jennifer. "I really mean it. You took great care of me and I really do appreciate it!"

"You're welcome, Jack," she replied sincerely as she wrapped her arms around his neck and hugged him tight. "I'm so glad you are okay. Now get out of here! I have sick people to take care of!"

They laughed. Sara loaded his flowers onto a cart the gift shop manager loaned her. Jennifer paged a volunteer to wheel it down to the patient loading area while Sara pushed Jack down the hallway towards the elevator.

"I could get used to this," Jack teased as she rolled him through the open doors.

Sara just smiled and pushed the button to the lobby. She was relieved that Jack was okay. She could not remember a time when she had been so frightened. When the elevator finally reached the ground floor Sara wheeled him over to her car. The patient loading area was fairly empty this morning so there was no need to rush.

She helped Jack get into the car while the volunteer filled the back seat and the trunk with flowers and the rest of his belongings. In no time at all Sara pulled into Jack's driveway. She started to walk him into the house to be sure he didn't lose his balance.

"This really isn't necessary," Jack said gruffly.

She looked at him sternly.

"Do I need to call the doctor already, Detective Russell?" Sara responded with her firmest nurse's tone.

Jack grunted. She laced her arm through his and immediately felt his muscles relax. He patted her arm gently as they made the short trip to the sofa. Jack smiled to himself. He loved a strong woman. Three trips later Sara was finally done unloading the car. The aroma of fresh flowers quickly filled Jack's living room.

"Now *this* is a cheery place!" Sara declared when she finally finished arranging the vases.

Jack agreed.

"Would you like a tour of the house?" Jack asked, glad he had taken the time to clean a few weeks ago.

"We can do that later," she replied. "I have a surprise for you right now."

"Really?" Jack said. "What is it?"

"I've been doing some research on you, Jack Russell," Sara declared proudly. "You just sit here for a bit and lunch will be served shortly. I have something very extravagant to prepare and I don't need you underfoot!"

With that Sara promptly turned and marched into the kitchen. A short time later Jack heard the clanging of pans and the clanking of silverware and glasses. A very flavorful smell soon floated into the living room. Sara finally returned to announce that lunch was served. She ushered Jack into the dining room.

When he saw the spread laid out for him, Jack laughed so hard that his head started to hurt. Sara had prepared his favorite lunch in the world – grilled cheese sandwiches with ham and tomato and creamy tomato soup. She even found the little crackers he liked so much, the ones shaped like little fishes.

"Thank you, Sara," Jack said gratefully. "This is a great surprise!"

Sara blushed. She was glad Jack was pleased.

"After what you've been eating these last few days, I'm afraid shoe leather might taste good to you!" she exclaimed.

Jack chuckled. Sara laid her napkin neatly over her lap and shyly placed her hand over his.

"I'm glad you're home, Jack," Sara said sincerely as she looked into his eyes. "And I'm very glad that you are okay!"

"Thank you, Sara," Jack said, touched by her concern. "I'm glad to be here with you!"

CHAPTER 39

Under Sara's watchful eyes, Jack followed Dr. Lundgren's orders completely. By the end of his second week at home, he was desperately itching for something to do besides watch television and read. Recovery hadn't been all bad, though, Jack had to admit. True to her word, Sara treated Jack to her superb culinary skills.

"You're spoiling me, Sara," Jack teased as they polished off the leg of lamb Sara had prepared for tonight's dinner.

With Jennifer's help, she had discovered all of his favorite foods and the entire time Jack was recovering at home she purposefully never made the same meal twice.

"I could get used to this!"

Sara smiled and patted his hand.

"And you'll get used to helping with the dishes, too," she joked as she gave him a wink.

Jack grinned. He was sure she knew he would have been happy to help. However, Sara wouldn't let him lift a finger around the house until the doctor released him from his care. Tomorrow Jack would see the surgeon for what he hoped would be the last time. He was anxious to get back to work – and back to the investigation.

The Chief insisted that Dan not discuss the case with Jack until he was able to return to work. Although Jack was mildly annoyed by that, he respected the Chief's decision and didn't try to pry the details from his friend.

"Let's stop at the Thai place for lunch before your appointment later," Sara suggested after she stopped in to make breakfast the next morning.

"That's a great idea," Jack said. "Shall we give Dan and Jennifer a call and see if they want to join us?"

Sara blushed and shrugged her shoulders.

"I already did that!" she said, somewhat sheepishly.

Jack grinned and shook his head.

"You're way ahead of me, Sara Bronstein!" he said jokingly.

"And don't you forget that, Detective!" she exclaimed with a smile.

Sara had arranged to meet Dan and Jennifer at one o'clock. Jack and Sara stopped to pick up some dry cleaning on the way to the restaurant. After running a few more errands, the couple pulled into the parking garage at almost exactly one.

"I don't like to be late," Sara lamented.

Traffic had been a bear and her frustration was starting to show. She felt bad that her errands made them run a few minutes late for meeting their friends.

"Don't worry! I'll show them my scars," Jack joked. "They can't get mad at an invalid!"

Sara rolled her eyes at him as they walked hand in hand towards the entrance. Dan and Jennifer were already seated. Dan waved at them and Jack and Sara walked over to the table.

"Wow! You look fantastic, Jack!" Jennifer exclaimed. "You've done a great job, Sara," she added. "I think he's put on some weight!"

The four friends laughed as their waitress approached the table with a tray loaded with soft drinks and water glasses.

"We've already ordered pretty much one of everything," Dan declared jovially. "I'm sure you'll find something you like."

The foursome talked and laughed as they waited for their food. Finally, the waitress brought out their steaming selections.

"You weren't kidding, Dan!" Sara exclaimed when the last dish was placed in front of them. "Who is going to eat all of this?"

She shook her head. They all laughed.

"Well, the leftovers will be going back to headquarters with me this afternoon," Dan said. "We've been pulling some late nights trying to tie up all the loose ends of the Swanson case."

Jennifer elbowed her husband hard in the ribs.

"Owww!" Dan exclaimed, looking at his wife with surprise. "What was *that* for?"

"You don't follow instructions very well, Daniel Meyer," his wife chided. "You aren't supposed to talk about the case in front of Jack!"

"It's okay, Jennifer," Jack said, coming to Dan's defense. "In roughly," he paused dramatically to look at his watch, "two hours I expect to be cleared for full duty."

"Well, you aren't cleared yet!" Jennifer declared. "Eat your lunch and then we'll see what the doctor has to say. Personally, I think you need another two weeks off!"

"I agree!" Sara adamantly bobbed her head.

"Please," Jack begged. "*Please* don't tell the doctor that! I can recite the entire program guide on television. A man can only take so much time off!"

They all laughed. Jack had never been the type to sit around. No one was surprised that he was a little stir crazy. Even still, at Jennifer's insistence the topic of conversation was turned away from the case and the four laughed and ate until they were full. Dan groaned as he laid down his fork.

"I hope I can stay awake this afternoon!" he declared as he rubbed his stomach.

Once the leftovers were packed up and the check was settled, Dan returned to headquarters with the take out bags tucked under his arm. Jennifer walked back to the hospital to finish her shift and Jack and Sara quickly made the three mile drive to Dr. Lundgren's office.

"I hope this is it," Jack said nervously as they walked up the stairs to the office.

Sara knew he was getting a little anxious about being away from work for so long.

"I hope so too," she said supportively. "But if it isn't just remember the doctor is looking out for you. If you aren't completely better, you could make things worse for yourself by going back too soon."

Jack sighed. He knew she was right. He just couldn't say it out loud right now.

"Hello, Detective Russell!" a bright voice exclaimed when they walked into the office.

Hannah Jansen was Dr. Lundgren's receptionist. She was a young, pleasant woman with a friendly smile. In a lot of ways she reminded him of his secretary.

"How are you, Hannah?" Jack asked.

"I'm doing well, thanks," she replied pleasantly. "The question is how are *you*?"

Jack smiled.

"I feel good, thanks," he responded with a wink.

Jack and Sara sat down and waited for a few minutes until the medical assistant called for Jack.

"This way, Mr. Russell," she said crisply.

Sue Thomas was very capable and professional. She had a no nonsense way about her that Jack appreciated. The petite brunette escorted him through the hallways to the examination room. Once the door was closed and the patient was seated on the examining table, she checked his vital signs.

"So far so good!" she announced with a smile. "Now - how have you been feeling?"

"Pretty good," Jack said. "Getting better every day!"

He wasn't going to mention the headaches or the dizziness he felt two days ago when he was in the shower. He was positive they would pass eventually. Sue looked at him inquisitively. Jack was sure she had read his mind. She nodded slightly and tapped her pen on his chart.

"Any dizziness or nausea?"

Yep, Jack thought to himself. *She read my mind.*

"No nausea," he answered honestly. "I was dizzy two days ago in the shower but it passed right away and once in a while I still get a headache or two. I don't think it's anything to be worried about."

"How about where your stitches were?" she asked matter-of-factly. "Any discomfort?"

"Once in a while," he said reluctantly.

Jack was starting to lose his confidence that he would be returning to work. He brushed away the disappointment and forced a half smile.

"Alright," she said slowly as she looked directly at him.

Sue paused for a few moments to make some notes in his medical chart. When she was done she looked at him and smiled.

"Let's have you remove your shirt," she said. "The doctor will be in to see you shortly."

She closed the door behind her and Jack mechanically started to unbutton his jersey. The chest wounds were still a little sore when he dressed, but he really *was* feeling much stronger. He laid the shirt on the table behind him. After a few minutes, there was a sharp knock. The door promptly flung open and the physician stepped into the room.

"Jack Russell," Dr. Lundgren said boldly. "How are you doing?"

Jack smiled as he shook the doctor's outstretched hand. After taking a moment to glance at the chart the surgeon looked squarely into his patient's eyes.

"So you were dizzy?" the doctor asked. Jack nodded.

"How long did it last? A minute? A few minutes?"

"Just about a minute or so," Jack answered. "Maybe not that long. It went away pretty quickly."

"And you're still having headaches?" he inquired.

"Once in a while, yes," Jack replied. "But not at all like they were in the hospital. An aspirin or two knocks them right out."

Lundgren made some notations in Jack's chart. When he finished he stepped closer to the table to examine Jack's head. After poking around where the lump had been, he stopped to make notes in the chart again. Eventually he moved back to the table to examine the areas on Jack's chest where Lundgren and another surgeon had sewn close to a hundred stitches.

"These wounds have healed nicely," he commented.

Jack winked.

"I had an excellent surgeon!" he said slyly.

Dr. Lundgren smiled.

"Do you still have any sensitivity around where the stitches were?" he asked.

Jack shook his head.

"Some tenderness once in a while, but I don't notice it until I look in the mirror."

Jack looked hard at the doctor, trying to read his expression.

If Dr. Lundgren doesn't play poker, he should, Jack thought to himself.

"Good," the surgeon said. "The sensitivity will eventually go away. Does it keep you from doing your normal daily activities like showering or dressing?"

"Not at all," Jack replied honestly.

"Okay. That's very good. Now here's what I think."

The doctor sat down on the chair next to the examining table and turned his attention to his patient. Jack drew a deep breath, not sure he wanted to hear what the doctor had to say.

"Your chest wounds have healed nicely," the older man began. "Keep putting liquid vitamin E on them and the scarring should be minimal. You have good skin tone, which helps."

He paused for a moment. Jack felt the color leaving his face. He wasn't sure how to prepare for what the doctor was going to say next.

"Now, as for your head," Dr. Lundgren paused for what seemed like an eternity.

"I'm concerned that you're still having some dizziness and headaches, but it isn't all that uncommon after the concussion you experienced. Still, in your line of work, I can't release you until I know for sure that this has resolved."

The surgeon noticed that Jack's shoulders dropped slightly.

"However," he added. "I'm sure you are anxious to return to work. Am I right?"

"Yes," Jack replied, confident that the doctor understood how he felt.

The doctor nodded.

"Okay. Then here's my recommendation. I will release you to light desk duty. That means no running, no jumping over tall buildings, and absolutely no diving to take down the bad guys. Can you do that without too much trouble?"

Lundgren looked over his glasses at Jack with a hint of a smile on his lips.

"Yes, I can do that," Jack replied with a slight grin and a nod.

He let out a sigh of relief. He was pretty sure he would have gone crazy if he had to stay home one more day. Thankfully the doctor spared him that cruel sentence.

"And no driving for now as well," the doctor continued. "I don't want you behind the wheel of a car until the headaches are gone and you have no more dizzy spells for at least two weeks."

Lundgren waited for a nod of acknowledgement from Jack before he finished the notes in his chart. Jack put his shirt on quickly. When he turned to leave, the older man shook Jack's hand firmly.

"I'll see you again in two weeks," he said.

Jack followed the surgeon out of the room. He returned to the reception area where Sara was waiting for him. She looked up and smiled warmly.

"So?" she asked expectantly. "What did the doctor say? Can you go back to work yet?"

Sara nodded as Jack briefly explained the doctor's orders. She didn't tell him but she was pleased that he still had limitations. Sara knew his head injury had been severe and her training as a nurse told her he needed more time to heal. The couple left the office with Jack clutching his light duty medical release papers firmly in his hand like a first prize ribbon from a fair.

CHAPTER 40

The next day, Dan swung by to pick Jack up for his first day back at work. As soon as he saw his friend pull into the driveway, Jack walked outside and greeted him with a smile. Dan immediately noticed the brown bag Jack was trying to conceal under his jacket.

"What kind of contraband are you sneaking into the office on your first day back?" Dan demanded with a hint of a smile.

Jack just laughed.

"I brought your favorite strawberry pastry to say thanks for being my personal chauffer for the next two weeks," he replied. "I didn't even eat any of it!"

Dan laughed. He appreciated the gesture but it wasn't necessary. Their friendship ran deep. There wasn't anything they wouldn't do for each other. As they drove down the streets towards the station Dan filled Jack in on what was happening with the investigation.

"I'm sure you already know this, Jack," Dan said. "Wilson died in the emergency room before I had a chance to interview him. He took three bullets to the chest. He lost so much blood he went into cardiac arrest on the gurney."

Jack knew that Wilson died as a result of the altercation with the police from follow up stories on the late night news. To say he was disappointed about that would be an understatement.

"I heard that he had died from the news on TV while I was in the hospital," Jack confirmed. "I had hoped to talk to Wilson myself. I thought if I talked to him it would help to make some sense of everything that happened. Wilson's death was just a tragic ending to an already tragic life."

Dan nodded his head in agreement.

"I spoke to the DA about Miles Winston and his role in all of this," Dan continued. "Cindy Reagan is going to review all of the documentation and make a recommendation. I got the impression that she didn't think there was any intentional wrong doing on Winston's part. With almost everyone involved being dead, there may not be any reason to pursue it anyway. There are no winners here, so it's pointless."

Jack sighed. He was frustrated by the loopholes afforded to attorneys. He had a great deal of respect for the job they have to do, but it seems like they go too far over the line at times. Jack felt strongly that this was one of those times, but he knew the deal. They would have to accept her decision.

"Where are we with the evidence?" Jack asked.

"The crime lab is still working on processing the books and papers we recovered from Wilson's room. If you remember, the handwriting was, well, atrocious!" Dan declared. "The preliminary reports they sent over from the walls indicated that the blood was from all three of the Swanson sisters as well as his own. Most of it was his. DNA confirmed that he *was* Swanson's son."

Jack sat quietly for a moment, letting Dan's words sink in.

"How did Wilson manage to get back into the hospital after that brutal attack with no one noticing?" Jack asked. "He had to have been drenched in blood!"

"We may never know that, Jack," Dan replied. "My guess? He had a change of clothes with him. That must be how we got photographs of him at the crime scene with no blood on his clothes. The bloody outfit had to have been stashed someplace."

"It was too far for him to have made it back to the hospital to change and get back in time to watch the activity at the house," Jack mused. "Maybe he went back to where the clothes were hidden after all the commotion was over. He must have used the blood from the clothes to draw on his walls. Maybe he tossed them into the hospital incinerator when he was done."

Jack tapped his foot slowly, considering this possible scenario. It made sense, in a sick sort of way. No traces of blood were found on any of the clothes in his room.

"Were you able to establish a connection between Wilson and the Swanson family yet?" Jack asked.

"I put the rookies on that," Dan replied. "Apparently one of the Swanson sisters hired him to clean out their basement. From what the guys were able to find out from their financial records, Wilson worked for them for about two months before the murders. That was the first record Austin and Shane could find of him having any contact with the family. My guess is he probably stole the photos from the house when he was there prior to the murders."

"So the whole time they thought he was helping them he was actually figuring out his plan of attack," Jack said softly.

"It looks that way," Dan replied, sharing his friend's anguish.

The two men drove along in silence for a few minutes. Dan waited patiently for Jack's next question. He knew this was a lot for his buddy to process on his first day back. Meadowbrook had never seen a crime like this before. He hoped they never would again. Jack sat quietly trying to put himself in Tim Wilson's place.

"I wonder what must have gone through Wilson's depraved mind during those long two months before he made his fateful move," he said thoughtfully as he stared out the window.

"I've been wondering that myself," Dan replied.

Finally they were at the parking garage. Dan maneuvered his car into his assigned space and the detectives were quickly on their way upstairs to Chief Sheppard's office. As soon as Jack rounded the corner Judy Lane was out of her seat. She planted a kiss on his cheek and promptly wagged a menacing finger at him.

"Jack Anthony Russell!" she exclaimed dramatically. "Don't you *ever* get shot again, do you hear me?"

"I will do my best, Ma'am!" he exclaimed with a grin.

The worry in her face touched his heart. He hugged her and thanked her for her concern. Chief Sheppard walked out of his office and greeted the detective warmly.

"So," he said cheerily. "You're finally back! And not a minute too soon! Lisa Vick just called a few minutes ago to see how you are! Looks like you're going to be another front page story!"

Jack groaned. The Chief and Dan laughed as Judy rolled her eyes at him. That made the detective smile.

"Come on in," the Chief said, motioning for the detectives to enter his office.

"Hold my calls, please Judy?" the Chief asked.

"Of course," she replied graciously.

They sat down and Dan continued to brief Jack on the progress of the investigation.

"One thing I don't understand," Jack said. "Where did someone like Tim Wilson get Rohypnol?"

"We wondered that, too," Dan said. "Several bags of pills were found in one of the boxes in his room. Most of them were things like aspirin and antacids. But one of them was an empty evidence bag from the case involving that serial rapist Bill Peters."

"How did Wilson get his hands on that?" Jack asked, shocked that anything like that could even happen.

"There's only one theory we've been able to come up with to explain that," Chief Sheppard said solemnly. "The bag must have been left behind accidentally when Peters was released from the emergency room the night he was apprehended."

"Wilson must have found the bag of pills when he cleaned the treatment room," Dan added. "It was labeled pretty clearly. Somehow he found out what it could be used for, most likely on the internet – or in the pages of one the mystery books he filled his head with."

"Leaving that evidence behind was a careless mistake if that's what happened," Jack said soberly.

They all agreed.

"I have Kline and Peterman looking into that," the Chief replied. "We need to make sure that nothing like that ever happens again!"

Dan and Jack nodded.

"And the gun? Where did the gun come from?" Jack asked.

"It was registered to Mr. Biglow, the guy who gave Wilson his job at the hospital," Dan replied.

"He used it to shoot rats around the hospital, which is illegal," Dan continued. "When his gun and crate of ammunition disappeared, Mr. Biglow thought maybe his boss found out what he had been doing and confiscated them. He never even reported the weapon missing or stolen."

"And the knife we found in his desk?" Jack inquired.

"Forensics determined that it was used to stab holes in a number of the photographs and articles glued to the walls. The only DNA on it was Wilson's," Dan responded.

Jack just shook his head as he looked down at his hands. The Chief paused for a moment, waiting for Jack to look up again. When their eyes met, he started to speak.

"Winston finally told us why Swanson decided not to keep his son," Chief Sheppard announced.

Jack shifted slightly in his chair and waited for the Chief to continue.

"Apparently his parents went bankrupt caring for one of his siblings who had a handicap of some sort," Sheppard said. "The child lived for about seven years, racking up hundreds of thousands of dollars in medical bills. Swanson was about eleven years old when the family lost their home. A few months later, his mother committed suicide."

Jack moaned softly and shook his head. The Chief paused for a brief moment then continued on.

"Swanson was afraid that Melody was too fragile to handle such a needy baby," he said. "She had a history of depression and their high profile life was already very challenging for her. Apparently he was trying to protect her in a twisted sort of way."

The Chief raised his eyebrows as he turned his head slightly to one side.

"He truly thought the baby would die soon after he was born," Dan added. "Winston never told him that his son was still alive. The two men never spoke of him again after Swanson signed away their parental rights - at Swanson's insistence."

Jack sighed and rubbed his eyes. What a strange series of events had come together to create this perfect storm. Unfortunately, it cost three innocent women their lives. After almost an hour Jack was finally up to speed on the investigation. The Chief welcomed him back one more time, and the two detectives left to meet Stephanie Bright at Jack's office.

His secretary was delighted to have her boss back. Stephanie had already filled his office with fresh flowers. His favorite coffee was perking happily in honor of her favorite detective's return. A small tray of breakfast pastries and fruit rested squarely in the middle of Jack's desk.

"Obviously, this is where I belong today!" Dan declared when his eyes fell on the mounds of food.

Jack and Stephanie laughed. Stephanie assured her boss that she was only a phone call away. She closed the door behind her when she left his office.

"She's great," Dan commented. "You're lucky to have her."

Jack nodded his head in agreement. Lately he had begun to realize what a lucky man he really was. Dan and Jack sat down to review the documents that had just arrived from the crime lab. Judging from the stacks of boxes that were piled up around his desk, Jack was sure it was going to be a long first day back.

CHAPTER 41

As they read through the material recovered from Wilson's room, the detectives found notations in his journals about a book that the young man had apparently modeled his actions after. *Sweet, Sweet Justice* was a best seller written by young adult author Charles Emory. They remembered seeing those words scrawled in blood on one of the walls when they searched Wilson's room at the hospital.

"Let's get the rookies on this, Jack," Dan suggested. "We can have them check it out to see what the storyline is about."

"Great idea," Jack replied. "Wilson got that *Sweet, Sweet Justice* idea from somewhere. I don't think he was capable of coming up with what he did all by himself."

Dan agreed and placed a call to Austin James. The junior detectives were seated in Jack's office less than thirty minutes after Dan contacted them, eager for their next assignment in the investigation. As soon as Jack said the words, Shane knew immediately where Wilson had first seen them written. He described the poster of the Statue of Liberty he had seen at Conlin's Bookstore and Coffee Shoppe the day they followed him.

"I saw the poster that day, Detective Russell!" Shane exclaimed. "I'm sorry. I didn't realize it had anything to do with our case!"

"I saw it too," Austin chimed in. "It didn't seem to be significant at the time."

"You couldn't have known, guys," Jack reassured them. "You were never inside his room before we sent you to tail him. We're going to need you to go through every page of that book. We want to know how much of what Wilson did followed the storyline and how much he came up with on his own or from other sources."

The rookies agreed to the assignment and left the office to return to the bookstore. Jack and Dan pursued their quest to make sense of the boxes of Wilson's unorganized records.

"There's one thing I can't stop thinking about," Dan said to Jack when they decided to break for lunch.

"What's that?" Jack asked.

He noticed the puzzled expression on his friend's face.

"The 911 call. Who made it? Was it Wilson or was it somebody else?"

Dan rubbed his eyebrows as he asked the questions.

"We can listen to the tape again," Jack suggested. "I couldn't really tell when we listened to it before, though. Maybe something will sound different this time."

They agreed to listen to the recording again after lunch. With the amount of reading they still had to do the detectives decided to grab a quick sandwich from the cafeteria and return to Jack's office to eat. On the way back with their lunches, Jack and Dan stopped in at the evidence room and signed out the 911 tape.

After they finished their meals, Jack popped the tape into the cassette and cued it to the time the call came into the dispatch office the night of the murders. The third time he played it Dan shot up in his chair.

"Did you hear that?" he exclaimed with excitement. "In the background! That's the clock in the courtyard near the courthouse! I'm sure of it!"

Jack listened carefully to the recording again two more times.

"You might be right!" he agreed, looking triumphantly at his friend. "Now, what's around that area?"

They started listing off the occupants of the offices that were near the county courthouse and the buildings immediately situated around the clock.

"Right around the main courthouse there are mostly offices that belong to judges, lawyers, child advocates….." Dan paused.

"*Lawyers!*" Jack exclaimed. "And who do we know *might* have had a reason for making that call?"

"Miles Winston!" Dan blurted out. "It *had* to be Miles Winston!"

The detectives listened to the tape several more times. If that was Winston's voice on the recording he muffled it masterfully.

"We should pay him another visit!" Dan declared.

"No time like the present, I say!" Jack exclaimed. "Let's go see what he has to say about this!"

Jack was still disturbed that the DA was leaning towards not pursuing sanctions against Winston for his handling of Swanson's son. He completely disagreed with that, but Jack knew he had to pick his battles. The detective would have to put his personal feelings about the whole thing aside. He reminded himself that sometimes you have to lose a battle to win the war.

"If Winston *did* make the 911 call," Jack asked Dan, "do you think he knew that Tim Wilson was the perpetrator all along?"

Dan sat silently considering Jack's question.

"I don't know. How could he have?" Dan mused.

"I'm not sure. Do you think it's possible that Winston knew that Wilson was Swanson's son?" Jack asked. "Was this just another one of their secrets?"

Dan sighed and shook his head.

"Where will all of this end?" Dan wondered out loud. "Do you think we'll ever know the whole truth?"

Jack just shrugged. By the time the detectives arrived at Dan's car, their frustration was running high. They avoided talking about the case on the way to the attorney's office. When they walked into the reception area of the law firm, Robyn Lightwood looked up to greet them. Before she could speak Dan put his hand up to silence her.

"No need to announce us," Dan said softly, placing his index finger against his lips.

Jack and Dan quickly walked down the hall to the office where they sat with Miles Winston the last time they met with him. The graying attorney looked up wearily from the file he was reviewing when Jack and Dan walked in. His face was chalk white and as lifeless as stone.

Off to the side of the desk Jack noted a tumbler that was half full of what he suspected might be scotch from the open bottle on the credenza. The detectives sat down in front of him as Winston laid the folder he was holding on his desk.

"Gentlemen," Miles said steadily as he looked at the two men.

They nodded in response to his guarded, mechanical greeting.

"It's good to see you up and about, Jack," Winston said. "You're looking well."

"Thank you, Miles," Jack said briskly. "I appreciate that."

"What can I do for you today?" Miles asked, almost as if he didn't really want to know.

"We're just wrapping up the details of the Swanson investigation," Dan said evenly. "We have a couple of things we need to get straight."

Miles never blinked. He waited silently for one of the detectives to speak.

"You know, Miles," Jack said. "You had a lot of 'insider knowledge' about the Swanson's, what with handling all of their financial and legal affairs."

Winston nodded.

"More than anyone else you had a direct interest in what happened to those girls."

Jack watched Miles as the attorney closed his eyes and slowly lowered his head. Even though he was frustrated by the attorney's actions throughout the case, Jack felt a flood of empathy for this once formidable man.

"Miles," Jack asked gently, "did you make the 911 call to the police that night?"

Silence blanketed the room for a brief moment. Tears slowly started to flow down Winston's pale cheeks. His shoulders shook as he sobbed for several minutes. He finally composed himself enough to speak.

"Yes, Detective," he said softly. "I made that call."

"How did you know about the murders?" Dan asked evenly.

Winston took a deep breath.

"I had been trying to call the house for almost the entire day," Miles began guardedly. "I needed Beth to sign some papers for the estate. No one answered. I knew something had to be wrong because someone was always there with Madeline. She couldn't be left alone since the accident."

He paused for a moment to regain his composure. After clearing his throat he started to speak again.

"When I got there, I rang the bell and knocked several times," he said. "No one answered so I used my own key to let myself in. That's when I saw them lying there!"

Miles laid his head in his arms and began to sob uncontrollably again. Jack and Dan looked at each other, wondering how they should respond. Compassion rushed over them as the two men waited for Winston to calm down enough to continue. After several minutes he was able to go on.

"With all of that blood," he said, "I was sure they were gone. I never walked in the room far enough to see if they were still alive. I drove back to my office immediately and used a calling card to make the 911 call from here so it couldn't be traced. I'm *sorry*. I am *so, so sorry!*"

Neither detective was sure what he was apologizing for. That question was answered with Winston's next revelation.

"I suspected for a number of years that Tim Woods might have been Megan's twin brother, but I never knew for sure," Winston declared. "They looked nothing alike but his mannerisms and the expression in his eyes were very similar to Melody's. I noticed him standing outside the property line at their home on several occasions, and once he even showed up at a fundraiser Michael and Melody were hosting. Woods seemed oddly fascinated by the Swanson family. Every single time I tried to speak to him he ran away."

Winston paused for a moment to catch his breath.

"I didn't know he was so sick. *I just didn't know*!" Winston declared angrily. "Even after that night I didn't realize he was the one who killed them. I never said anything about him to anyone. Maybe if I had this wouldn't have happened! This is my fault! This is *my fault*!"

Jack and Dan could see that the attorney was on the verge of collapsing. The weight of these secrets had finally become too heavy of a burden for the aging man to carry alone. He clearly needed professional intervention.

Dan stepped out of the office and called 911. When he returned, Jack was kneeling by Winston's chair, his hand on the grieving man's shoulder. The despondent attorney continued to sob uncontrollably. There were no words to comfort him.

Is there any punishment worse than what we inflict upon ourselves out of guilt? Jack wondered woefully to himself.

Finally the sound of sirens floated up to the seventh floor. Jack stood up to clear the way for the paramedics. Before either he or Dan could see what the attorney was doing, Miles Winston swiftly opened his desk drawer and pulled out a small handgun. He pointed it squarely under his chin and pulled the trigger.

BANG!

In the blink of an eye his suffering was over.

CHAPTER 42

The funeral service for Miles Winston was held at St. Bartholomew's with over a thousand people in attendance. Father Walter officiated at the heart wrenching celebration of the life of a man who had been a prominent figure in the legal community of Meadowbrook, Virginia. Dozens of his family members, friends and colleagues spoke words of honor and tribute on behalf of a great man who had left this world too soon. He would be dearly missed.

The day after the burial, Jack and Dan met with the Chief to fill him in on what had transpired when they visited the attorney the day he ended his life. Chief Sheppard listened intently as Jack described their conversation right down to the moment that Winston pulled the trigger. His eyes softened as he sensed the pain of his detectives.

"This is not your fault, men," he said compassionately.

"Miles Winston made a choice to live with so much secrecy. I'm very sorry it ended this way for him, but there wasn't anything more you could have done. You are not responsible for the decision he made."

The detectives let their mentor's words sink in. They wanted to believe that he was right. Somehow it just didn't feel right. Maybe it would be different after some time had passed. Maybe.

"I want you both to take a couple of days off," the Chief continued. "This has been a tragic turn of events. You need to take a break from it all. Spend some time with those beautiful ladies

I've seen you with. Have some fun. That's a direct order!"

Jack and Dan forced smiles as they thanked the Chief for his support. They left his office with heavy hearts. Sheppard knew they felt responsible for Winston's death. It was understandable, even expected in situations like this. He also knew that nothing he said right now would take away their pain. A little time removed from the case would do them both some good. Dan called Jennifer to let her know the men would be taking a few days off.

"Why don't you come and get me when my shift is over?" Jennifer suggested. "The kids are going to spend the night at your mom and dad's. I'll call Sara. Maybe she can put together some sandwiches and fruit for dinner. It will be a great evening for a picnic at the park! That jazz band we like is there tonight!"

Dan ran her idea by Jack, who agreed to the plan half-heartedly.

"Okay, Jennifer," Dan said. "Jack's in, too. Give Sara a call. We'll pick you up after work."

Both men knew Jennifer's heart was in the right place. Neither of them felt up for much of anything but they didn't want to disappoint her. By the time they left headquarters it was almost time to pick her up. Dan headed the car towards Meadowbrook General.

At a little after five o'clock they arrived at the hospital to see a smiling Jennifer chatting with another nurse near the front door. When she saw them she quickly said something to the other woman and waved to Dan and Jack as she ran down the steps.

"What a crazy day I had!" Jennifer said while she crawled into the back seat. "That crazy old Mr. Dawson took off his hospital gown and ran down the hallway naked! It took four of us to get him dressed again!"

Jennifer attempted almost successfully to replace their solemn moods with her light-hearted chatter. Jack struggled to concentrate on her story, but his mind kept wandering back to other less pleasant matters. When Dan finally swung the car onto Winchester Street, Jack started to feel his spirits lift a little.

Sara walked out onto her porch when they pulled into the driveway. She motioned for them to come inside. The three friends climbed out of the car and walked along the sidewalk in silence. When they had almost reached the front steps, Sara greeted them all warmly.

"I hope you don't mind," she said a little apologetically as she ushered them inside. "I've changed our plans!"

"What do you have in mind?" Jennifer asked.

She was sure the guys didn't care. It was pretty obvious they were only putting on a brave face for them anyway.

"I thought we could eat here," Sara said. "I've already put everything out in my back yard. It's nice and cozy, and we have our own grill master on hand to do the cooking!"

She smiled sweetly and batted her eyes at Dan. He grinned in return.

"Everything else is ready to go," she announced.

She escorted her guests to the back yard where the patio had been converted into an elegant outside buffet, complete with soft music and twinkling lights. Dan and Jack sprang into action to get the meat ready to toss on the waiting grill. While the men bickered over which steak sauce to use, Jennifer hugged her friend.

"This was a wonderful idea!" she said gratefully. "They weren't at all excited about going out!"

"I didn't think they would be," Sara said. "This way if they want to talk about it they can, and if they don't, we can play cards or dance or just do something else."

"They have to do what they have to do to get through this," Jennifer said sadly. "I want to fix it for them but I can't!"

"I know. Me, too," Sara replied sadly.

When the steaks were finally grilled to perfection, the chefs proudly carried the plates to the waiting table, where they were joined by the ladies. The couples talked and laughed while they ate dinner, avoiding the subject that hung over them like an umbrella. Dinner was a great distraction and the four of them welcomed the chance to think about anything but the events of the last several days.

When they finished eating and the table was cleared off, the foursome played cards for a few hours, enjoying the friendly competition. After losing three games in a row, Dan and Jennifer decided their luck had run out. It was time for them to go home.

"You can leave Jack behind," Sara joked. "He can help me clean up!"

They all laughed, knowing that cleaning anything was not one of Jack's strongest qualities. Besides, Jennifer and Sara had pretty well taken care of that already. Dan and Jennifer thanked Sara for the nice evening. When the couple was pulling out of the driveway, Sara turned to Jack.

"You're pretty quiet tonight, Detective," she said gently.

Jack shrugged.

"Not much to say, I guess. I'm sorry."

Sara placed her hand in his and gave it a quick squeeze.

"It's okay. I understand."

Jack smiled at her. He knew that she did.

"Would you like to take a walk with me?" he asked casually.

She nodded.

"Absolutely! Just let me get my sweater."

She rushed into the living room to remove a garment from the closet near the front door. When she returned, Sara placed it over her shoulders with Jack's assistance. Silently they strolled down the streets of Sara's neighborhood hand in hand.

Every once in a while one of them would comment on someone's yard or the bright moon that was out and the other would simply agree. After about two hours they ended up back at Sara's front yard.

"It's getting late," Jack said. "You should probably take me home now."

Sara was sorry to see the night end. She didn't want Jack to be alone.

"Okay," she agreed reluctantly. "But I do have a guest room. It isn't *too* girly!" she teased.

Jack thought about staying for a moment. Maybe it wouldn't be a bad idea. At least then Sara wouldn't have to drive back by herself.

"Okay," Jack said. "I don't want to be any trouble, though!"

"Oh, Jack," Sara said sincerely. "It's no trouble at all. Besides, I don't think you should be by yourself tonight!"

Jack hated to agree, but the company would be a welcome distraction. He didn't feel like talking, but he didn't want to be by himself either. Sara seemed to understand that.

The couple walked into her house still holding hands. Sara returned her sweater to the closet. After she turned on the gas fireplace she switched off the lights and sat on the sofa next to Jack. Sara rested her body against his as they cuddled together wrapped in a light blanket.

"This is nice, Sara," Jack said softly as she snuggled against him.

He gently kissed the top of her head. Silently they watched the flames dance gracefully until they were both fast asleep.

CHAPTER 43

Three days later Jack and Dan were back at work. They were still somewhat shaken by the recent chain of events, but the time off had been a healthy distraction. It was time to tie up the loose ends of the case.

When they arrived at Jack's office the senior detectives were greeted enthusiastically by the rookies. The younger officers were excited about their report on the book they had been asked to examine.

"The similarities are chilling, Detectives," Austin observed.

He recited several passages described in the work of fiction that were almost exactly like the events of that brutal night.

"Wilson had emulated almost everything he read. He took everything the guy wrote literally!" Shane exclaimed, his eyes wide with dismay. "It's almost like Wilson became the character in the book!"

Jack and Dan looked over the report, noting many of the details the young detectives were referring to. Jack sighed when he realized how much one twisted young man had learned just by reading a simple murder mystery. He wondered if the author would ever know that his graphic research had cost innocent people their lives.

"Congratulations on another fine job, men," Jack declared as he shook their hands.

Dan nodded.

"Your assistance has been greatly appreciated," Dan added. "Our next project is to read through all of this material."

Dan waved his hand towards the boxes piled up in Jack's office that contained the loose papers and notebooks recovered from Wilson's room at the hospital. Austin's eyes grew wide as they took in the large amount of material that was waiting to be reviewed. Jack couldn't help but laugh at the expression on his face.

"It's a little intimidating for sure," he said with a smile. "We are trying to put them in some kind of organized sequence in order to create a timeline of events leading up to the murders. Would you like to help? We could sure use it!"

Austin and Shane were pleased that the detectives had requested their assistance again. They agreed to the task and the four men began moving the boxes into a large conference room so they could spread out. When the last box was moved, the four men began the painstaking task of reading through Wilson's handwritten journals.

Before long Jack realized that Wilson had meticulously documented the graphic details of every minute he had spent with the Swanson sisters the night he took their lives. What Jack had been reading was making him nauseous. He thought about what it was doing to the rookies. Austin and Shane had never been involved in a case this violent as far as he knew.

"Men," Jack said gravely. "I need to say something."

Dan, Austin and Shane each laid the papers they had been reading on the table in front of them and turned their full attention to Jack. He looked intently at the rookies, trying to discern their reactions to what they had read so far. He waved his hand slightly at the young officers.

"You two have never worked a case this extreme before, am I correct in that?"

Both men confirmed his statement with a slight nod of their heads.

"Okay, then. What you are reading are the deranged ramblings of a mentally challenged adolescent in a man's body. It is violent and extremely graphic. If you don't want to do this, neither Dan nor I will think less of you. It's completely up to you."

Jack looked at both Austin and Shane, who returned his gaze, then looked at each other, and back at Jack again. They sat quietly for a few moments, pondering Jack's words. Finally, Austin began to speak.

"Well, sir," he replied. "I have never read anything so twisted in all of my years reading murder mysteries *and* studying at the academy."

"That's right," Shane agreed. "I know evil is out there, but this is worse than I expected."

Jack nodded empathetically.

"This is the worst we've seen, too," he said reassuringly. "If it's too much you let us know. There won't be a problem if you don't want to finish."

Austin and Shane sat silently for a moment, pondering the senior detective's words. Finally, Shane cleared his throat.

"Sir," Shane said firmly. "Thank you for your concern. But I worked hard to get into this division. I'm not going to turn back now because it's a little rough."

"That's right!" Austin chimed in emphatically. "I agree with Shane. We're all in!"

Jack smiled broadly. Out of the corner of his eye he noticed Dan grinning from ear to ear.

"Well, then," he said. "That settles it. Let's get back to work!"

The four men focused once again on deciphering the twisted story hidden in the words carelessly scrawled on the crumpled pages of Wilson's journals. Page after page they uncovered clues into the mind and soul of Tim Wilson.

They painstakingly compared their findings, trying to piece together the events that led up to the night the Swanson sisters were murdered. Nearly a week passed before the four men completed their review of all the journals.

Once they finished detailing the sequence of events leading up to and including the night of the murders, the men somberly packed the material in cartons that would eventually be stored in evidence lockers deep in the bowels of headquarters. As Austin placed the last carton on top of one of the stacks of boxes, Jack cleared his throat.

"This is the roughest case I have ever worked on," Jack stated somberly. "I appreciate having each one of you working with me. I know it's been a challenge, but your dedication and excellent police work helped close this case. Thank you."

"The only thing left to do is to prepare our final report and present it to the Chief. I will prepare the report, but I'd like each of you to be with me when I present it to him. Each of you played a significant role in this investigation."

Austin and Shane were visibly pleased to be included. Dan smiled to himself, remembering how good it felt the first time he helped to close a big case. He looked at Jack, who smiled and slightly nodded his head.

"Just let us know when it is and we will be there!" Austin exclaimed excitedly as he and Shane stood up to leave.

Shane nodded his head in agreement. When they left the room they were practically beaming. Jack chuckled. He thoroughly enjoyed working with these two young officers.

"This was definitely a big twisted mess of a case," Dan said as he stood up. "I'm glad it's finally over. If you want help with the report for the Chief, let me know. For now, I'm going home to hug my wife and kids."

"Sounds like a plan to me," Jack replied, wiping the fatigue from his eyes. "I'll walk out with you."

Jack flipped out the lights and locked the door as the tired detectives left the conference room. They avoided talking about the case as they made stops at each of their offices. Wearily the two men made their way down the stairs to the parking garage.

After saying goodnight to his partner, Jack walked slowly to his car. Finishing the report was the end of the nightmare, he knew, but Jack dreaded having to write it. What he needed was a good night's sleep – and maybe a beer or two – to prepare for the job ahead of him.

"Beer and sleep. Now *that*," Jack said out loud, "is the best idea I've had all day!"

294

CHAPTER 44

Jack managed to complete the final report on the Swanson case by the end of the next day. He arranged a meeting with the Chief for the following morning.

Finally, Jack thought to himself, *the Swanson family can rest in peace."*

Even still, no matter how many times he reviewed his notes Jack could not fathom how depraved Tim Wilson had become. He was a nameless, faceless drifter who came when he was called to clean up someone else's mess. Wilson had been a time bomb just waiting to go off and no one around him noticed.

What a sad, tragic life, Jack thought to himself as he waited for the others to arrive for their meeting.

By ten o'clock on the dot Chief Sheppard, Dan, Austin and Shane were seated and ready for Jack to begin. Judy Lane was also present to take notes for the Chief.

"Good morning, everyone," Jack began. "As you know we are here to review the final report of the Swanson murders. Chief, I took the liberty of including Officers Austin James and Shane Cook in this meeting. Their assistance was an extremely valuable part of our efforts to close this case."

"Excellent!" the Chief exclaimed boldly as he looked over his glasses at the young officers. "Good work, men!"

The rookies just smiled nervously as Jack continued.

"I hope you have all had the opportunity to read the report."

He scanned the room looking for confirmation, which he received from everyone.

"Good. Are there any questions?"

"Yes, Jack," Chief Sheppard said. "I have a few."

The Chief's furrowed brow told Jack his superior was as troubled.

"I know Tim Wilson was clearly mentally challenged," Sheppard began.

Jack nodded in silent agreement. The Chief cleared his throat.

"Are you sure there wasn't another person involved in these murders? It's just so hard to believe that someone with the maturity of a fourteen year old could pull this off by himself."

"We've all struggled with that, too, sir," Jack responded gently. "There is no evidence, DNA or otherwise, to suggest he had an accomplice. Wilson was very highly functioning and physically very strong. He was also capable of following directions. Unfortunately, those directions came from murder mysteries. He followed the storyline of a book. And that, unfortunately, resulted in the death of three innocent girls who never even knew he was their brother."

Jack paused a moment to let his words sink in.

"Around the age of eight or so," Jack continued, "his adoptive mother told him it was the Swanson's who did not want him. It appears that knowledge may have caused him to become obsessed with finding the family that rejected him. From what we were able to discern from his journals, all he wanted was for them to tell him they were sorry for abandoning him."

The Chief looked up abruptly from the report he was holding, his cheeks flushed with anger.

"He wanted an *apology*? *An apology*? And this bloodbath was the result?" he exclaimed.

"I'm afraid so," Jack replied. "He spent a lot of time writing about making them say they were sorry. Somewhere along the line when he was growing up he developed a passion for murder mysteries. He spent hours at the library and in book stores reading novels centered around violent crimes. In fact, many of the details of this case mirrored a book called *Sweet, Sweet Justice* that he actually may have used as a guide."

"Wait a minute," the Chief said. "*Sweet, Sweet Justice*. Where have I heard that before?"

"It was written on the wall in his room at the hospital," Jack replied.

The Chief sighed deeply and closed his eyes for a moment.

"That's right," he said, shaking his head. "I remember now. Please, Jack. Continue."

"Wilson described what he did in detail in his writings," Jack said. "People were always referring him to others who needed odd jobs completed because he was such a good worker. He met the Swanson girls when someone referred him to them to do repairs around their house. Unfortunately, that gave Wilson access to their home – and to them."

"I see," the Chief said. "At what point did he decide to kill them?"

"Actually, sir," Jack answered, "we don't believe he ever *intended* to kill them. We aren't sure he even understood that he took their lives."

The Chief laid his report on the table. He took off his glasses and laid them beside the glass of water in front of him. He looked at Jack, trying to process his words. Finally he began to speak, slowly and carefully.

"Help me to understand this, Jack. He shot them, each one of them multiple times, but didn't think that might kill them?"

Jack nodded his head.

"That is correct. I know this is hard to comprehend, Chief, believe me. We've all struggled with this."

Jack paused, giving Sheppard a chance to process what he was hearing.

"From his journals, it appears that he did not understand that shooting them would kill them. He taped their mouths shut but couldn't understand why they wouldn't talk to him. When they were all either dead or unconscious, he thought they were sleeping. He even turned the chairs on their sides because he thought that might make them more comfortable."

He waited for the Chief to look at him before he went on. Finally their eyes met. Jack could see the anguish in his mentor's face. He shared his pain.

"And you know this from his journals?" Sheppard asked softly.

"Yes, sir," Jack replied confidently. "We examined every page he wrote."

The Chief sighed and bowed his head. He had read Jack's report from cover to cover several times and still had trouble processing it.

In all of his years as a police officer he had never come across a case as senseless as this one.

Three young women, beautiful, talented, and loved by everyone murdered by a man who only wanted them to say they were sorry. Sorry for something they had nothing to do with. And by a man who did not understand that they would die when he pumped them full of lead. *How could this be?*

Silence blanketed the room. Jack sat down, waiting for a signal from the Chief. Finally, Chief Sheppard raised his head and began to speak earnestly.

"The details of this case must not be disclosed to the public. The Swanson family must be allowed to rest in peace with their reputations untarnished. In spite of what you have uncovered, we must not allow scandal to diminish the good that this family has done in our community for decades. Is this understood?"

The Chief looked hard around the room until he saw an acknowledgement from each person present. He stood up and turned to Jack.

"Jack, you and your team have done a great job. Thank you for your efforts. Keep up the good work!"

With that, Chief Sheppard left the conference room, followed closely by his secretary. Jack and Dan looked at each other, then at the rookies. The young officers looked a little shell shocked.

"Well, gentlemen," Jack said. "What do you think?"

Austin's face was pale. Jack could tell he was a little shaken. Shane also looked distraught. Finally, he turned to Jack.

"I still don't get it, sir," Shane said softly. "How is it that Wilson was smart enough to follow the instructions in a book that he read, but he couldn't understand that he was hurting them?"

"We may never know that, Shane," Jack replied gently.

He wondered how to explain it to Shane when he couldn't understand it himself.

"That's right," Dan said. "What was going on inside the mind of Tim Wilson was dark and deadly."

"Yeah," Austin exclaimed angrily. "And three women who never even knew who he was are dead. Where is the 'Sweet, Sweet Justice' in that?"

"I don't know, Austin," Jack replied somberly. "I just don't know."

CHAPTER 45

The official story on the Swanson investigation as relayed by Meadowbrook Daily News reporter Lisa Vick was that a vagrant named Tim Woods killed the girls in a psychotic rage. Thankfully, none of the gruesome details were released to the press, including the details of who Tim Woods really was.

Tim Wilson was never mentioned in the article. No one in the community had any idea that the two men were one and the same. No one even wondered what ever happened to the unusual young man.

"His identity as Michael Swanson's son was hidden in his death just like it was in his life," Jack said to Sara after he read the front page story. "All he ever wanted was recognition as a part of their family. Now he will never get it."

Sadly, Sara had to agree.

A few days later, a sharp knock on his office door drew Jack's attention away from the reports he was working on. He looked up and saw a beaming Dan Meyer standing in his doorway.

"Let's go!" Dan ordered. "We're going to Madelyn's for dinner tonight to celebrate your return to full duty. And you owe me a steak! Jennifer and Sara are meeting us there."

Jack didn't need a second invitation. He stood up and put his jacket on. He smiled at the thought of seeing Sara.

"This paperwork will get finished tomorrow," he announced.

"That's the spirit!" Dan replied heartily.

The two friends talked and laughed casually as they walked to the sports bar. Sara and Jennifer were already seated at their table when the men arrived. Jack kissed Sara lightly on the forehead before he sat down next to her.

A few moments later Sonya arrived with menus. Dan and Jack flirted with her in their usual manner. She laughed with them and left to get their beverages. The conversation was lighthearted until Lisa Vick entered the bar.

"Jack," Sara nudged Jack as he was talking about the playoff game with Dan. "Isn't that Lisa Vick?"

Jack glanced in the direction Sara was looking and sighed. He wondered if he could duck under the table so Lisa Vick wouldn't see him. Too late. Their eyes met. The reporter smiled broadly and made her way over to their table.

"Well, Jack Russell," Lisa said brightly. "How nice to see you doing so well!"

"Thank you, Miss Vick," Jack replied.

He waited for her dagger-like questions to begin tearing him to shreds. To his surprise she smiled at him pleasantly instead.

"I suppose you've heard I will be leaving the newspaper," she said, a look of triumph shining in her eyes.

Jack and Dan were stunned. They had always assumed she would be around to plague them forever. Curiosity got the better of him. Jack cleared his throat.

"Why, no, I hadn't heard. Have you taken another position somewhere?" he asked, pleased that he actually sounded like he was interested.

"I have, as a matter of fact," she gushed. "Governor Langford practically *begged* me to take a position on his staff as a media correspondent. I guess he finally realized that, with my ability to uncover the truth, I would be an asset to his office. I start in a week!"

Her face was flushed, her eyes bright with excitement.

"Congratulations," Jack said, almost as if he meant it. "Your familiar face will be missed around headquarters!"

"Well, I'm sure we'll be seeing each other from time to time," she said with a wink. "We'll have to stay in touch!"

Jack did not respond. He did not want to promise something he was certain he would not follow through with. Lisa Vick never noticed. She wished them all goodnight and returned to the people she was dining with.

"Wow!" said Dan. "What was the Governor thinking?"

"Maybe she knows something he doesn't want made public," Jennifer said wryly.

The four sat with their heads low as conversation turned to the investigation.

"I still don't understand why that boy's mother told him the Swanson's didn't want him!" Jennifer exclaimed. "He was already mentally handicapped! The torment of knowing who it was that abandoned him was probably what pushed him over the edge!"

They all nodded in silent agreement.

"What's really sad," Sara added, "is that he was obviously more intelligent than anyone gave him credit for. How differently things might have turned out if the Swanson's had raised him!"

"We will never know what he could have been under different circumstances," Dan said. "There is a lot we may never understand. Wilson was like a child in a man's body. He learned enough to reason out *what* to do, but never developed the maturity to understand the consequences of his actions. I'm glad it's over, but I feel bad that it ended the way it did. It didn't have to be that way."

"I can't imagine what it was like for Miles Winston to carry all those secrets with him for so many years," Jennifer said woefully. "I wonder what would have happened if he hadn't involved Langford and his wife."

"I don't know what to think about all of that," Jack said sadly. "The Langford's chose to be involved every step of the way. Melody Swanson was their friend."

"On one hand," he continued, "I think providing medical care for the baby and allowing him to be adopted was the right thing to do. But it was done so underhandedly. Melody Swanson had a right to know her son was still alive. Who could have predicted all these years later that a secret like that would cause all of this heartache?"

The foursome sat quietly for a minute, pondering the gravity of the chain of events that gradually brought the Swanson legacy to its tragic conclusion.

"It's always better to face the truth," Sara finally said. "Sometimes it's a difficult thing to do, but it's better to know what you're up against than to battle against the unknown."

The others nodded in agreement. Their solemn conversation ended abruptly when Sonya arrived at their table with a platter full of piping hot wings.

The truth? Jack thought to himself as their attention turned to the feast being laid out in front of them.

The truth, Sara Bronstein, is that I'm falling in love with you!

EPILOG

The stillness in the hallway echoes coldly, but the patient doesn't notice. Silently she sleeps, with machines breathing for her, feeding her, meeting her every physical need.

It's been almost two years since the hospital transferred her to the convalescent home. Never once has she opened her eyes, or even uttered a sound.

Tenderly the nurse adjusts the pillows around her motionless head and arms. She checks the young woman's vital signs. No change. No sign that she is even in there.

It's quite heartbreaking, really. The transporter who brought the patient over from the hospital years ago said the girl nearly drowned and was declared brain dead.

The nurse sighs. Keeping her alive this way almost seems cruel. The owner of the facility decided to care for her as long as she lives. He is hoping that her family will come looking for her. Year after year she sleeps, like a princess under a dark spell. Will no one come to rescue this damsel in distress?

The nurse checks the IV's and rubs moisturizer on her arms and legs. She raises the mechanical bed to help the circulation in the poor dear's limbs. If only they knew her name, she thought. Someone must be missing her.

After making notes in the chart the nurse turns to leave the princess to her never ending dreams. Suddenly, she feels a tug at her skirt. Thinking her uniform is caught on the side of the bed, she reaches down to brush it loose. To her surprise, the hand of the fair maiden is holding firmly onto her crisp white apron.

"Call Doctor Brennan!" she yells frantically, her shrill voice piercing the stillness.

"She's awake!"

www.ingramcontent.com/pod-product-compliance
Lightning Source LLC
Chambersburg PA
CBHW070808180626
46818CB00001B/169